I0741758

Also by Marian D. Schwartz

Realities
The Last Season, The Story Of A Marriage
The Writers' Conference
Sara Barefield

HARRY DANCED DIVINELY

A COLLECTION OF GIFFORT STREET STORIES

MARIAN D. SCHWARTZ

Gristmill Publishing, L.L.C.

Harry Danced Divinely is a work of fiction. The characters and events portrayed in this book are the product of the author's imagination. Any resemblance to actual persons, living or dead, events, or places is entirely coincidental and not intended by the author.

HARRY DANCED DIVINELY

A Collection of Giffort Street Stories

Marian D. Schwartz

Copyright ©2013 by Marian D. Schwartz

All rights reserved.

ISBN 978-0-9886076-6-8

V

Gristmill Publishing, L.L.C.

In Memory of My Parents

Contents

A PERFECT NANNY

I have never understood what triggers memory, how a slight movement of the body—a quick tilting of the head or a brief pursing of the lips—can bring the past back. I had forgotten Meddie. She was as much a part of my childhood as the towering elm trees that graced Giffort Street, where I was raised. Meddie and the trees are gone now, and I am a grandmother, which I hadn't imagined I would ever be in the nineteen fifties when I was growing up.

I remembered Meddie while I was visiting my daughter, Caroline, and her family in Brooklyn. After working part time for three years, Caroline had been offered a full time job. She and her husband, Ted, were looking for someone to live-in, to do light housekeeping and to watch Laurie and Brian, my grandchildren, until they came home from work.

Ted was home the Saturday morning they scheduled the interviews, and I was invited to sit in. I had every intention of being as uninvolved and unobtrusive as possible; there is nothing worse than giving one's opinions where they may not be welcome. Miss Poynton was the third woman they interviewed, and they started arguing as soon as she left. "Why didn't you hire her?" Ted said, frowning so intensely that his black eyebrows almost met above his nose.

"I wasn't sure," Caroline said.

"Miss Poynton was the best prospect we've had. She might have been a perfect nanny, and you let her leave without a word of encouragement!"

"There was something about her, a reserve, an

attitude…"

"I don't understand."

"There was something about her," Caroline repeated with a shrug. "It's hard to explain."

"Well, try."

"I don't know," she said. "Really, I don't want to be difficult, but as badly as we need someone, I'd go back to working part-time rather than hire Miss Poynton."

They stared at each other, momentarily speechless. I knew that Caroline had worked hard to convince Ted that their family would benefit from her taking a full time job. "You can't mean that," he said.

"Yes, I do," she said.

"Did she say anything about the bedroom?" Ted was sensitive about the room. It was both a guest bedroom and a study, and he was relinquishing it reluctantly. One of the women they had interviewed didn't care for the color of the walls, which were painted a soft green. Hospital green, she'd said. Ted was offended, for he had picked the color and painted the room himself.

"Miss Poynton commented on its northern exposure, which she said was perfect for growing African violets."

Caroline didn't add that Miss Poynton had offered to teach Laurie how to grow violets. "I learned how to care for plants when I was a little girl" she said, walking about the room, the heels of her sensible black shoes making clicking sounds on the wood floor. "I couldn't have been more than five years old, like Laurie. A maiden aunt taught me. I can still remember how excited I was when my first plant blossomed. The secret is in the humidity, you know, that and the steady north light." She paused by the room's single window. I noticed that her blue eyes were unusually pale, the color of ice.

Ted sighed with exasperation. "Caroline, be reasonable. Miss Poynton was a miracle walking through our front door."

"Maybe she's too good to be true," Caroline said.

"I give up!" He marched into the living room, heavy-footed with anger.

Caroline looked at me. "Well…?"

I didn't know what to say. My reaction had been strong, almost visceral to the innocuous Miss Poynton. "I need to think about Miss Poynton while we make lunch," I said.

While I set the table and helped make sandwiches, I tried to remember everything I could about the interview. The doorbell had rung at precisely eleven o'clock. It was Miss Poynton, wearing a navy blue suit that had a spray of lilies-of-the-valley pinned to the lapel. The suit was lintless, and the flowers, which were made of organdy, looked as if they had been dipped in starch. So did Miss Poynton. She was a small woman in her early-to-mid sixties who smelled faintly of lavender. Her thinning gray hair was neatly combed to conceal her scalp, her face was free of makeup except for a bit of blush high on her round cheeks, and her posture was perfect. Miss Poynton had a no-nonsense spine that remained straight whether she was standing or sitting.

She told us about herself, practically conducting the interview on her own. She had quit her job as a bookkeeper to nurse her only living relative, a sister, through cancer. The company she had worked for didn't have a pension plan, and all that Miss Poynton had to support herself were Social Security checks supplemented by a rapidly dwindling savings account "I have abundant energy," she said when Caroline questioned her age with regard to the demands of the job, "and after staying at home with my sister, I don't believe I'd enjoy working at a desk again. It's nice when each day is just a little bit different in routine from the day before." Her remarks were delivered with a brightness that reminded me of a woman in a television commercial for detergent exclaiming over the whiteness of her wash.

I was carrying a pitcher of iced tea to the table, still sorting through the details of Miss Poynton's interview, when my grandson, Brian, bounded into the kitchen. Brian is eight and big for his age. He generally leaps before he looks; this time was no exception. The tea sloshed but didn't spill, a lucky save. Caroline saw the near accident. "Brian," she said, "you must walk up to people instead of over them."

"Sorry," he said, proudly offering a lopsided airplane for my inspection. "Is that lady still here? I'll show it to her, too. Dad already saw it."

Then I knew. After Caroline introduced Miss Poynton to the children, she conversed pleasantly with both of them. But when Brian walked up her to show her a sticker he was planning to put on his airplane, Miss Poynton seemed to pull her shoulders back. It was not so much a movement as it was a stiffening, a setting of her bones. I had seen that gesture before, when I was a child. It was another woman's response to a boy. The woman was Meddie, and the boy was my brother, Will.

I put the pitcher on the table, told Brian that his airplane was wonderful, and walked to the kitchen sink. Although it was warm and sunny, I felt a sudden coolness in the air, and as I stood staring out the window, I could have sworn I smelled the verdant spring of Giffort Street instead of warming Brooklyn asphalt.

Meddie was always the first on Giffort Street to know that spring had arrived. She was the Whittakers' housekeeper, and during our bitter winters Meddie hibernated in the Whittakers' house, venturing forth only when Bernice Whittaker drove her to the store to shop for groceries. Meddie insisted upon picking out the staples herself, and she entrusted no one in the Whittaker household with the selection of meat, vegetables, and fruit. I suppose the arrangement was logical since Meddie did all of the cooking, but I wondered about it as I was growing up. It seemed to me that Meddie had enormous power, deciding what the Whittakers ate every night.

But my earliest memories of Meddie were in the spring. Long before the air lost its iciness, Meddie would come sailing down Giffort Street under an arch of elms in her black coat, a tall, gaunt woman with fine hair of an indiscriminate brown that was pulled back and held in place in a bun at the nape of her neck. Whatever the condition of the sidewalks, her stockinged feet were encased in white rubber-soled oxfords. She carried a black purse topped by a strong metal snap on one arm, and on the other arm a deep satchel made of black cloth. One could always tell if Meddie were coming or going by the size of the satchel. If she were going, the satchel was flat; it invariably bulged on a return trip.

My mother saw Meddie first every year. "I saw Meddie today," she would tell us in March. "The crocuses must be up under the snow by the side of the garage." Will and I would run outside and carefully brush the snow away. Sure enough, tender green blades had poked through the hard ground. To this day I remain convinced that Meddie, through a sense denied to other mortals, could divine the exact moment the crocuses were ready to have their winter covers lifted.

Meddie seemed to know everything that went on on Giffort Street, which was as great a mystery to me as her divination of the crocuses. She never conversed with the adults on our block except to say hello, and then only if spoken to first. Her greetings were always crisp, crisper to some than to others, and to the males of the street she would merely nod an acknowledgment, her full lips compressed. She was out every day during the nice weather, traveling up and down the street on one errand or another, always wearing stockings and immaculate white oxfords, carrying her purse and satchel, a large-boned woman moving silently under the elms.

Occasionally Meddie did not return a greeting. If she continued her silent passage without an acknowledgment, everyone on Giffort Street was immediately alert; we knew that something was amiss in that individual's household. The something could be anything: an argument, an extra-marital affair, an evening of drunkenness. Meddie always seemed to know before anyone else. I once overheard my mother say that Meddie knew the Heusslers' marriage was in trouble six months before Adele Heussler made an appointment with an attorney. Meddie had ignored Adele for an entire summer.

The houses on Giffort Street were built during the nineteen twenties. They were spacious, two-story homes with full attics, each architecturally different except that most had either a sun room or wide veranda in front. Many, like ours, also had a sun porch off a second floor back bedroom. Although the lots were narrow, the street had a graciousness that I have not seen duplicated in new suburbs advertising acreage. The graciousness could have come from the magnificent elms standing like sentinels at the curb, their branches forming a wondrous natural arch high above the street; or it could have been because the houses were separated by long driveways leading to double garages in the back; or it could have come from the people who lived there, their pride in the street after having lived in smaller houses on narrower lots.

The Whittakers lived next door to us in a green cedar-shingle house that had white trim. Their back sun porch had been enclosed at Meddie's insistence when the older Whittaker daughter, Candace, was a toddler. Meddie, so the story went, found Candace peering dangerously over the side, one small leg raised in a tentative effort to scale the railing. She grabbed the child, carried her safely inside, and waited stone-faced for Arnold Whittaker to come home from work. The rest was Giffort Street legend. Meddie ordered Arnold to call workmen immediately: the porch was to be enclosed at once or she, Meddie, would leave the Whittaker household. Bernice Whittaker could not envision her life without Meddie, and Arnold loved Bernice, so the porch was enclosed within the week.

Now that I think about it, Candace's innocent escapade on the back porch was probably her most adventurous childhood experience. Candace was three years older than I, a rather plain girl who had remarkably white skin and large, somber brown eyes that were as flat and expressionless as buttons. She had an air of conviction about her, as did her sister, Margaret, who was five years younger. Margaret was blond and delicately-featured like her mother, but Bernice Whittaker had a vivaciousness that her youngest daughter lacked. Both Whittaker girls were very proper. During the years we were growing up, I never saw them wearing clothes that were soiled in play; their hair was always combed, their hands were always clean, and there was never a scratch or black-and-blue mark on their smooth white shins.

Nor did I ever hear the Whittaker sisters called by anything other than their given names. Margaret was never Meg, Maggie, or Peggy; Candace was always Candace. I once overheard Bernice Whittaker tell my mother that Meddie believed people should be called by their given names. "It is proper," she said, quoting Meddie, "that people be called by their proper names."

Aside from Bernice and Arnold, no one on Giffort Street knew Meddie's proper name, and I doubt that even they remembered. Meddie was simply Meddie. She came to live with the Whittakers when Candace was born. Bernice had had a difficult delivery and was forbidden by her doctor to climb stairs. Arnold hired Meddie while Bernice was still in the hospital, and when he brought her home to Giffort Street, Meddie accompanied them, carrying Candace. Meddie ran the household and cared for the baby while Bernice convalesced. After Bernice regained her strength, Meddie moved upstairs to the maid's quarters on the third floor. "I was so lucky that Arnold was able to find Meddie," Bernice often said. "I don't know how I could manage without her."

Besides their daughters, there was no one more important to the Whittakers than Meddie. Arnold owned a chemical company, and Bernice was forever busy with committee meetings and luncheons; they were both avid golfers and dedicated bridge players. Their enjoyment of their life and each other was infectious; they never lacked for invitations, which they easily accepted. Their freedom depended upon Meddie, and with Meddie they never had to worry: their girls were safe. "After marrying Bernice, hiring Meddie was the smartest thing I ever did," Arnold often said, his broad face widening into the smile of a man sincerely happy with his mate and his life.

Bernice came to our house late in the afternoon at least once a week to have coffee with my mother. If I were home, I deliberately stayed within earshot of the two women, pretending to read or do homework so I could listen. I learned a great deal about Giffort Street during those afternoons, for Bernice never arrived without a tidbit of gossip or an observation made by Meddie.

Bernice loved to talk, and she was at her best when she talked about the Whittaker household. It would usually be a funny story told well, something silly that had happened to herself or to Arnold, but one winter afternoon she talked about her daughters. I wasn't interested at first because I didn't like Candace and Margaret, but when Bernice lowered her voice, I strained to hear.

The Whittaker girls weren't getting along. "They have been squabbling," Bernice said. "Since Candace turned thirteen she's been complaining constantly, always about Margaret. 'Margaret was in my room' or 'Margaret messed up my papers' or 'Margaret took something that belonged to me.'

"I've asked Margaret to leave Candace's things alone, but it hasn't helped. 'Everything I do bothers Candace,' she says. 'Ask Meddie. Candace has gotten mean.'"

Bernice wrung her manicured hands. My mother nodded sympathetically.

"I know it's their age difference," Bernice said. "Margaret is only eight. She can't appreciate what's happening to her sister. I tried to explain, but it's so difficult to discuss hormonal changes with an eight year old." She shook her head. "We had no choice. We had to space them to keep Meddie. When Candace was two, I casually mentioned that she needed a brother or a sister. Meddie threatened to leave. 'I can't take care of the house and Candace if there is another child,' she said. 'It would be too much. Everything must have its proper attention'

"So I asked her when, and she told me that Candace would have to be ready to go to school. Arnold was disappointed, but I was frantic. You see, we had already started trying, and I remembered how weak I was after I had Candace. I didn't tell Arnold, but the doctor said it could happen again. Then I found out that I wasn't pregnant. I was so relieved because it would have meant losing Meddie, and Meddie is such a treasure.

"We waited until Candace was four before trying again, not realizing that the age difference would be important. But it is," Bernice said. She ran her fingers through her blond curls, then brightened. "Meddie was so pleased that we had another girl, so pleased. Even Arnold didn't seem to mind, although I do believe that every man would like to have a son. Of course, Arnold has never said so. He's always been as proud as he could be of his daughters.

"Arnold and I consider Meddie a member of our family. So do the girls. When they were little, they insisted that Meddie give them their baths, not us. Even now they never miss saying goodnight to her privately. I know most people think that Meddie is rather cold—maybe austere is a better word—but they don't know her as we do. Sometimes I hear her talking softly with Candace and Margaret as a mother would. And when they were babies, she crooned to them and played with them as if they were her own. You know," Bernice said, "devotion like Meddie's is a rare thing. I have never trusted anyone, with the exception of Arnold, as much as I trust Meddie."

I was ten years old when I overheard that conversation. The part about Candace and Margaret loving Meddie didn't interest me; as for Meddie, I couldn't imagine her loving anyone. But the part about the spacing of the Whittaker girls was fascinating. My knowledge of the facts of life didn't include the possibility that children could be planned as carefully as a vacation. I decided to wait a few days, then ask my mother so she wouldn't connect my questions with Bernice's visit.

My questions weren't asked until months later. Hours after Bernice left our house, my father was killed in an automobile accident. He was driving home from an emergency call at the hospital when a car driven by a drunk driver veered across the road, killing him instantly.

The Whittakers knew about my father's death before I did. Someone must have notified them during the night, for when I awakened the next morning and went downstairs, I found Meddie in our kitchen instead of my mother. To my knowledge, it was the only time she was ever in our house. Now I realize that Meddie's presence showed the esteem Bernice Whittaker had for my mother, but the sight of Meddie that morning made me flee the kitchen in alarm. "Elizabeth," she called kindly, coming after me. I ignored her and, unseeing, collided with my uncle in the hall. It was then that I formally learned of my father's death. But to this day I believe that I really knew when I saw Meddie standing in our kitchen.

My mother, who had been a nurse, went to work a year after the accident. At the time she explained her decision, Will was fourteen and I was eleven. She told us that my father had left enough insurance to cover the cost of our education and that she didn't want to touch the money. "It is important for both of you to have a good start in life," she said. "Your father had to struggle financially to get through medical school and he wouldn't want that to happen to his children. He meant to take out more insurance, but he just didn't think…" My mother bit her lip, then composed herself. "You'll go directly to the Whittakers' after school, Libby. Meddie will be there, and you are to stay until Will comes home."

"Oh, no," I said, rebelling at the thought of spending afternoons with Margaret and Meddie. "Please let me have my own key. I can take care of myself. Besides, Will comes home late every day. He's always practicing football or basketball or something."

My arguments failed. "This is hard enough for me," she said firmly. "If you're with Meddie, I won't worry."

"But," I started to say.

"I expect your cooperation, Libby," my mother said. There was a weary resignation in her voice that stopped me from arguing further. Will tried to be especially nice to me for the remainder of the day, but it didn't help. I was feeling too sorry for myself to respond to his kindness.

What I remember most about my afternoons at the Whittakers' was my boredom, endless minutes spent waiting for Will. Margaret never dawdled after school. She went directly home to Meddie, so I could no longer stay in the playground or walk home slowly with my friends, talking and laughing. Whenever I arrived late, Meddie would be standing at the back door waiting for me. "Elizabeth," Meddie said each time, calling me by my detested proper name, "I have been concerned. I hope you weren't detained by a teacher."

I wasn't an exemplary child like Margaret or Candace, but I was usually well-behaved, yet Meddie always made me feel as though I had transgressed. Still, it would have been easier for me to tell her that I had been held after school by a teacher than to admit the truth, that I was late simply because I was having a good time. As a result I tried to be prompt, and when I wasn't, I apologized without an explanation.

I was uncomfortable in the Whittakers' house, unsure of how to act or what to say, so I followed Margaret, adapting myself to her routine. First, we washed our hands. Then we had our snack. Meddie's sparseness didn't extend to food. She was an excellent, sometimes inspired cook, and the plates of cookies, sweet rolls, and cakes she set before us with glasses of milk were the high point of those afternoons. After our snack we settled down with our homework.

In the beginning I tried to play with Margaret, but it was impossible. She was a moody girl who had a smugness that infuriated me; everything she did had to be perfect. If we played a game, she had to be the winner. Once we played jacks on the green linoleum kitchen floor. "You're out," I said when Margaret was on threes.

"No, I'm not!" she said, clutching the red ball.

Then I heard a voice behind me. "If Margaret says she didn't drop one, she didn't drop one. It is not polite to make accusations, Elizabeth."

Meddie stood over me, stern and straight-backed. I couldn't defend myself, although I was positive that Margaret was out. I felt my face redden. Margaret picked up the rest of the jacks with a victorious smirk on her face. We never played jacks again.

After that I brought books to read and sat by a window where I could glance out for the sight of Will, easily recognizable at a distance by his long, athletic strides.

While I waited, Margaret practiced the piano, recopied her notebooks with precision neatness, or worked on her stamp collection. Candace came home after we were settled. She had something to eat, talked to Meddie for a few minutes in a voice too low for me to hear, then retreated to her bedroom. If she were in an expansive mood, she said hello, but more often than not she walked past me as if I didn't exist.

On afternoons when she was home, Bernice Whittaker tried to make me feel welcome in her breezy, friendly way, but she was usually busy, either making telephone calls, conferring on a household matter with Meddie, or taking a late afternoon rest before an evening out. Bernice was too engrossed in her own life to notice my discomfort.

The first time Will came to get me he knocked on the back door. Meddie was standing at the stove, stirring the contents of a heavy saucepan. "Yes," she called out.

Thinking that her acknowledgment was an invitation to enter, Will opened the door and walked up the steps into the kitchen. I happened to look at Meddie before turning toward Will. Meddie's shoulders stiffened; the movement was not so much a stiffening as it was a setting of her bones. "Yes, William," she said, studying his feet as if he had tracked the dirt of the world directly into her kitchen.

I felt a sudden coolness in the room, a chill that cut through the heat from the oven and the pot that Meddie was tending, which had come to a rolling boil. Will stepped back, his narrow face aflame. "I believe that Elizabeth is ready," Meddie said as she removed the saucepan from the stove.

I picked up my books, and we left silently.

I would have forgotten the incident had it not been

for Will. After that day he waited for me outside, knocking and calling my name. When the weather became bitter, I asked him why he didn't come into the back hall to wait for me. "Meddie won't let me leave unless my boots are on and my coat is buttoned," I said on a frigid December day. "If you wait in the back hall, you won't have to stand out in the cold."

"I don't mind."

"But you'll get sick," I said.

Will transferred his books from under his right arm to his left, pulled his leather glove off with his teeth, and reached into his trouser pocket for his key. "No, I won't," he mumbled, the glove still in his mouth.

"I'll tell Mother," I said.

Will unlocked the door. "Don't, Libby. She's having a tough time as it is."

"Then why won't you wait for me in the back hall?"

"It's better this way."

"Why?"

Will shrugged. "I don't know," he said. "It's just better, that's all."

He didn't get sick, and the matter wasn't discussed again. Will continued to wait outside for me until the spring, when my mother relented and let me have my own key.

I didn't see the Whittakers often after that. Since my mother wasn't home during the day, Bernice's visits became infrequent. I had passing contact with the Whittaker girls and Meddie: we passed each other on the street or in school, said hello, then moved on. During those years Candace became very popular. Boys called for her constantly, and every Saturday night there was a different car parked in the Whittakers' driveway, another boy who had come to take Candace out. Her popularity mystified me, for Candace was neither pretty nor vivacious. But she was smart. Candace did well in high school, and she was accepted at every college where she applied. In her senior year, she was more aloof than ever: I can still picture her walking on Giffort Street, chin high, her small features set with satisfaction.

I wasn't interested in being as smart as Candace, but I did want to be as popular. I was a freshman in high school and anxious to be liked, so I asked Will about Candace. "You don't want that kind of popularity," he said.

"What kind?"

"Candace's kind," Will said, walking away before I could question him further.

Several months later, I overheard Will's friends talking. I was doing my homework at the kitchen table; the boys were playing basketball in our backyard, and their voices traveled through the open window. A car had just backed out of the Whittakers' driveway. "There she goes again," one of the boys said. Between the thumping of the basketball, I heard another boy's voice. "You can do almost anything to her, almost anything…"

I knew they were talking about Candace and strained to hear more, but Will warned them to be quiet. "Hey, cool it," he said, making a motion with his head toward the Whittakers' house. The boys stopped talking and continued playing. The basketball thumped against the concrete, hit the backboard, and swished through the net, over and over again in an irregular rhythm, for the remainder of the afternoon.

I couldn't believe what I had heard. If I had understood correctly, the boys were saying that Candace was fast, that she was a loose girl. But it didn't make sense. I knew that certain girls had reputations. I also thought I knew what the girls did to earn their reputations, yet I had never heard a rumor about Candace, anything to indicate that she was one of those girls. Further, I was sure that Meddie would know if Candace were doing things she shouldn't be doing. Meddie knew everything. The whole business became too contradictory for my adolescent mind to handle. I wasn't even sure that the boys knew what they were talking about. They were the same age as Candace, but she had been dating college boys for quite some time. I finally concluded that, if Candace were indeed doing the things that the boys had intimated, she was able to get away with it without suffering a bad reputation because she was so smart.

Candace spent the next four years at Radcliffe and graduated with an honors diploma in one hand and a substantial diamond ring on the other. She returned home with her fiancé, a young man fresh out of Harvard Business School named Roger Hornung. Roger, with some helpful introductions from Arnold Whittaker, soon had a number of job offers. He took a position as a junior executive with a local chemical company and settled into an apartment where the couple planned to live after they were married.

When our invitation to Candace's engagement party arrived, I put it aside without a thought of attending. It was my first summer home from college. I'd had a taste of independence and liked it, so when my mother insisted that we go, I balked. "I haven't seen Candace in years," I said, "and I never cared for her anyway. Go without me. Really, I won't be missed."

I relented and went to the party, not for the Whittakers but for my mother. Will wouldn't be coming home that summer. He was working at a hospital before starting medical school in the fall, and we both felt his absence deeply. Also, Mother had been alone during the past winter. Although she didn't complain, I knew that it was hard for her, coming home every night to an empty house. She had aged. There were new lines in her face, and her hair, which had turned prematurely gray after my father died, was completely white. Her happiness when I agreed to attend made me feel ashamed of my selfishness.

The party was held at the country club where the

Whittakers played golf. It had been an estate, and as my mother and I walked up the flower-banked path to the Tudor clubhouse, I was struck by the beauty of the place, brightly lit and glowing with rustic charm in the darkness. The night air was calm, sweet with the fragrance of midsummer. It was an evening made for lovers. I remember pausing in front of the massive oak door, wishing for a romance of my own.

Once inside, my romantic notions vanished. My mother was whisked away by friends, and I was left facing Meddie. "How are you Elizabeth?" she said. Her eyes, darker than ever, seemed to bore right through me.

"Fine, thank you," I said, uncomfortable as always under her scrutiny. "And you?"

The same," said Meddie in a tone which made me feel that I had asked a question of a highly personal nature. "I trust that you will continue to do well in your studies. Your mother has such high hopes for you and your brother. It has not been easy for her now that both of you are gone for most of the year. She is lonely."

Meddie turned and walked away without waiting for me to reply. Stunned, I remained where I was standing. Her outburst—more words than I had ever heard the laconic woman speak at once—made me feel like a child who had been admonished without knowing why. Later, I saw her moving in tight-lipped silence among the guests, as if searching for signs of misbehavior. Had it not been for the fact that she was wearing white leather pumps instead of her white oxfords, Meddie appeared no different than she did during the day, moving silently down Giffort Street under the elms.

Candace's engagement didn't change her. Still somber eyed, she seemed the same as she held the arm of her fiancé with the same air of conviction she had always worn. "This is Roger," she said when she introduced me to Roger Hornung. She spoke as if Roger were an object rather than a person, a possession or a prize hard won, yet she had been hanging onto his arm all evening, so I assumed that her behavior gave true indication of the feelings her eyes didn't express.

I had had glimpses of Roger Hornung entering and exiting the Whittakers' house and was interested in getting a closer look. Roger was of medium height and build; he had brown hair, brown eyes, and wore tortoise-shell glasses. Although he had a pleasant face and friendly manner, his clothes and bearing made him appear stuffy, almost priggish. That night, as I had seen him before, Roger was wearing a three-piece suit with a watch chain dangling from his vest. All that was missing from his ensemble was the umbrella I had seen him carry, whether or not rain was forecast. At a time when the Beach Boys music was popular, Roger was conspicuously different from other young men his age; he seemed to be the perfect mate for Candace. "Pleased to meet you, Elizabeth," he said, extending his hand after Candace introduced us.

"Libby is the name I'm comfortable with," I said, smiling as disarmingly as I could.

"Then Libby it is," said Roger. "It suits you better, you know."

Candace's lips tightened. "Come, Roger," she said, tugging on his arm. "There are still so many people for you to meet."

"Nice seeing you," Roger said as Candace led him away.

Candace and Roger were married early in December. My mother attended the wedding and told me about it when I came home for Christmas break. "It was a gorgeous wedding. Bernice and Arnold outdid themselves. I think the nicest part was seeing the two of them, so happy with each other after all these years. I hope Candace and Roger are as happy. They certainly have a wonderful example in Bernice and Arnold," Mother said. Then she frowned.

"Don't you think they'll be happy?" I said. "Roger seems so well suited for Candace—figuratively as well as literally." I started to laugh.

My mother didn't smile. "I had the strangest notion when I walked down the receiving line after the ceremony. They were all there—Arnold, Bernice, Candace, Roger, Margaret, Meddie, Roger's parents. Meddie was standing between the two girls. There was something about the three of them…it was almost as if Candace and Margaret were Meddie's girls, not Bernice's. Neither one has a trace of her mother's personality."

Our conversation was interrupted by the ringing of the telephone. It was Will calling from the airport; he had surprised us by taking an earlier plane. The Whittaker girls were forgotten.

The following summer I saw Candace and Roger going in and out of the Whittakers' house frequently. I was often outside in the evening, as were many of our neighbors. Almost a third of the Giffort Street elms had been painted with large white X's by the city forestry department; they were marked for removal, the victims of Dutch elm disease. A committee formed to hire tree experts in an effort to save the remaining elms. Our tree was still miraculously healthy, but the Whittakers' elm was in the throes of dying, its leaves limp and yellow.

Candace wasn't interested in the fate of the trees. She and Roger had decided to buy a house. "I wasn't meant for apartment living," she told me early one summer evening. "The noises, the odors from other people's cooking. Some nights I can't eat dinner. I'm not accustomed to living this way. It's…it's distasteful."

Roger and Candace spent their evenings searching for a perfect house in the suburbs, then reported their findings to Bernice, Arnold, and Meddie. Candace was dissatisfied with every house she saw: either there weren't enough bathrooms or the kitchens were too small. Roger said little, but one night he lingered outside instead of following his wife. "It's a shame about the trees," he said, surveying the sad elms. "I never realized how much grace trees add to a street. Candace and I have started looking at new houses; she's decided that she doesn't want to live in a place that's been lived in by someone else. But all the houses seem to be alike, one after another painted white. Sometimes you don't even know what street you're on. You just see white houses looking naked without a cover of trees."

"You can plant your own trees," I said.

"I suppose so," said Roger. He sighed and thrust his thumbs into his vest pockets. "But it takes a long time for a tree to mature. A child can grow into adulthood before a tree has grown sufficiently to give full shade. I guess each thing in nature takes its own time."

Roger stood gazing at the dying elms so sadly that I didn't know what to say.

When I came home from college the following summer, half of the elm trees on Giffort Street were gone. So was Meddie. "No one knows where she is," my mother said. "Bernice and Arnold are frantic. They went to pick up Margaret from college last weekend, and when they returned, Meddie was gone. She didn't leave a note. Not a clue. Nothing. They came home and found her room empty. There wasn't a trace of her in that house. The police came, but they said there was no evidence of foul play, so they won't investigate. The woman simply vanished! Can you imagine that, after so many years?"

"Maybe she felt the Whittakers didn't need her anymore," I said, oddly affected at the news. It didn't seem possible that Meddie wasn't there. She had always been there.

"Of course they need her. The girls aren't home, but Meddie did all of the cooking and the cleaning. Bernice is absolutely lost. They've eaten out every night this week."

It wasn't long before the Whittakers hired a cleaning woman. "I couldn't give Meddie's room to someone else," Bernice said late one afternoon in our kitchen. She had begun to age in earnest and had had her blond hair lightened to platinum, but Arnold still gazed at her adoringly. "I've gone over it and over it in my mind, and I'm more confused than ever. Why did she leave? It just doesn't make sense."

"She could have had private reasons," my mother said. "Meddie always seemed to know what was happening before anyone else. Maybe she sensed that she was going to become ill."

"We would have helped her," Bernice said. "Meddie was a member of our family. She carried Candace home from the hospital, for goodness sake. The girls are crushed. They don't understand it any more than Arnold and I do."

The face of Giffort Street changed that summer. More trees were marked for cutting. The familiar figure of Meddie, carrying her purse and black satchel, moving silently up and down the street in her white oxfords, was gone. It seemed that the people who lived on the street changed, too. They spent more time in their backyards or retreated into their homes, as if they felt vulnerable without the shade of the elms.

My mother decided to sell our house. "I debated putting it on the market after you left for college, but I just wasn't ready," she said. "Now that the elms are going, it's time that I go, too. I couldn't bear to see our elm cut down."

Our house was sold to a young couple who had three children. Since we both worked during the day, my mother and I spent evenings and weekends sorting what seemed to be endless paraphernalia that had accumulated in the basement, attic, and closets. I was going through my closet on a steamy Sunday in August and decided to quit; it was too hot to work a minute more. Armed with a book and a glass of lemonade, I went out on the porch off my bedroom to relax on a chaise lounge.

The air was still, heavy with heat. I heard a car ignition turn off in the Whittakers' driveway as I opened my book. A murmur of voices drifted up from the Whittakers' kitchen. I ignored them and settled in for my sunbath. The murmurs grew louder. There was the sound of female weeping and deep, agitated male voices. The sun was becoming oppressive. I began to perspire heavily and debated whether to go inside when I heard Arnold Whittaker yell, "What are you trying to tell us Roger? What in the hell are you trying to say?"

It was hard to believe that anyone would yell at meticulous Roger Hornung, who, I was sure, was wearing a three-piece suit on the hottest day of the year, certainly not Arnold Whittaker, whom I had never heard yell. I picked up my book and glass and started to go inside when Roger's voice, in a cry of frustration, spilled into the steamy air. "Sir, have you ever fucked a log?"

***

Bernice came over the day before we moved, several weeks later, to say good-by. She sat in our kitchen looking lost beneath a fading summer tan, a woman whose perfect life had slipped away without a warning. She was nervous and spoke to my mother agitatedly, seemingly unaware of my presence as I packed our remaining dishes into cardboard cartons. "Candace and Roger are separated," she said. "They will be divorced. Arnold and I had no idea, no idea at all. We thought they were happy."

"Sometimes these things happen," my mother said. "Candace is young, she can begin again."

"Begin what?" Bernice said, disconsolate.

"She has a good job teaching, and eventually she'll find someone else. I know you and Arnold are upset, which is natural, but you're acting as if her life is over."

Bernice's face seemed to dissolve. Suddenly she looked old despite her carefully applied make-up and platinum-blond curls. "No, you don't understand. I'm not sure that I understand, either. Candace…Candace can't love a man. She can't give of herself."

"She's hurt," my mother said. "It's temporary."

"No, not hurt," Bernice said, weeping. "Damaged. Candace is damaged. So is Margaret. We took them to a psychiatrist. He explained it to us. When they were little, they developed ideas about themselves, attitudes about their bodies. They can be touched, but they won't allow anything or anyone to touch them. They can't respond.

"I couldn't believe it. I told him how popular Candace was in high school, how boys were always calling for her. He wasn't surprised and said that she probably acted the same with those boys as she did with Roger. She allowed them to do things to her in order to be accepted; she used her body to get what she wanted, and she let the boys use it to get what they wanted. But she didn't respond, ever, because she couldn't.

"The psychiatrist told us that the girls were profoundly influenced during their formative years. He said it was almost as if they were forbidden to have sexual feelings, that they were trained to keep them inside, to suppress them until the feelings died."

"Can they be helped?"

"Only Margaret. He said there is a slight chance for Margaret but not to count on it. All those years," she sobbed, "all those years Meddie bathed them and cared for them. They always insisted upon Meddie. We thought it was wonderful that the girls were so fond of her. How could we have known? How? She was a tireless worker. She had no family that we were aware of; no one ever called or wrote to her. She never talked about herself, so we assumed that she had nothing to say. And she gave of herself to the girls. How were we to know what she was telling them behind the bathroom door? No one knew."

As I closed the last carton, I remembered a late afternoon in the Whittakers' kitchen years ago. Will knew. He knew it in the setting of Meddie's bones.

THE QUEEN ANNE BEDROOM SET

The trouble between Stan and Adele Heussler might have started when Adele backed Stan's car into their house; or it might have started when they bought the Queen Anne bedroom set…

There wasn't a better housekeeper on Giffort Street than Adele Heussler. She was a plump, auburn-haired woman whose bright brown eyes were forever searching for fingerprints and black heel marks and particles of dust that escaped her cleaning rags. Although Adele couldn't seem to stay on a diet, she never broke her household routine. The Heusslers' laundry was always washed on Monday and ironed on Tuesday; their yellow kitchen was scrubbed and waxed on Friday, and the books on the living room shelves were removed and dusted weekly, whether they needed it or not. The Heusslers' home smelled of furniture polish and Murphy's oil soap, and even on gloomy mid-winter days the double-hung windows of the neat gray-and-white side-entrance house sparkled like table crystal. It was commonly known that the Whittakers' laconic maid, Meddie, who never conferred with anyone over anything, asked Adele her opinion of new cleaning products and respected her advice on the removal of stains. Meddie, however, ignored Stanton Heussler so pointedly that the very air seemed chilled when she walked past him. The neighbors knew this, too, and they wondered about it. Stan appeared to be a devoted husband and father. He was a short, burly fellow with a broad nose and a strong chin who had the habit of rising on his toes when he became excited, particularly when he wanted to emphasize a point. Other than that rather unusual mannerism, he was generally thought of as an easy-going fellow. He was a sales representative for a power tool company, and his territory was the largest in the Northeast. He traveled often and had occasional lapses of fidelity, which he was able to rationalize until he returned home; the sight of his hard-working wife and well-ordered house filled him with such remorse that he usually consented to whatever Adele asked, whether it was a request as simple as taking out the garbage or one as expensive as remodeling the kitchen. Adele assumed that Stan's easy acquiescence came from a kind and generous nature, as did everyone else except perhaps Meddie, who kept her suspicions about Stanton to herself.

On a Monday morning in March, Stan left the house at six thirty to drive to the airport. He forgot to reset the alarm, and Adele didn't awaken until eight o'clock. She jumped out of bed, put on a rose chenille bathrobe, then ran to the children's bedrooms and told them to hurry downstairs to breakfast. Tommy Heussler, a sturdily-built eight-year-old, knocked over a full glass of milk reaching for a piece of toast. The milk splashed on him and ran over the table, soaking his sister, Gail. While the children went back upstairs, Adele wiped up the mess, calling to them to change quickly or they'd be late for school. Tommy came down first. Before Adele could stop him, he ran out the door hatless, though the temperature was below freezing and he had just recovered from an ear infection. Gail came down later. She was a chubby strawberry blonde who looked cherubic until she opened her mouth. "I wanted to wear my blue dress today," she said. "I promised Lucy. We decided on Friday to wear blue dresses. Now she'll be mad because I'm wearing my jumper, and there's hardly any blue on it. It's all Tommy's fault. I bet he did it on purpose."

"It was an accident," Adele said, starting down the

basement stairs with milk-soaked kitchen towels. "He had to change, too."

"No, he meant it!"

"You'll be late if you don't get moving." Adele paused on the steps. "And wear your boots."

Gail stamped her foot. She didn't want to wear boots. No one in the entire fourth grade wore boots when there was hardly any snow on the ground. Besides, she didn't want to walk to school by herself. "If I have to wear boots, I'll really be late," she said. "They're too hard to get on over my new shoes. Can you drive me?"

"I'm not dressed."

"You can put your coat on over your robe. No one will know."

Adele sighed. She didn't want Gail to be late. It offended her sense of order, which included punctuality as well as cleanliness. "All right," she said, "but I hope no one sees me with my bathrobe hanging out from under my coat."

When Adele slid the garage door open, she saw with dismay that Stan had taken her Chevrolet to the airport and had forgotten to back the Buick into the garage. Like all Giffort Street driveways except for those on corner lots, the Heusslers' driveway narrowed from a wide concrete expanse in front of the double garage to a single car width when it jogged around the house. Adele had difficulty maneuvering the bulky white Buick when she was driving forward; she could barely see over the steering wheel, even when she sat on a cushion. She eyed patches of ice that gleamed menacingly under a thin dusting of snow and was tempted to tell Gail to walk, boots or no boots. But then Gail would almost certainly be late for school.

"I want you to look out the back window and tell me how I'm doing," Adele said after they were in the car. She turned the key in the ignition, put the Buick in reverse, stuck her head out the window and accelerated slowly while Gail watched, perched on her knees on the front seat.

"How am I doing?" Adele said after she had jerked the car out of the garage, braking every foot or so.

"Fine," Gail said.

"How am I doing now?" Adele said, her head still out the window as she approached the jog in the driveway.

"Fine," said Gail, who was becoming bored with the whole business. She glanced down and spotted a candy bar wedged in a corner of the back seat. If she stretched, she might be able to reach it.

"How am I doing" Adele said again. Despite the cold, perspiration was forming on her upper lip.

Gail was hanging over the front seat, her rump in the air. She looked up, and from that peculiar angle judged that her mother was heading straight for the fence. "You're going to hit the Mastersons' fence," she said, stretching to reach the candy bar.

If Adele had glanced in the rear view mirror, she would have seen that she had plenty of room; the Buick was several feet away from the fence. But she reacted to Gail's warning by immediately slamming her foot on the brake. Gail pitched forward—head first, legs flying—into the back seat as the car slithered sideways on the ice. There was a loud crunch as the back bumper caught a corner of the house before the car slid to a stop. "Are you all right?" Adele said anxiously, turning to check on Gail.

"I guess so," Gail said, disgruntled though she had finally managed to capture the candy bar.

Her heart pounding, Adele peered tentatively out the car window to assess the damage. She saw that the end of the bumper was scratched and bent, and there were pieces of cedar shingle lying on the driveway. "Oh, no," she said, "I've put a hole in the house!"

After she dropped Gail off and pulled the Buick back into the garage, Adele stood at the side of the house shivering in her fur-collared storm coat, her rose chenille bathrobe hanging over her boots, staring dismayed at the damage she had done. A corner of the house had been partially ripped away; gray siding was splintered around a hole that exposed the underlying frame like a gaping wound. She stooped to pick up jagged pieces of shingle, wondering how she could tell Stan that she had not only bent his bumper, but that she had torn away a chunk of their home.

Another woman might have gone back to bed or sat with the morning paper and a soothing cup of tea to relax after the accident. But not Adele Heussler. It was Monday, and there was work to be done—beds to be stripped, breakfast dishes to be rinsed, the laundry to be sorted and washed. Adele cleared the breakfast room table, put the dishes in the dishwasher, and poured herself a cup of lukewarm coffee, looking wistfully at an almond pastry ring sitting on the kitchen counter. She had promised herself over the weekend that she would stick to her diet this time. But it had been such an awful morning— disastrous, really—that a small piece wouldn't hurt. She sliced a thin wedge of the nut-covered pastry, popped it into her mouth, then cut a large piece that oozed almond filling. She consumed the pastry greedily with her eyes half-closed. A low, sensuous sound escaped from her throat, a hum of pleasure, of guilty delight, that would have shocked her had she been aware of it.

The telephone was ringing when she stepped out of the shower. She wrapped herself in a towel and ran to answer, but the line was dead when she picked up the receiver. "This is ridiculous!" she said, slamming the wet receiver into its cradle. She went back to the bathroom, modestly holding the towel closed though she was alone in the house, projecting the unfortunate events of the morning into a run of bad luck. But then she thought of Stan and the children and the wonderful life they had and dismissed her suspicion as foolish.

The telephone rang again at noon while she was folding laundry. It was Phoebe Stedman. "I called early this morning but no one answered," Phoebe said. "I didn't think you'd be out on a Monday."

If it had been anyone but Phoebe, Adele might have laughed and told about her wet dash from the bathroom. But the sound of Phoebe's voice, melodious and self-assured, made Adele bristle. It was just like Phoebe to hang up after three or four rings without giving a person a chance to answer. "I had to take Gail to school," she said.

"I don't know if anyone has told you, but Jack and I are getting a divorce."

"Oh…it's…I'm sorry," Adele said, stunned at the news.

Phoebe laughed. "You make it sound as if one of us is dying. It's a shame, but it isn't a tragedy. Anyway, I'm calling about our bedroom set. We've decided to sell it. Are you interested?"

Adele had seen the set once, at the Stedmans' last Christmas party; the furniture was so magnificent that she could still picture it vividly. "Yes," she said. Then, not wanting to appear too eager, she added, "Are you sure you want to sell it? The set is beautiful, the kind of furniture that one keeps."

"If the marriage keeps," Phoebe said lightly. There was an edge of bitterness in her voice that Adele, in her excitement, didn't notice. "We're asking twenty-five-hundred dollars, two hundred more than we paid. I think it's a fair price. We got a tremendous buy on it, and antiques of that quality are constantly appreciating. I'm throwing in the mattress and box springs, too. We had to have them custom made because the bed is an odd size. The mattress is firm, and there isn't a spot on it. It's in perfect condition. Unless you object to sleeping on a mattress that's been used."

"Oh, no, it will be fine," Adele said, already

planning to have a new mattress made. "Stan is out of town and won't be back until tomorrow night. I'm sure he'll want the set, but I won't be able to give you a definite yes until I talk to him."

"Then call me Wednesday morning," Phoebe said before hanging up.

Adele found it difficult to concentrate on her remaining Monday chores; her head was swirling with thoughts of Phoebe, the Stedmans' divorce, and the Queen Anne bedroom set. The set was elegant. There were two chests, one slightly larger than the other, with scroll tops that had carved urns in the center; the four-poster bed had a canopy. She had seen a bed like it in a museum in New York City, and a book she had bought describing the collection stated that the bed was rare.

She wondered why Phoebe had called her. They had known each other since they were children, but they had never been close. They were as different as people could be. Phoebe had always been slender and vivacious, and people clustered around her like petals clinging to the center of an exotic flower. She wasn't beautiful, but she was striking-looking with her large dark eyes and lustrous black hair. Needles of jealousy pricked Adele's memory. Their families had summered at the same beach. Adele pictured herself, plump and freckled, her nose a tender, peeling pink, sitting alone on the sand watching Phoebe, who tanned to a glowing honey brown, flirting with admiring boys who followed her like ants trailing spilled sugar.

So Phoebe was getting a divorce. It wasn't surprising. Marriage was a serious business, yet it hadn't changed Phoebe a bit. She was the same as she had always been, as capricious as a butterfly. Even with cleaning help, Phoebe couldn't keep her house in order. Adele smiled with self-justification as she recalled a tiny cobweb she had spotted in a corner of the powder room at the Stedmans'

Christmas party. Her recollection took some of the sting out of her other memories of the party; she had made a fool of herself that night, carrying on nonstop about the Stedmans' house and their beautiful bedroom set. Phoebe certainly had a flair for decorating.

By Tuesday, Adele was no longer thinking about Phoebe. She spent part of the day ironing and in the afternoon prepared Stan's favorite dinner—stuffed pork chops, homemade apple sauce, and chocolate cake. While she worked, humming tunelessly, she mentally arranged and rearranged the Queen Anne furniture in her bedroom until every piece was placed to her satisfaction. She was glad that the room was spacious (it was the full width of the front of the house) because the possibilities seemed endless, and nearly all of them were pleasing. Her reveries would have been blissful if it weren't for the hole in the house. Occasionally the accident of the morning before intruded in her thoughts, spoiling her pleasant daydreams like a sudden thunderstorm dampening a picnic. How, she wondered, could she tell Stan about his car and the damage she had done?

* * *

It was dark and starless when Stan Heussler came home. He parked Adele's car in the garage and walked slowly toward the house, trying to recall whether he had checked his clothing for lipstick stains and traces of perfume before he packed. Stan had spent Monday evening in Pittsburgh with a waitress, a tall, leggy blonde; she didn't leave his hotel room until dawn. He had packed in a rush, anxious to be on time for his first appointment, a breakfast meeting with one of his best customers. His day had been both successful and exhausting, and he had slept on the plane coming home, his dreams a happy hodgepodge of new orders and the delights of the blonde waitress,

Gladys. It didn't occur to him that he might have been careless until he turned onto Giffort Street from Hewett Avenue. He usually checked his clothes and sent any items needing special attention to the hotel laundry with money and instructions to ship the clothing home. Over the years there had been occasional packages from hotel laundries sent to the Heusslers' house, which Adele thought was not only considerate, but a measure of the high regard people had for her husband. She had never heard of anyone but Stan receiving forgotten shirts, handkerchiefs, and underwear from hotels, all freshly laundered.

The aroma of baking pork chops greeted Stan when he entered the house, instantly enveloping him in guilt. Without removing his coat, he raced upstairs with surprising quickness for a man of his bulk and disappeared behind his bedroom door, where he tore open his overnight case. Then, in a frenzy, like a man looking for a ticket to salvation, he searched through his dirty linen for evidence of his indiscretion. A low, nervous whistle escaped his lips when he spotted a red lipstick smudge on the corner of a handkerchief. Perspiring, he stuffed the handkerchief into his pants pocket until he could dispose of it later when he took out the trash.

Adele had intended to tell Stan about her Monday morning accident before she talked about the bedroom set. To act otherwise would be cheating, she had reasoned, like cleaning a room without moving the furniture. But when they were sitting alone in the living room after the children went to bed, she found it impossible to broach the subject. She wanted that bedroom set so badly, and Stan seemed to be in such a receptive mood. He had acted unusually glad to see her when he came home, and he had eaten his dinner with relish, though it was obvious from the heavy shadow of his beard and the puffiness under his eyes that he had had a long day. She had also been afraid that the children might talk about the hole in the house, but neither child mentioned it. "Phoebe Stedman called," she said after fussing for a while with a milk-glass candy dish filled with cellophane-wrapped sour balls on the maple table next to her chair. There were pieces of milk glass scattered around the room—fluted candy dishes, a cigarette box, and candlesticks—that were as comfortingly monotonous as the pale blue walls and carpeting. "She and Jack are getting a divorce."

Stan shifted nervously on the overstuffed sofa, conscious of the problems he would have had if he hadn't confiscated the lipstick-smudged handkerchief, while Adele continued. "They're selling their bedroom set," she said, so intent on winning his approval for the purchase that she didn't notice his reaction. "You remember the set, don't you? We saw it at their Christmas party when Phoebe took us through the house. It's magnificent, and it's perfect for our bedroom."

Stan didn't remember the set; wood furniture looked pretty much the same to him, whether it was colonial or provincial. He liked machines. They were the first family on Giffort Street to have a television set, a clothes dryer, and a dishwasher. He had bought them himself, the newest, latest modern gadgets. And now she wanted used bedroom furniture. "What's wrong with our bedroom set?" he said.

"Nothing," Adele said, "but it can't compare to the Queen Anne bedroom set. We can give our bedroom furniture to Gail. She still has the chest in her room that we bought when she was a baby. It's time we replaced it."

"I suppose so," he said. "How much are they asking?"

"Twenty-five hundred dollars."

"Twenty-five hundred dollars!" he said, leaping off the sofa. "I could trade in my Buick for a new Cadillac for that kind of money! It has under ten thousand miles, and there isn't a scratch on it."

Adele flinched at the mention of the scratchless car. "The set is at least one-hundred-years old. Phoebe said something about it being made around 1850 when she showed it to us."

"Well, this is 1950, and I could go to Rashman's tomorrow and buy the nicest bedroom set in the store for five hundred bucks," Stan said, rising on his toes to emphasize the ridiculousness of her reasoning. "It's crazy to buy old furniture for five times more than a new set will cost."

"Antiques are an investment," Adele said earnestly. "Phoebe could get more money for it if she wanted to."

"Then let her. Why did she call you anyway? You and Phoebe were never close friends."

"I guess she knew how much I admired it. I couldn't stop talking about the set the night of their party. I'll feel like a fool when I tell her that I don't want it since I practically said 'yes' when she called yesterday. She wanted to know as soon as possible. I should have tried to reach you last night."

Stan's eyes, which were small and dark, bulged with alarm. What if Adele had called while he was out of his room getting ice and what's-her-name, the waitress had answered? "No, no," he said, gesturing with his hands as if he were trying to rub the idea out of her head. "I don't want you to call me unless it's an absolute emergency. You know that. I would have been worried that something had happened to you or one of the kids. You did the right thing."

"But what will I say to Phoebe? Adele asked, her eyes welling with tears.

"Tell her we'll take the damn furniture," he said

Adele didn't mention the hole in the house until they were in bed. "I had a little accident yesterday," she began after the lamps were out. "Some shingles were ripped off the house, but Gail and I weren't hurt."

Stan's mind had already slipped into the fog that precedes sleep. "That's good," he mumbled. Minutes later he was wide awake. "How did the shingles get ripped off?"

"You forgot to back the Buick into the garage. I had to take Gail to school and skidded on the ice. It was awful. The car slid every which way, and Gail went flying head first into the back seat. It's a miracle she wasn't injured. But the house, I feel just terrible about the house!"

"Never mind the house! What happened to the car?"

"The bumper's slightly bent and there are a few scratches, but you can hardly notice them. It shouldn't be too hard to fix."

Stan gnashed his teeth. His Buick, his beautiful Roadmaster, scratched and bent!

"You're not angry, are you?" she said when he remained silent. Her voice sounded strained and small in the darkness. "I'm sorry, really I am. I picked up the shingles hoping I could save them, but they were splintered into pieces. Do you think we'll be able to get new ones that match?"

"Probably," he said, jerking the covers as he rolled onto his side. He lay awake long after she fell asleep, stewing over his car. Although he had always believed Adele to be incapable of deviousness, for the first time he began to have doubts about her. She was more concerned about those stupid shingles than she was about his car, and she didn't tell him about the accident until he agreed to buy that damn bedroom set. He wondered how extensive the damage to his Buick really was and whether he should get dressed and go out to the garage with a flashlight to check. But there was no point to it since that damage had already been done.

* * *

The Queen Anne bedroom set was delivered to the

Heusslers on the last Thursday in March. Adele hovered anxiously around the movers and was relieved when the furniture was finally in place, undamaged. She had the four-poster bed set up in the center of the long front wall between the windows, with the bed tables on each side. Stan's dresser, which was the larger of the two chests, was placed several feet away from a window on the left side of the room; her dresser was on the opposite wall near the closet. Although the set didn't come close to filling the room (there was still enough space for a pair of chairs, a table, and perhaps a small desk), its effect was overpowering. The pale green walls, deeper green throw rugs, and plain white curtains seemed to recede, to be obliterated by the extraordinary beauty of the black cherry wood and gleaming brass fittings. Adele gazed at the graceful pediment top of the larger chest with admiration, finding it hard to believe that she owned such magnificent furniture. She would definitely have to redecorate.

Instead of doing her usual Thursday grocery shopping, she spent the day polishing the furniture and lining the drawers. She wiped the wood gently, lovingly, starting at the top of the large pieces and working down to the graceful cabriole legs. She lingered over each piece, tracing the rich, undulating grain of the wood with her polishing cloth, then lined the drawers with heavy white paper, measuring and cutting until each lining fit precisely. When she was finished, she vacuumed the mattress; it was covered in gold ticking that had the look and feel of satin, and it was spotless, as Phoebe had promised. There was no need to have a new mattress made, she decided, walking to the hall linen closet where crisply ironed sheets and pillow cases were stacked in neat rows. The sheets and blankets fit skimpily over the mattress; she would have to buy new bed linens and have a bedspread and matching canopy made.

It was past three thirty when Tommy came into the bedroom. Adele was arranging Stan's shirts in the deep bottom drawer of his dresser. "What's for dinner?" Tommy said.

Adele jumped, startled at the sound of her son's voice, then turned and stared at him as if he were an apparition. "I'm hungry," he said, shifting his weight from his right leg to his left.

"Oh, no," Adele said, suddenly aware that she had lost all sense of time and had spent the entire day in the bedroom. There was nothing in the house for dinner except frankfurters and beans. Stan would complain all evening; frankfurters and beans gave him distress. As she rushed downstairs to the kitchen with Tommy close behind, she realized that she had forgotten to eat lunch. She hadn't thought about food all day, yet strangely, she wasn't hungry.

When Stan came home, Adele insisted that he go directly to their bedroom. "I can't wait until you see the set," she said, following him. "It's even nicer than I remembered."

They stood in the center of the room. The late afternoon light, cool against the green walls, played on the Queen Anne furniture, brushing the deep wood and brass drawer pulls with a patina so rich that it seemed almost alive to Adele. But Stan, looking first at the bed, then at the chests, saw nothing except twenty-five-hundred-dollars-worth of old furniture sitting on squatty legs. He had been quieter than usual since her accident. He had arranged to have the house and car repaired without comment, and she, anxious to forget the matter, had escaped into her housekeeping routine as if nothing had happened.

"Well," she said, looking at him expectantly, "what do you think?"

He scowled and pursed lips; his mouth was small and thin, incongruous with his broad features. "I think I'd like a beer."

Adele lingered in the bedroom after he left. Her

disappointment in his reaction, which had at first crushed, then bewildered her, finally turned to anger. He had no appreciation for fine things, no appreciation at all! She went downstairs glad that that they were having frankfurters and beans for dinner.

The weather turned warm over the weekend. The temperature jumped from the low thirties to the mid-sixties, and a heavy rain that began late Saturday and continued through Sunday washed the final traces of winter from Giffort Street. Gritty snow mounds that had lined the curbs disappeared, and sagging gray snowmen dissolved in Giffort Street backyards, their withered carrot noses and coal eyes sinking into soggy winter-brown grass. On Monday the sun was out again. The air smelled sweet and the buds on the elm trees swelled with the promise of spring.

Adele was up early Monday morning. She was frying French toast for breakfast when she heard Stan call "A-dellle" in a tone so calamitous that she knew she must come at once. She scurried out of the kitchen and ran upstairs with a metal spatula in one hand, the hem of her bathrobe in the other, wondering what could have happened.

Stan was waiting for her at their bedroom door dressed in a white undershirt and gray suit pants; a jagged piece of toilet tissue with a dark center of dried blood was sticking to his chin. "I need a shirt," he said, his face red with frustration. "I have an appointment with Elliot Brownell at nine o'clock and I have no intention of meeting him in my underwear."

"Your shirts are in the bottom two drawers of your dresser," Adele said, annoyed that he had made her run up the stairs for nothing. She thrust the spatula into his hand and went directly to the large Queen Anne chest.

Stan watched her, glowering, while she struggled with the drawers. She tugged on the brass pulls until they left ridges in her fingers, but the drawers wouldn't budge. "They're stuck," she said, turning reluctantly to face him.

"You're damn right they're stuck!" he said, pointing the spatula at her. "Any suggestions?"

She shook her head, too upset to think clearly.

"Well, I have one," Stan said, rising on the balls of his feet. Rotund in his undershirt, he looked like a top about to spin. "I'm going down to the basement for my hammer and chisel. I'll force those damn drawers open!"

"No!" Adele cried. She back up and pressed her body protectively against the chest. "I'll figure something out."

"What?"

"Your shirts are in the washing machine now…"

"All of them?" he interrupted. "You mean *all* the shirts I own are either incarcerated in that piece of junk or soaking in the wash? I'm probably the only man on Giffort Street who got up this morning and discovered that he didn't have a shirt to wear, thanks to his wife!"

Adele had more than her share of insecurities, but there was one area in which she had never doubted herself: she took care of her family as well as any woman alive. The color drained from her face. "You'll have a shirt!" she said, storming out of the bedroom.

She was halfway down the stairs when she smelled something burning. "The French toast!" she cried, racing to the kitchen. Quickly, she turned off the burner and placed the frying pan, smoking and sizzling, on a metal hot pad in the center of the stove. After she opened the double windows above the sink to let out the acrid smoke that had filled her immaculate kitchen, she set out cereal bowls and a box of Rice Krispies for the children's breakfast, then went to the basement where she stood in front of the Bendix, watching Stan's shirts through the round window of the machine while they sloshed and spun through the final wash.

The Heusslers didn't speak to each other again that morning. Adele ironed Stan's white shirt as if she were imagining it on his back, flattening the garment with such fury that the ironing board teetered dangerously from side to side. When she was finished, she gave him the shirt wordlessly and retreated to the basement until she heard him leave the house.

Whenever Adele was nervous or upset she turned to food for solace, but by the time Stan left the house, her indignation had grown far beyond a craving for sweets. There wasn't a woman on Giffort Street who worked harder than she did, and it was clear to her that her efforts were unappreciated. Instead of reaching for a piece of candy, she looked in the yellow pages of the telephone book for cabinet makers and started making calls. The fourth man she spoke with, a fellow named Gilbert Thomson, seemed to know a great deal about antiques. After she described the Queen Anne bedroom set, he agreed to look at the drawers that afternoon, though he generally didn't bother with minor repairs.

Adele did her usual Monday wash while she waited for Gilbert Thomson. She stripped the children's beds, folded underwear warm from the dryer, and ironed Stan's shirts and put them on hangers to avoid trouble on Tuesday. But rather than make a cherry pie as she had originally planned, she decided to serve JELL-O for dessert instead.

Gilbert Thomson didn't arrive until almost five o'clock. He was tall and spare and had sharp, clean features. "Sorry I'm late," he said, brushing a shock of gray hair off his forehead. "I couldn't get away earlier."

"I'm glad you could come," Adele said, ushering him past the living room up the stairs.

Gilbert Thomson's blue eyes sparkled when he entered the Heusslers' bedroom. He had climbed the stairs reluctantly after he had glimpsed the colonial furniture in the living room, sure that he was wasting his time. But the

Queen Anne bedroom set more than surpassed his earlier expectations. He walked directly to the bed and ran his hands down a post, then stooped to examine the cabriole leg and pad foot. His fingers, which were long and calloused, moved knowledgeably over the beautifully carved wood. "Where did you get this set?" he asked, rising.

"A friend sold it to me," Adele said, disconcerted. Thomson's eyes were darting around the room, and his interest in the bed disturbed her. "I called about the large chest. The bottom two drawers won't open, and my husband's furious."

He went to the dresser and tried the drawers. They wouldn't budge. Then he carefully pulled the top drawer out of the cabinet and placed the contents, stacks of brown and black socks, on the floor. He turned the drawer on its side and examined the dove-tailed joints; they were clearly the work of a master cabinetmaker, and the drawer guide was nothing short of perfection.

"Can the bottom drawers be fixed?" Adele said, irritated that Thomson was lingering over a drawer that worked.

"There's nothing wrong with them," he said, sliding the drawer back into the chest.

"Then why won't they open? They worked fine last week."

"Last week?"

"The set was delivered last Thursday."

"That probably explains it," said Thomson, who had been puzzled by the sticking drawers. "Wood is kind of like people in that it becomes accustomed to its environment. Solid hardwood like this usually isn't affected too much by humidity, unless there isn't enough and the wood starts to dry But this set was moved from one place to another, and we had a drastic temperature change and heavy rain over the weekend. The wood must have swelled, though it's rare in furniture of this quality. The drawers will be working fine by the end of the week."

"But I need them to work now—today," she said, trying to get his attention.

"That's impossible," Thomson replied in a faraway voice. He was examining the top of the chest. He hands moved across the arches until they met on the center urn, which he studied with his fingertips, as if he were memorizing the delicate carving.

"But my husband threatened to open the drawers with a hammer and chisel!"

"What?" Thomson said. He looked at Adele as if she had just blasphemed.

"If you can't get those drawers to work, my husband will force them open," she said, her cheeks flushed with agitation. "He thinks this furniture is overpriced junk."

Gilbert Thomson studied Adele as carefully as he had examined the Queen Anne furniture. He noted her high color, her nervous wringing of her hands, and her over-bright eyes. "I don't know how much you paid for the set," he said, intent on preserving the furniture since it was apparent to him that she didn't know the value of what she had. "But I can get you at least five thousand dollars above my commission and have it out of here by the end of the week."

Five thousand dollars not including his commission. The set was worth more than double what they had paid for it. Adele took a deep breath. "We'll keep it," she said.

Stan was halfway down Giffort Street when he saw Gilbert Thomson's station wagon back out of his driveway. He wondered who had been visiting so close to dinner time and asked Gail. "Some man," Gail said, her eyes fixed on the television.

"Why was he here?"

"I don't know," she said, moving closer to the screen. "He was upstairs with Mom in her bedroom."

Adele said nothing about the visitor during dinner. She served pot roast, potatoes, and carrots with her usual efficiency and dished out raspberry JELL-O for dessert. "Where's the whipped cream?" Tommy said, scowling at the gelatin as if he'd been cheated.

"There is no whipped cream," Adele said.

Stan waited for Adele to say something about the man who had been in their bedroom, but she sat quietly all evening in a corner of the living room thumbing through a book about antiques. Her silence disturbed him. There had been a man in his house, in his bedroom, and he wanted to know about it. But he would be damned before he would ask her. He went upstairs to check on the dresser drawers. They were still stuck. What had that man been doing in his bedroom with his wife—in broad daylight while his children were watching television—if the drawers hadn't been repaired? The muscles in his chest tightened with suspicion. He traveled more than most men, yet not once had she ever initiated sex, not even when he had been away for as long as two weeks. She had to be getting satisfaction somewhere, he reasoned, his mind so twisted with growing anger that he completely forgot about Adele's reticence in bed, her self-consciousness and extreme modesty that had continued from their wedding night throughout the years of their marriage. He had done everything he could to protect her. She had no knowledge of his infidelities, not even the slightest hint, and this was his payment! And in his own bed with his children downstairs!

On Tuesday morning Adele awakened refreshed after nine hours of untroubled sleep and told Stan that he would find fresh shirts hanging in the closet. "Then the drawers are working?" he said, knowing very well that they weren't. He had had a sleepless night; his eyes were bloodshot and his voice was gravelly.

"The drawers will be working by the end of the week," she said, buttoning a full, flower-print bathrobe.

"And you might be interested in knowing that the set is worth more than double what you paid for it."

Stan sat upright in bed. "Who told you that nonsense?"

"I had it appraised yesterday," she said, with a note of triumph in her voice. "An expert on antiques, Gilbert Thomson, told me he could get over five thousand dollars for the set, plus his commission."

"I don't believe it!" Stan said, wondering if she were using this Gilbert as a cover-up for her other activities, about which he now had little doubt.

"It's true. You can call him yourself. He was here late yesterday afternoon. You missed him by only a few minutes."

"Really?" he said, torn between his desire to believe her and the strength of his doubts.

"Really," she said. "I'm going shopping today to look for wallpaper and carpeting."

"What wallpaper and carpeting?"

"The wallpaper and carpeting for our bedroom."

He threw back the covers and leaped to his feet. "I didn't agree to wallpaper and carpeting."

"The room needs redecorating. I don't know how you can possibly object since I've already doubled your investment."

He stared at her, incredulous. "I thought…I thought we discuss large purchases before making decisions."

"No," she said, "you buy what you want, and I have to ask your permission to get what I want."

"That's not true," he said, rising on his toes.

"Yes, it is. You bought the dishwasher, the disposal, and the dryer because you wanted them. You shopped without me and picked the models you liked."

"But you use them," he said, rocking back on his heels as though he couldn't believe what he was hearing.

"Not well enough according to you," she said,

stalking out of the bedroom.

Adele spent the week shopping. She pored over wallpaper books, agonizing over papers until she finally selected one that had wildflowers scattered randomly against a white background. She ordered matching fabric for draperies and vacillated between carpet samples, unable to decide between a Wedgewood-blue plush and a soft rose sculptured design. It was difficult for her to make decisions. Ordinarily she brought wallpaper books and carpet samples home for Stan's approval, but their relationship was strained to the point where neither one knew what to say to the other.

While Adele waited for Stan's apology, full of self-righteousness, he became increasingly distant. He could not understand why she felt so abused when he had done everything he could to make life pleasant for her. Thousands of women would be grateful to have a husband as considerate as he was. He planned an unnecessary trip to Pittsburgh at the end of April. Since Adele wasn't grateful for his attention, he would spend time with that waitress, who certainly knew how to make a man happy.

The dresser drawers opened on Friday, as Gilbert Thomson had predicted. Adele would have been elated if it weren't for the fact that she and Stan weren't speaking. Not only were the drawers working, but she had lost five pounds. She had never lost that much weight in such a short time, and without any effort. It must be the simple meals, she thought, visualizing herself a perfect size eight. If that's what it took, there would be no more fattening foods in the house.

* * *

The trouble between the Heusslers might have ended if it hadn't been for Meddie. Adele met the Whittakers' maid on Thursday, better than a week after her

Tuesday morning outburst. Meddie, wearing white oxfords and a severe black coat that matched her black purse and black satchel, entered the Blue Start Supermarket as Adele was leaving. "Hello, Meddie," Adele said, pausing near the door with a cart full of groceries. She hadn't seen Meddie in months and waited for the woman to return her greeting, but Meddie walked past her without a glance of recognition.

Meddie's snub paralyzed Adele. She stood trembling while people pushed grocery carts around her until she finally left the store, ashen. Late that night, unable to sleep, she told Stan what had happened. "I saw Meddie today," she said after she had awakened him. "She walked past me without saying hello."

When Adele had nudged him on the shoulder, Stan had become instantly aroused. He had been miserable for over a week and was eager to reconcile. "Forget about it," he said, reaching for her breast.

Adele pushed his had away. "Forget about it! How can I forget about it? Don't you understand? I'm the only woman on Giffort Street that Meddie has ever conversed with besides Bernice Whittaker, and now she won't even say hello."

"So what," he said, reaching for her again. "That scarecrow has never talked to me, and I've managed to survive."

Adele moved to the edge of the bed. He was right: Meddie had never said hello to him. And now Meddie wasn't saying hello to her. Soon everyone on Giffort Street would know. She would feel humiliated in front of the neighbors, and it was probably all his fault.

Stan inched closed to Adele "I don't know why you're so upset. You're carrying on as if Meddie is someone important. She's nothing but a nanny and a maid."

Adele felt his hand move down her back and began to sob. She had hoped that he would at least try to understand, but all he was interested in was sex. "Why are you crying?" he said, his ardor cooling as she continued to weep.

"You don't understand!"

"You're damned right I don't understand! I'm your husband. You haven't talked to me in days, but that doesn't seem to bother you. Instead, you're crying over that witch who lives across the street because she didn't say hello. I've done everything I can to make you happy. You have a beautiful home, two fine children, and the most expensive bedroom set on the block. And what have I gotten in return? Silence and skimpy dinners! You haven't baked a cake or a pie all week. I've had it! I was willing to overlook everything that's happened—the scratches on my car, the bent bumper, the hole in the house, your remarks about the appliances, the money you're spending to redecorate with profits we haven't made—but now I'm not sure that I can. I'm owed an apology, and I expect one!"

Adele didn't apologize. He had been insensitive and uncaring, demanding and unreasonable. She had always tried her best to please him, and he had not shown any appreciation. None. Meddie got more respect at the Whittakers' than she did in her own home. And now he wanted an apology. Well, he wouldn't get one from her!

The rift between the Heusslers widened from a crack into a chasm as the weeks passed. They spoke to each other only when necessary, and then with exaggerated politeness. Their anger spread through the house like an infectious disease. Soon the Heussler children, who were generally well-behaved, though spoiled, began to bicker. They picked on each other constantly as the days grew longer and hotter. Adele continued to lose weight. Dieting became an obsession: she counted calories as rigorously as she had once scrubbed floors. By mid-August, she had lost thirty-seven pounds and could wear a size six. Her face lost its plump prettiness; there were cadaverous hollows around her eyes, and her collar bones protruded. She started to have her nails manicured every week and hired a cleaning woman to do the heavy housework with money left over from her household allowance. They no longer ate pies and pastries, and she prepared salads, chicken, and broiled fish instead of meat. Spots on the walls and floors that the cleaning woman missed bothered her, but she didn't have the energy to clean them herself. She blamed her lethargy on the summer heat and spent entire afternoons in her bedroom, lying on the Queen Anne bed. The soft rose carpeting and clusters of wildflowers soothed her nerves, which were raw from the children's squabbling. She gazed at the Queen Anne bedroom set for hours, awed by its beauty. The furniture seemed impervious to time, to trouble, to an impending feeling of doom that followed her step-by-step like her own shadow.

Stan traveled as often as he could. He went to Pittsburgh, to Cleveland, to Erie, and spent nights with barmaids, waitresses, and secretaries. The women became a confusion of names and faces to him, of irritating giggles and unfamiliar bodies. He slept badly, often awakening in the middle of the night in strange hotel rooms longing for the smell of Murphy's oil soap and furniture polish. It seemed to him that his life had narrowed to the confines of his suitcase, which was a jumble of dirty socks and wrinkled shirts. He craved peace and order, but when he came home he was greeted by the noise of his children's fighting and the sight of his wife, wasting away before his eyes. Everything had changed. Gone were the rich desserts, the aroma of roasting meat, the clean smells of oil soap, furniture polish, and wax. Only the elms, standing in leafy silence at the curbs, remained the same. There were moments when he thought he would do anything to restore the tranquility that had become a dream to him. But then he would remember what had happened, how unfairly Adele had treated him, and his anger would come rushing back.

He would not apologize. Instead, he planned another trip.

The Heussler children went back to school the Wednesday after Labor Day. Adele shooed them out the door, still bickering about the raisin toast they had fought over at breakfast, and went down to the basement to start the wash, which she had postponed doing because of the holiday. After she emptied the contents of the clothes chute into an oversize wicker basket, she sorted the clothing by color into smaller baskets, checking each piece for stains that needed special attention; the stained items were piled separately on the floor. She was almost finished when she noticed a smudge on the shoulder of one of Stan's white shirts. Wondering how he could have gotten a spot in such an odd place, she walked to the windows over the stationary tubs and held the shirt up to the light. It was a lipstick stain, nacreous pink and nearly two inches long. She dropped the shirt as if it were contaminated. She had had a premonition that something was going to happen, but she hadn't expected this. Weeping, she climbed the basement stairs, grasping the railing for support like an old woman. When she was calm enough to speak without sobbing, she called their lawyer. He was with a client, the secretary said. Adele insisted that she had to see him and made an appointment for one thirty that afternoon.

It was impossible to remain in the house after she showered and dressed. Adele felt his presence everywhere, his and the nameless woman whose lipstick stuck to the shoulder of his shirt like an epaulet. She tried to imagine the woman, whether she was blonde or brunette, fat or thin, but couldn't. Then she recalled the packages they had received from hotels over the years, freshly laundered shirts and underwear that Stan had *forgotten*. How stupid she had been! How naïve! She ran out of the house as if someone were chasing her and drove downtown, though it was only ten o'clock.

Adele wandered aimlessly through department

stores, her eyes glazed; she walked past several people she knew without seeing them. It was close to noon when she stepped out of a half-filled elevator in Rickard's department store and felt someone's hand on her arm. It was Phoebe Stedman. "We were in the elevator together," Phoebe said, "but when you didn't say hello, I began to wonder if it was really you. At first I wasn't sure because you've lost so much weight. Have you been ill?"

Adele withdrew her arm. "I've been dieting," she replied stiffly.

"You've certainly been successful," Phoebe said. "Are you downtown for something special?"

"I…I have an appointment with…with the doctor."

"Soon?"

"At one thirty."

"Then we'll have time for lunch."

"I'm really not hungry," Adele said, anxious to get away, "and I have a few errands to do."

"Oh, come on, Adele," Phoebe said. "I'm moving to Phoenix on Friday, so this is the last chance we'll have to get together. We can take the elevator up to the Garden Room and be seated before the lunch rush."

Before Adele could protest further, Phoebe stepped into an open elevator. Adele followed reluctantly, wondering how she could get away without being rude. The elevator doors closed. Miserable, Adele tried to think of another excuse, one that Phoebe would have to accept, but her mind wouldn't function. "Eighth floor, Garden Room," called the elevator operator. Adele's shoulders sagged. "That's us," Phoebe said, stepping forward.

A hostess led the two women to a corner table that was set against a white trellis from which artificial roses hung in perpetual bloom. An ivy plant in a yellow ceramic pot was centered on the green tablecloth. After a waitress took their order, Phoebe lit a cigarette. "How are Stan and the children?" she said.

"Fine," Adele said, feeling ill. She had to talk about something—anything—but Stan and the children. "When did you decide to move to Phoenix?"

"A couple of months ago. My parents have been living there for five years; the climate has helped my father's arthritis. Donna and Joanne are living with them now so they could start school at the beginning of the term."

"Didn't Jack object? Won't he miss the girls?"

Phoebe inhaled deeply on the cigarette. "I doubt it," she said. "He's too busy playing with his secretary."

Adele watched Phoebe crush the cigarette in an ash tray. Her motions were aggressive, nervous. It occurred to Adele that she had never seen Phoebe smoke before. "Won't you miss your friends?" she said, noticing that Phoebe's makeup was applied too heavily. She was still striking-looking, but there was a brittleness in her face that reminded Adele of a mask.

Phoebe laughed. It was a forced laugh with none of the vivaciousness that Adele had always envied. "Divorce changes things," she said, lighting another cigarette. "My friends are willing to see me as long as their husbands aren't around. Going out to lunch when I can afford it and afternoons of bridge are my big social activities now. It's the old story of the threatening, unattached woman grabbing whatever she can. The worst part is that I'm not interested in their husbands, although nearly all of them have managed to proposition me anyway."

The waitress came to their table carrying a julienne salad for Adele and a club sandwich for Phoebe. "Coffee, ladies?" she said.

"Yes, please," Phoebe said.

After the waitress left, Adele picked at her salad, embarrassed. "I've made you uncomfortable, haven't I?" Phoebe said, studying Adele.

"N-No," Adele said.

"Sure I have," Phoebe said, her eyes narrowing. "You've always been such a prude, Adele. Let me tell you something: most of the marriages in this city aren't any better than mine was. Jack and I fought a lot, but some of my friends' husbands have been cheating on them for years. They don't talk about it, but they know, and so does everyone else."

Adele's face turned a sickly white. "Then why don't they divorce them?"

"Because they're smarter than I am," Phoebe said. "Do you know what my life is like? Do you have any idea? This is 1950, but I feel as though I'm living in the Middle Ages. I stay home night after night or go out with losers, men who have never married because no one will have them. It's so damn lonely. There are no decent men around, not for a thirty-six-year-old woman with two children, unless I want to lure someone away from his wife, which would be too messy. It just isn't worth it. I may be divorced, but I'm not cheap. I still have my self-respect, and I intend to keep it. I suppose, if I live long enough, I'll meet a widower, but at that point I probably won't want to be bothered. That's why I'm moving to Phoenix. I'm going to use my settlement money to set myself up as a decorator. I'm pretty good at it, and I'll have something to do besides wait for my alimony check. Originally I had planned to finish college so I could teach, but when I went to pick up an application and saw all those kids in bobby socks and penny loafers, I turned the car around and drove home. I don't know why I'm telling you this. I guess I've kept it inside so long that it had to spill out."

While Phoebe was speaking, Adele slowly realized that all of her troubles had started with Phoebe's call offering to sell her the Queen Anne bedroom set. And now Phoebe was giving her a reading into her future. "Why…Why did you offer to sell the Queen Anne bedroom set to me?" she managed to ask.

"Oh, that," Phoebe said, picking up a triangle of sandwich. "I really don't know."

"You must have had a reason," Adele said. "You could have gotten double the price from someone else."

"I guess so," Phoebe said, dabbing her napkin at a speck of mayonnaise that was clinging to a corner of her mouth.

Adele leaned across the table, clutching the green tablecloth. "Then why me?"

"Well, if you must know, I felt that you deserved it."

"What do you mean, *I deserved it*?"

"You irritated me. You were always so sensible, and everything you did had to be perfect. When we were growing up, I felt that you looked down on me because I didn't measure up to your standards. I can still remember those looks of disapproval on your face."

Adele gasped. "Those weren't looks of disapproval. It was envy. You were so thin and so popular. I would have given anything to be like you."

Phoebe smiled ironically. "It really doesn't matter anymore, does it?" she said, the rancor in her voice gone. "You wanted to know about the bedroom set. Jack and I had our troubles like any other couple, but we managed to survive them until we bought the Queen Anne furniture. Everything fell apart after that. We were at each other's throats until we had no choice but to separate. I suppose it would have eventually happened anyway, but at the time I blamed the bedroom set. Then I thought of you and your immaculate house, your well-mannered children and your adoring husband. Your perfect life. It seems crazy now, but I honestly believed that that antique furniture…"

Adele didn't wait for Phoebe to finish. She opened her purse and extracted a five dollar bill from her wallet, which she placed next to her plate. Then she fled, moving as quickly as she could around crowded tables, avoiding waitresses balancing trays, until she reached the entrance of the Garden Room. "Excuse me, where can I find a telephone?" she asked the hostess.

"In the alcove opposite the elevators on your right," the hostess said.

Adele ran past clusters of shoppers waiting in front of the elevators and entered the first unoccupied booth. After she closed the door, she looked in the telephone directory for the lawyer's number. "This is Mrs. Heussler," she said when the secretary answered. "Please tell Mr. Carswell that I won't be keeping my appointment. I'm sorry for any inconvenience I might have caused him."

Before the secretary had a chance to reply, Adele replaced the receiver. She flipped through the directory again and put another dime in the slot. Her call was answered after the fifth ring. "Hello, Mr. Thomson," she said, sighing with relief. "This is Mrs. Heussler. I don't know if you remember me, but I own a Queen Anne bedroom set. You came to my house in April to look at drawers that were sticking."

"Yes," Thomson said, "I remember."

"I've decided to sell the set."

"Are you sure?"

"I'm positive," she said, "and I want it out of the house as soon as possible."

Adele didn't drive directly home. Instead, she stopped at the Hewett Avenue Meat Market and ordered extra-thick pork chops. Then she went to Creigle's bakery and bought a chocolate cake and a dozen Parker House rolls. Her step was as light as a young girl's as she carried her packages to the car.

AN AUTHENTIC HERO

Everyone who lived on Giffort Street knew the Kenway boys, Rodman and Dale. Rod Kenway was the Giffort Street celebrity. He was a rugged-looking, powerfully-built young man who had a self-assured smile and an athlete's grace, and no one who watched him playing ball in the street as a youngster was surprised at his success. His picture was often in the evening paper, not only on the sports pages for his exploits on the football and baseball fields, but also in the local news section as a leader among his peers. It seemed as natural for Rod Kenway to win awards as it was for the sun to rise in the morning. On a street where children sensed at an early age that they were expected to exceed or at least match the achievements of their ambitious parents, Rod Kenway was an undisputed winner; there wasn't a man or woman who lived on Giffort Street who wouldn't have been proud to have him for a son. But if these same people were asked which Kenway brother they were partial to, it would be Dale. "That Dale," they would say, the expressions on their faces softening, "he's a decent kid. A really decent kid."

Dale Kenway was two years younger than Rod. He was small-boned and had even features that were unremarkable except for his eyes: his left eye was a startling blue, his right eye a dreamy brown. Dale was happy with the world as he found it; he had time to putter and time to dream. He spent hours building model airplanes out of balsa wood and paper, not because he wanted to become a pilot, but simply because he enjoyed constructing the planes. He liked the clean lines of their skeletons, the perfection of their form after he painstakingly covered and painted them. The finished airplanes were suspended on thin wires attached to the ceiling over his bed; he spent hours lying on his back looking at them, his brown eye soft and hazy, his blue eye the color of a clear summer sky. When he wasn't building airplanes, Dale was tinkering with machines. At one time or another he must have fixed every lawnmower on Giffort Street. He could listen to a car engine and know immediately if the carburetor needed adjusting. His mechanical ability was like a sixth sense, coming to him as easily as he breathed.

Grace and Frank Kenway didn't know Dale had dropped out of college before the end of the second semester of his freshman year until Dale received a draft notice late in the spring of 1951. College had been their idea. It was not so much an idea as it was an assumption. Frank Kenway had worked nights to put himself through college; since he was a college graduate, his sons could not achieve less. Rod was playing football at Princeton. They knew Dale wasn't a candidate for Princeton, but they were aghast when he told them that he wanted to be a mechanic. Dale saw that it was useless to argue, so he went to the local university and tried to like it. His grades were respectable, but he was unhappy. He wasn't learning anything he wanted to know. Hegel's philosophy and the tribal practices of the Arapesh wouldn't help him put new brake linings in a car. He stayed as long as he could, then wrote a letter to Dean Gerald Anderson, telling him that he had decided to leave. The letter, like Dale, was courteous and respectful. Dean Anderson wrote back, regretting Dale's decision and telling him that he would be welcome to return in the future if he so desired. Dale discarded the letter; he had no intention of returning.

Dale worked in a garage until his draft notice came. He left the house early in the morning, changed into coveralls, and returned in time for supper, his hands and fingernails scrubbed as clean as he could get them. The only one in the household who knew what Dale was doing was Grandpa Tarpin. Joe Tarpin was an irascible man who had strong opinions, which he was quick to express. When Dale told him, the old man was both pleased and upset. "You'll have to tell your parents," he said, flattered that the young man had confided him. He also felt justified, for he had warned Frank and Grace that it was a mistake to insist that Dale go to college.

"I want to wait," Dale said. "If I'm made a full mechanic before I tell them, maybe they'll accept it."

"Never! Your father is going to be mad as hell. He wants his sons to go to work wearing suits and ties. He's wrong, of course, and I'll be the first one to tell him," Grandpa said, a grin spreading across his bony face in anticipation of the moment. There was nothing he liked better than proving his son-in-law wrong. "I bought this house with money I earned in the plumbing business, and I'm proud of it. I had dirty hands and clean paychecks. But you have another problem, and that one isn't going to be easy to solve."

"What?" Dale said.

"The Korean War. You dropped out of school, so you're prime for the draft."

"I hadn't thought about that."

"You'll have to think about it now," Grandpa said. He turned abruptly and limped upstairs to his room before Dale could see tears in his eyes.

Dale went to work in a daze after the draft notice came. He couldn't stay home. His mother's eyes welled with tears when she looked at him, and his father was so furious that his jaw puffed up as if he'd had a tooth extracted whenever the draft notice was mentioned. Rod was back from Princeton and called his friends for advice, but they had none to offer other than getting Dale a physical exemption, which the Kenways would have to arrange. Grace wanted to call every doctor in the city. She was a pale, high-strung woman whose thin face was creased with worry. Frank forbid her to call. "But he could get killed," Grace said, weeping. She felt protective toward Dale, almost defensive about him, as if his eyes were somehow her fault. Both Frank and Rod had blue eyes; hers were brown. Dale had certainly inherited his small frame from her, a handicap for football.

"He won't be killed," Frank said too quickly, his voice lacking conviction. He was as concerned about Dale as Grace was, but he would not show any sign of weakness. Frank Kenway was a determined man. He had worked hard to establish a successful insurance agency and, like many men, had rationalized his drive, telling himself and others that he labored for his family until he believed it. He had plans for his sons, and now Dale had invited this disaster by going against his wishes. Dale had dropped out of school without his permission--without even consulting him! Since Dale had made the decision on his own, he would have to live with the consequences.

The Korean War became real to the people who lived on Giffort Street when they heard that Dale had been drafted. Until that time the war had been remote, a matter of newspaper headlines and radio and television reports of battles fought on the other side of the world. Everyone agreed that the Communists had to be crushed like the Japanese were six years earlier, but the war didn't seem real until Dale received his draft notice. He had grown up on Giffort Street; he was one of their own. Memories of World War II were stirred, still vivid and rosy with patriotism. We had won and we would win again. Nearly everyone on Giffort Street stopped at the Kenways to wish Dale well before he left for basic training. Silently, they hoped he would come home safely.

Grandpa Tarpin, who was usually so hungry for company that he waited for the mailman everyday just to chat for a minute or two, stayed in his room while the neighbors came and went. He sat on an old maple rocker that rested on a hooked rug, staring at his disfigured left foot. No one in the family, not even his daughter, knew exactly how his foot had been maimed. For a man who loved to talk, he was uncharacteristically quiet about his injury. The most he ever offered was that he had lost his toes in Cuba during the Spanish-American War. Grandpa stared at his foot for hours, rocking and thinking. He forgot about the mailman and looked up with rheumy brown eyes, as if awakened out of a dream, when he was called for meals.

* * *

Dale suffered through basic training. He thought that hell must be a lot like Kentucky in August. He broiled under the strong summer sun, longing for the shade of the Giffort Street elms. The humidity was unbearable; he felt as if he were drowning in sweat, and his skin was raw from insect bites. On nights when he didn't fall asleep instantly, his body numb with exhaustion, he lay on his cot trying to picture the airplanes that hung over his bed at home, but sometimes he could see nothing but the beams of the barracks in the moonlight, rough and ugly overhead. He would swallow hard then, and the muscles in his face would tighten.

The men in his company were young, most of them in their late teens. They came from the North and the South, from city streets, small towns, and farms. They were a feisty bunch, eager to prove themselves men and quick to sense weaknesses in each other. On the second day of basic training, Curtis Clay, a beefy boy from Mississippi who had an acne-ravaged face, noticed Dale's eyes at morning mess. "Ya'll look at them eyes," Clay said, pointing at Dale, "one blue and one brown. Ah had me a dawg like that once, a mongrel named Sam. One eye was yaller an' the other was brown. Sam was scart of his own shadow. He'd bark at it like crazy, then chase after it until his tongue hung out, not known' that he was chasin' after his own self. Dumb dawg. We figgered he was that way 'cause of his yaller eye. He was no good for nothin'."

Everyone at the table turned to stare at Dale. "Ain't you got nothin' to say?" the Southern boy prodded.

Dale continued to eat his oatmeal, which was gray and lumpy. No one else at the table was eating.

Clayton's face broke into a mean grin. "Since you ain't got nothin' to say, Ah guess you won't object if we call you *dawg eyes*."

Dale put his spoon down and looked at Clay, his brown eye defensive, his left eye a piercing blue. "My name's Kenway," he said, "Dale Kenway."

Curtis Clay had an inbred dislike of Northerners, especially city Northerners. He had never met any until he had arrived at Fort Knox, but he had heard enough about them back home: Northerners were slick and tricky and stole from their own mothers whenever they had a chance. He sized up Dale and figured that he had at least sixty pounds on him. "Ah think Ah'm goin' to call you *dawg eyes* anyway," he said.

Clay continued to taunt Dale. He enlisted the help of another Southerner, a farm boy from Arkansas named Vernon Walker, who had a hulking body topped by a disproportionately small head. Clay and Walker called out "dawg eyes" constantly, then guffawed as if they had said something uproariously funny. Several of the smaller fellows in the group began to snicker with the Southerners while the others watched expectantly, measuring the situation as if it were a length of lighted fuse attached to a bundle of dynamite. Dale tried to ignore them. He bore their taunts silently, never acknowledging Clay, Walker, or their chorus of followers until the end of the first week when Clay stepped in front of him in the shower. "Ah got me some soap to clean them dawg eyes," Clay said, thrusting a bar of soap in Dale's face. "Maybe if Ah lather 'em up good Ah can get them eyes the same color."

No one in the shower room moved. They stopped washing themselves and stood with water hissing over them, watching Dale and his tormentor. Clay reached for Dale's head. Dale ducked. Then, his heart pounding so hard that it felt as if it were going to break through his chest wall, Dale lunged at Clay, smashing him in the nose with his right fist. Clay stumbled backward and slipped; his flesh hit the wet floor with a SMACK. Dazed, he put his hand under his nose and saw that it was covered with blood. "Get 'em, Walker!" he yelled.

Walker grabbed Dale from behind, pinning his arms back, while Clay scrambled to his feet, blood streaming from his nose. "Hold the bastard for me," he said. "Ah'm goin' to pound the shit out of this dawg-eyed motherfucker!"

Between them, Walker and Clay weighed four hundred pounds to Dale's one hundred thirty-seven. Still, no one moved. But every eye was riveted on Dale and the Southerners. Clay started to punch Dale in the stomach and would have killed him if a muscular, black-haired youth hadn't interfered. His name was Hugh Trahern. He moved quickly, springing the others into action as if they had been waiting for his command. After they freed Dale, Trahern crouched in front of Walker and Clay, his dark eyes flashing, motioning with his hands for the Southerners to come at him. As soon as Clay and Walker were facing him squarely, Trahern leaped with his arms outstretched and smashed the sides of their heads together. There was a CRACK like a gun report before they slid unconscious to the floor. Trahern walked around their bodies and stepped under a spigot to finish his shower without a word, as casually as if he had swatted a couple of flies.

Later Dale saw Trahern alone and thanked him. "I don't like an unfair fight," Trahern said. He had a distinct New York accent.

"You took the two of them at once."

Trahern shrugged. "That was different."

"Why?"

"Because they're stupid. All I had to do was line them up so I could bang their heads together. Those goons did most of the work for me."

Dale became uncomfortable. "You make it sound easy," he said, feeling that Trahern was patronizing him.

"It was. The bone over the ears is the thinnest part of the skull," Trahern said, as if that bit of information were common knowledge. "You just have to be careful that the blow isn't too hard or you're in trouble; you want them dazed, not dead. With those two, I didn't have to worry. They're knuckleheads."

The soreness in Dale's gut lasted a week, but it was easier to live with than the constant harassment he had endured from Clay and Walker, who no longer bothered him. They kept to themselves and stayed a safe distance away from Trahern.

Trahern became the leader of the group. Although he wasn't the largest or the strongest, the others admired him for his coolness under pressure; nothing seemed to rattle him. The sergeant, a thick-necked fellow who toed out like a duck when he walked, began to resent Trahern and one day at target practice stood next to him, deliberately trying every tactic he could think of to break Trahern's concentration. Trahern shot one bull's eye after another, as if he were alone on the range with the target. When Dale froze on the infiltration course after a live bullet zinged past his head, missing him by inches, Trahern called out. "They don't want to kill us, Kenway. They're saving us for the Commies." Dale started moving again and managed to crawl on his belly to the safety zone at the end of the field.

Basic training lasted sixteen weeks. During the second half, Dale and Trahern were among those selected for the Armored School. They were trained to use the big tanks, huge mechanical snails with tremendous fire power. Dale hated it. He would have liked to work on the tanks, not operate them, but he had no choice so he fired the high-velocity guns until his ears ached from the blasts and his insides were as cold as death. Driving the tanks was no better. Deep inside the entrails of the machines he felt sick, as if he had entered a netherworld filled with terrible secrets from which there was no return. When he climbed out, his clothes were soaked with perspiration and his skin was ashen. "The tanks really bother you," Trahern observed late one morning as he and Dale were walking back to the barracks. Trahern's G.I. haircut had grown out into thick black curls that framed his grime-streaked face.

"Yeah," Dale said, embarrassed. He had been pushing himself, following the officers' instructions as best he could, hoping no one would notice how miserable he was.

"I look at it this way: if I have to fight, I want the odds to be in my favor. I'd rather be in a tank than out in a field with no protection."

"You're right," Dale said. He didn't add that he would rather be home than in a tank.

Dale had a two-week leave in the beginning of December before he was shipped to Korea. The Kenways celebrated an early Christmas. They hung a wreath on the front door, decorated a tree, and exchanged gifts, but their heart wasn't in it; they were thinking about Korea and the mounting death tolls. Although they tried to conceal their anxiety with forced gaiety and fixed smiles, their private fears for Dale's safety hovered over them like a cloud. Grace wept while she prepared a turkey for Christmas dinner, and Frank sat slack-jawed behind his office door, regretting his stubbornness. He hadn't realized how unbearable his loss would be if Dale was killed in the war. Grandpa Tarpin couldn't sleep. He wandered through the house at night, limping from room to room until his legs trembled and his foot ached with phantom pain so fresh he could have sworn his missing toes had just been severed again. Rod came home from Princeton and went to the library every day to work on term papers that were due after Christmas recess. He couldn't sit at the desk in the bedroom he and Dale shared. Rod felt guilty without knowing why, as if he had unwittingly contributed to his brother's decision to drop out of college. Dale walked for hours on the familiar snow-covered streets of his childhood—on Giffort, on Carlson past the elementary school, on Hewett where the store windows glittered with tinsel and lights—as if he were seeing them for the first time. Or the last time. The neighbors who happened to observe him from their windows, a slight, solitary figure in an Army jacket walking under the stark December elms, averted their eyes. They didn't know why, exactly. Some sensed that they were intruding upon Dale's privacy. Others would have liked to invite him in but didn't know what to say. Suddenly the glossy memories they had of victory in World War II began to lose their sheen. Dale was such a decent kid. He was worth ten Communists. One hundred Communists. One thousand Communists. What were they doing in Korea? Who gave a damn about the 38th parallel anyway?

* * *

Dale left for Korea on a boat packed with five hundred G.I.'s; there wasn't a familiar face on board. Soon the air in the hold became stifling, explosive with bravado and unarticulated fear. They were soldiers. They would kill. They might be killed. Dale awakened in his narrow berth at night hyperventilating. He didn't want to die. He didn't want to kill anyone. He listened to the heavy breathing of the men around him as he gasped for air as if he were suffocating.

After the boat docked in Japan, Dale was assigned to a unit in Korea. He arrived on a gray, bitter morning and was transported to his company. As he approached the camp, Dale spotted a figure in the distance, a G.I. walking on the frozen ground with an unmistakable stride, springy and confident. Dale's lungs expanded. The G.I. was Trahern.

The Kenways received four letters from Dale. *Korea is hilly,* he wrote, *and very cold, like the worst days of winter back home, but there isn't as much snow. A buddy I went through basic training with is in my platoon. His name is Hugh Trahern...It's been snowing almost every day, not a lot, just enough to make everything white except the food and the clothing...they're green...I've gotten so used to the helicopters and the whacking sound they make that I hardly notice them anymore...It's freezing here. Last night Trahern proposed a toast to the man who invented central heating. None of us knew his name, but we all raised our coffee mugs and cheered like crazy. It's the thought that counts...*

There were some things Dale didn't write. He thought about girls constantly, especially Sue Hastings, a petite, high-breasted brunette he had taken out a few times before he had dropped out of college. She was a sophomore now, probably dating juniors and seniors. He imagined her at fraternity parties wearing a cashmere sweater and pearls, flirting with admiring boys whose lives revolved around Saturday night beer blasts instead of tanks and guns. The image began to torture him. He tried not to be bitter. He still didn't want to go to college, but he didn't want to be freezing his ass off in Korea, either. He was a virgin. More than anything he didn't want to die before he had a woman, someone soft and pretty like Sue Hastings. He thought about soldiers he had seen, some missing arms and legs, others with their faces half-blown off. He saw blood from bullet wounds coloring the snow scarlet and wondered if he would be next, if his tank would be blown to smithereens, and visualized pieces of his body scattered in bloody chunks on the white hillsides. He thought about the Koreans and the Communists and fantasized them killing each other off, one by one, until they were as scarce as Martians. He didn't give a damn about them. All he wanted was to get back to Giffort Street where it was safe.

If it weren't for Trahern, Dale was sure he would have gone crazy. Somehow Trahern managed to joke about their predicament. When they ran to the tanks, Trahern would remark, "Another day, another dollar." or "This will be a short one, General's orders. We have to be back in time for lunch. They're serving lobster." or "Did you hear the news? They're requisitioning broads with big tits for every tank." The knots of Dale's fear would loosen then and he would laugh, forgetting for an instant that they might not return. One Sunday Trahern didn't joke. Hours after they lost two tanks and eighteen men, they were ordered back into action. Trahern's face was grim as he strapped on his helmet. "I'm sick of this fucking war," he said. "Don't those bastards know we're dying out here?"

"It isn't their asses," Dale said.

"Yeah, they sit with their maps drinking coffee while we get our heads blown off," Trahern said. Then he started to laugh. His laughter was low and sardonic at first, then rose in pitch.

"What's so funny?" Dale said, his spine stiffening with the realization that Trahern might be as scared as he was.

Trahern didn't answer; he was laughing hysterically. Dale grabbed him by the shoulders and shook him until his head bobbed. "I was just thinking," Trahern finally said between breaths, "about stuffing the brass and their maps into these goddamn tanks and sending them out for a Sunday drive. This fucking war would be over in an hour."

Dale killed a North Korean soldier at close range that day, a slender youth who looked no more than sixteen or seventeen years old. The boy was perched behind a rock on the side of a hill waiting for the approaching tanks with a grenade in his hand. He waited too long; perhaps he had trouble disengaging the pin. Dale saw him, his arm poised to throw the live grenade, and fired from the turret. The boy dropped the grenade with a look of surprise on his face as bullets tore through his chest. Within seconds the grenade exploded, showering the white hillside with blood and flesh. When they returned to camp, Dale vomited; he heaved until his face was as green as his uniform.

Two weeks later the Kenways were notified that Dale had been injured. They made frantic calls to Washington but were given little information until they received a letter from Dale's commanding officer. *A truck loaded with drums of gasoline went out of control as it made a turn on the outskirts of camp*, he wrote. *The truck overturned and the gasoline exploded. Without thinking of his own safety, Dale ran through the fire to pull a soldier out of the flames who had been standing nearby. As a result of his heroism, Dale suffered second and third degree burns. You can be proud of your son. His courageous act was that of an American soldier in the finest tradition. Dale will be awarded a United States Army Commendation Medal.*

"Dale's a hero!" Frank said in a booming voice after he read the letter. "He's going to get a Commendation Medal."

Frank, Grace, and Grandpa Tarpin were sitting at the breakfast room table. A weak winter sun shone through the windows of the room, which was wallpapered with cheerful country market scenes. Grace, however, was anything but cheerful. She sat at the table, sniffling. "What's the matter with you?" Frank said. "We should be celebrating. I'll take you out to dinner."

Grace pulled a tissue out of her apron pocket. "How can you even think of celebrating when Dale is lying in a hospital somewhere with second and third degree burns?"

"He's a hero," Frank said, waving the letter at her. He was tired of her tears. It seemed to him that she hadn't stopped sniffling since Dale had been drafted. "He's safe, and they'll fix him up good as new."

Grandpa Tarpin slammed his hands on the table and rose to his feet. "You're fools, both of you," he said before he walked away.

Dale was transported to a hospital in Japan for skin grafts on his legs, arms, and hands. The grafts on his limbs were successful, but the doctors became concerned when Dale's fingers started to fuse. Scar tissue formed on his hands that caused his skin, muscles, and tendons to contract, to bind together so that his fingers began to curl, claw-like, into fists. He would need surgery performed by a hand specialist.

Dale was sent to San Francisco to correct the contracture of his fingers. He called Frank and Grace from the hospital; a nurse helped him make the call. "I'm fine," he said. "They operated on my right hand yesterday. In a few weeks they'll operate on my left, depending on how well I do. Don't come to see me. I'll take a plane home when I'm released."

The nurse, a gray-haired, grandmotherly woman, replaced the receiver and watched him walk down the corridor to his room, a thin young man with unusual eyes. His left eye was so blue, she thought, shaking her head. She tried not to think about his other eye, the brown one. There was something about that eye that made her want to weep. It reminded her of grief, of loss, of knowledge too painful to bear. He was a boy, too young to look at the world through an eye like that. Later, when she brought Dale his supper, she found him sitting on his bed, staring at his bandaged hand.

Grace and Frank called Dale every other day for several weeks; each time he repeated that he was fine and would be coming home soon and that they shouldn't visit him. His responses were so repetitious and sounded so unlike him that Grace decided to call the surgeon who had performed the operations. "He's probably depressed," said the doctor, scanning Dale's chart. He was a coarse-featured, over-worked man who performed so many hand operations that he had difficulty remembering the patients the hands were attached to. "As I recall, your son mentioned that he wanted to be a mechanic. Depression is normal in cases like his. I'll have one of the staff psychiatrists look in on him. His prognosis is good. We think he'll have at least ninety-percent use of his fingers. If his progress in therapy continues, he'll be released in a month."

"Then why did he tell us he'd be home soon?" Grace said.

"A month isn't long," the doctor replied. "I told him before surgery that he'd be here for a minimum of six to eight weeks."

Grace thanked the doctor and hung up, stunned. "The doctor said Dale would be in the hospital for another month," she said, looking at Frank. "Why doesn't he want to see us?"

Frank shrugged; he was as surprised as Grace.

"Well, I'm going to visit him whether he wants to see me or not."

"No, you aren't," said Grandpa. "You're going to stay right here until he comes home."

"Don't talk to me as if I'm a child," Grace said. "I'm Dale's mother. I'm entitled to see him."

"Not if he doesn't want you to," Grandpa said. "Dale's not a little boy: he's a man who went through a terrible experience. He's earned the right to be alone."

Frank bristled. Moving into his father-in-law's house was the worst decision he had ever made. He had endured twenty-three years of Tarpin's meddling, and he'd had enough. "Dale is our son. If we want to visit him, we'll visit him. He's a hero! It will cheer him up when he sees how proud we are. Rod always plays better when we're sitting in the stands."

Grandpa's face hardened. "War isn't a football game," he said, jabbing a bony finger at them. "It's death and destruction. Dale has witnessed things no one should see, and being a hero won't change that. He doesn't need your cheers; he knows what he's done. It's obvious that he doesn't want you to visit him. Don't you two have any common sense? You wouldn't think of barging in uninvited on one of your friends. Give your son the same respect."

Chastened, the Kenways stayed home and continued to call Dale until he was released from the hospital.

* * *

When Dale came home on a Saturday in May, the azaleas were blooming and the elm trees wore veils of new leaves. Children were playing baseball in the street, using the elms for first and third bases. George Masterson was edging his lawn, Adele Heussler was washing her windows, and Lillian Levinson was digging in her flower beds. The Whittakers' nanny, Meddie, was walking down the street in her white oxfords, carrying her black purse and a bulging black satchel. Nothing had changed. It was spring and life on Giffort Street continued, moving in its seasonal rhythm, as sure and steady as the ticking of a clock.

Dale removed the airplanes that hung over his bed

the first night he was home. He cut them down with a red-handled wire cutter and watched them sink noiselessly onto his bed. When he was finished, he carefully packed them into cardboard cartons. The next morning he drove Grace's car to Father Devlin's Orphanage and gave the cartons to a pink-cheeked nun. "I can't let the children play with these," she said, admiring the planes. "They're so fragile and so beautifully made." She thought for a moment. "We have a glass display case. A store donated it years ago for a craft sale we had; they didn't want it back because the base is cracked. Perhaps we could put the planes in there."

She took Dale to a musty basement storeroom and showed him the display case. The top section was two feet wide, ten feet long, and three feet high. "It should be perfect, don't you think?" she said.

Dale swallowed hard and nodded; to him the dust-covered case looked like an over-large coffin.

Grace fussed over Dale. She prepared his favorite foods and watched him eat, measuring each mouthful he consumed with satisfaction. He was so thin, and his color was poor. She avoided looking at his hands and wondered about the skin grafts on his arms and legs. He said the grafts were healed, but she noticed that he wore long-sleeved shirts every day, buttoned at the cuff instead of rolled up as he used to wear them. Frank threw his arm around Dale's shoulders at least once a day, exclaiming, "You're a hero, an authentic hero!"

Dale responded with a smile that was more like a wince.

Frank tried to talk about the war. He wanted Dale to tell him about the fighting, the guns, the tanks, the Communists he had killed, the fire he had plunged through that had made him a hero. Frank wanted to share Dale's experiences, man-to-man, like he did with Rod. For years Frank's eyes had glittered with excitement while he had listened to Rod replaying football games, describing each call, run, and touchdown. Dale wouldn't talk; he would say nothing about the war or the man he had tried to save except that his friend had died. Only Grandpa Tarpin remained the same. He waited for the mailman every day and chatted with people who came to see Dale (if Grace didn't send him upstairs) as if nothing had happened.

Alone in his room, Dale flexed his fingers. It was impossible to fully extend the fingers of his right hand. He wondered if he could still fix cars. He decided to wait a while before he tried. It was almost better not to know. He rolled up his shirt sleeves and looked at the scars on his hands and arms. His skin was unnaturally pale, tight and shiny. It didn't bother him, but what would others think? Would they find him offensive, grotesque? Would a pretty girl like Sue Hastings be repulsed if he put his scarred arms around her? He'd thought of calling Sue every day since he'd been home, but he kept putting it off. She probably had a boyfriend, someone she'd met since last spring. He'd been gone for nearly a year. Everyone's life had continued; his had been interrupted, cut like a break in a reel of film. He'd always been able to fix almost anything. Now he felt helpless, unable to splice his life back together. He'd been told what to do for so long—when to eat, when to sleep, when to fight, what to wear, what to think--that he was lost without an order, a directive to tell him what to do next.

Dale's friends stopped by to visit, clean-cut fellows with crew cuts who slapped him on the back, saying, "You're a hero, a goddamn hero," as if he'd just hit a game-winning home run. They stayed for hours, talking about college, cars, and girls. Every so often they would pause and look at Dale with admiration that made him uncomfortable. He had difficulty concentrating on what they were saying. They were his closest friends. He had grown up with them, yet he felt different, older. When they asked him to go out for a few beers, he said, "Soon. I'll call you soon."

He didn't call.

The neighbors came to see him bearing gifts. Bernice and Arnold Whittaker arrived with a large dish piled high with sweet rolls "Meddie baked these for Dale this morning," Bernice said, handing Grace the sweet rolls. "She knew we were planning to visit and did this on her own. Isn't she amazing? There is nothing in the world like Meddie's sweet rolls."

Edna and Carl Harris came, each carrying a custard. Edna's custards were renowned on Giffort Street. They were smooth, golden masterpieces that Edna baked whenever there was illness in a neighbor's house. She was a large woman who wore chunky jewelry and audacious hats; her nature was as generous as her laugh, hearty and straightforward. "There is nothing like custard to build you up," Edna said, beaming at Dale.

Dale had been having trouble eating under Grace's watchful eyes. He stared at the custards, overwhelmed. "I know just how you feel," Edna said.

Adele Heussler baked a chocolate torte. "It'll taste as good as it looks," Stan Heussler said. Later Grace remarked to Frank, "Adele has really gotten heavy. I wouldn't be surprised if she gained back the weight she lost last year, plus more. Still, she looks better than she did when she was thin."

At first Dale was touched by the neighbors' kindness. They were good people, sincere people. But when he protested that he wasn't a hero, no one believed him. "It's just like you to be modest," they said. "Your father showed us the letter your commanding officer sent and we're proud of you." Night after night they came, talking about the war and the Communists, telling Dale how proud they were that he had been awarded a medal for his bravery. The more he told them that he wasn't a hero, the more convinced they were that he was. He sat quietly in the living room while Grace served coffee, sinking deeper into his chair, his narrow shoulders drooping under the weight of being a hero.

George and Prudence Masterson came to see Dale early on a Thursday evening the second week he was home. When Grace glimpsed them walking up the driveway, she looked around in panic, fearing that the house might not be in order. To her knowledge, the Mastersons had never visited anyone on the block. She saw that sections of the evening paper were scattered on the gray carpet around Grandpa's chair and hurried to pick them up. "I'm not finished yet," Grandpa said.

"The Mastersons will be at the door in a second. You can take the paper upstairs and read it in your room."

"And miss the Mastersons? Absolutely not! I won't budge from this chair. It's going to be an interesting evening," Grandpa chortled.

The doorbell chimed. "You'd better behave yourself," Grace said.

Prudence Masterson handed Dale a rectangular package wrapped in pale green paper. "It's *Kon Tiki* by Thor Heyerdahl," she said. "I haven't read it, but I understand that it is most inspiring. The woman at the bookstore assured me that it would be an excellent choice for a heroic young man. It's nonfiction, you know. I won't buy fiction: it's nothing but elaborate untruths, and it never ends the way you expect it to. I don't like being surprised."

"Thank you," Dale said. "I'm sure I'll enjoy it. But I'm really not a hero."

Prudence Masterson peered at Dale through her rimless eyeglasses. She had a long, serious face without a trace of humor in it. "Certainly you are," she said in a tone that precluded any disagreement. "You were even awarded a medal that proves it."

The Mastersons weren't settled in the living room for more than fifteen minutes when John and Marcella Laibrook arrived. Grace's eyes widened with alarm when she saw them at the front door. The Mastersons and the Laibrooks hadn't spoken to each other for years, ever since Janie Laibrook had toddled over to the Mastersons' and picked every one of their tulips. George Masterson had told Marcella that her child was ill-mannered and should be locked up until she learned to behave properly. Later, John Laibrook went over to the Mastersons' and threatened to have George Masterson locked up if he so much as set a foot on the Laibrooks' property. "The Mastersons are here," Grace whispered to John and Marcella.

"So are we," said John Laibrook. He was a tall man who had a paunch and the florid complexion of a drinker.

Grace chewed on her lower lip.

"Don't worry," said Marcella, who was holding a gift-boxed leather toiletry case for Dale. She was a smartly dressed, rather affected woman whose eyebrows were plucked into thin black lines. "I'll see to it that John behaves himself."

The Laibrooks walked into the living room and nodded to the Mastersons, who were sitting on the sofa as straight as fence posts. The Mastersons nodded back stonily. After the Laibrooks gave Dale his gift, they seated themselves diagonally across from the Mastersons in matching chairs that were upholstered a rose floral print. A chill descended upon the comfortable room. "I'll make coffee," said Grace, anxious to escape.

When she returned carrying a large tray, she was amazed to see George Masterson and John Laibrook talking amiably. "I've been watching him, too," John said. "He's a real scrapper."

"You're absolutely right," George agreed, leaning forward. The top of his bald head gleamed under the lamp light, and his face, which was as long and serious as his wife's, was more animated than Grace had thought possible. "Joe McCarthy will rout those Communists out, every one of them. Mark my words: within the next year or two McCarthy's name will be a household word. There won't be a man, woman, or child in this country who won't know who he is."

"I hope not," Grandpa said.

"You can't mean that," Frank said.

"I certainly do mean it! McCarthy should be stopped now before it's too late."

"Nonsense," George said. "Joe McCarthy is just what this country needs. We're fighting a cold war with those Communists. It's about time they learn we mean business. They're poking their noses into places they have no right to be. They're cockroaches, and we're going to rid ourselves of them once and for all!"

"I agree. Look at that mess they got us into in Korea. Our best young men, like Dale here, are being injured and killed because those damned Communists want to take over the world," Laibrook said, gesturing at Dale. "George is right: Joe McCarthy is just what this country needs. He's a real patriot."

Grandpa's face had grown red while the two men were speaking. He stood up. Grace shot him a warning glance, which he ignored. "Joe McCarthy is a dangerous man. He's a name caller, and they're the worst kind," Grandpa said. "He's calling people Communists to make a reputation for himself. He wants power and he doesn't care whose name he blackens to get it. Once a man is called a Communist, people will always have doubts about him, even if he proves that he isn't. That Nixon fellow from California insinuated that the Douglas woman he was running against was a Communist, and it cost her the election. Didn't you see those pictures of her in *Life* magazine--the anguish on her face? I'll never forget those pictures. She's no Communist. Nixon did a terrible thing to that woman to win an election. He doesn't have an ounce of morals! Neither does McCarthy!"

George Masterson leaped off the sofa and strode

across the room. "You're wrong," he said, standing challengingly in front of Grandpa.

Grandpa smiled devilishly. "What's to stop him from calling you a Communist, George?"

George's chin dropped. "How dare you! I'm not a Communist!"

"Prove it," Grandpa said, grinning at him triumphantly.

Dale excused himself and went upstairs to his room. He couldn't listen to another word about the Communists and Korea. He sat on his bed and looked at Rod's trophies; the bookcase next to Rod's bed was filled with them, six shelves of brass and silver trophies that gleamed in the semi-darkness. He remembered when each one had been added and how proud they had been, especially his father. Now his father was looking at him the way he looked at Rod, with that same hunger and boastful pride. The neighbors, too. Rod wouldn't be home for another week. He couldn't wait that long to be rescued. He went upstairs to the attic, brought down a suitcase, and started packing.

It was after midnight when Grandpa Tarpin heard Dale's door open. The old man had been unable to sleep. His confrontation with George Masterson had gotten his blood circulating better than it had in years. Oh, what a satisfying argument it had been! Oh, how he had loved that shocked look on George's face when he had dared him to prove that he wasn't a Communist! Grandpa heard Dale's footsteps on the stairs. He had been so busy thinking about George that he had forgotten about Dale. He hoisted himself out of bed and walked to the hall.

Dale was in the vestibule slipping his arms through a lightweight jacket when he heard Grandpa call his name. "Dale," the old man called quietly, limping down the stairs in baggy stripped pajamas, "where are you going this time of night?"

"I'm not sure," Dale said.

Grandpa spotted the suitcase. "You can't just up and leave."

"I have to," Dale said. "I can't stay here anymore."

"Come into the living room so we can talk a minute. It's kind of drafty here in the hall."

"There's really nothing to talk about."

"I think there is," Grandpa said. "Humor me."

Dale sighed, then climbed the vestibule stairs and followed Grandpa into the living room. "You must have a reason for leaving," Grandpa said, settling in Frank's chair. He put his lame foot up on the ottoman and leaned back as if he were relaxing, but his fingertips were white where they gripped the chair arms.

Dale stood with his back to Grandpa; he was blinking hard and his hands were clenched. "I can't take it anymore," he said. "Ever since I got home, everyone's been calling me a hero. Dad's the worst. He tells me at least once a day that I'm an authentic hero. He looks at me like I performed some kind of miracle. I feel like a fraud."

"You ran through a fire to save a man's life. That isn't something everyone would do."

"But I didn't save him. He died."

"It isn't your fault. You made the effort and that's what counts.'"

"No, you don't understand," Dale said, turning to face Grandpa. "I ran through that fire to save myself."

"What do you mean?"

"Trahern. I had to save Trahern. I couldn't have lasted another day in Korea without him."

Dale sat on the sofa, covered his face with his scarred hands, and started to sob. Grandpa sat quietly, listening to the coarse sounds, raw and painful as a fresh cut, coming from his grandson's throat. When Dale's sobbing eased, Grandpa said, "Tell me about this Trahern. He must have been special."

"He was," Dale said, speaking with difficulty, "but I

can't tell you much about him--about his family, his background, if that's what you mean. Trahern didn't talk about himself. Some of the guys bragged a lot. They talked about women they'd had, fights they'd won, that kind of thing. Trahern never said a word. He didn't have to prove himself. Somehow you just knew that he'd done as much-- probably more--than the rest of them. He had a sense of timing, a way of judging things, kind of like street sense. He knew when to move and when to back off. I saw him crack only once. It had been an awful day--tanks blown up, men dead. We were ordered out again. Trahern went crazy. He started laughing like a madman, but it didn't last long. After I shook him, he was all right."

"It sounds as if you were as cool as Trahern."

"I was scared out of my mind. I had to make Trahern stop laughing because I couldn't have climbed into one of those tanks without him. It probably sounds crazy, but I knew I'd come back if he was in there with me."

"So you think Trahern was the hero, not you?"

"I know it," Dale said. "Trahern was the brave one. Now he's dead and people are calling me a hero. Every time I deny it, they become more convinced that I am. Why won't they believe me?"

Grandpa pursed his lips and thought for a while. "Most of us live out our lives without doing anything special," he said finally. "Sometimes we do things we'd rather not admit to--petty things, mean things, things we are ashamed of that we don't want others to know about. So when we hear of someone who risks his life for another, we put him on a pedestal. He represents what we could be if we weren't selfish or afraid."

"But I'm not a hero," Dale said. "I can't live on a pedestal."

"Some people have had to live with a lot worse," Grandpa said, looking at his lame foot. "How would you like to be reminded with every step you take that you were a coward?"

Dale stared at Grandpa. "What?"

"My foot. I shot myself in the foot June thirtieth, eighteen ninety-eight," Grandpa said. "I had seen Colonel Wood and Teddy Roosevelt's men the day before. What a bunch they were--cowboys and Long Island polo players eager to play war. They had no idea of what they were getting into. I couldn't sleep that night. I knew I wouldn't be going with them, but I couldn't stop thinking about how insane it was. I wanted to go home. The next day I deliberately shot myself during a minor skirmish."

"Did anyone find out?"

Grandpa shook his head. "I was lucky. The Roughriders charged up San Juan Hill the next day. They were killed by the dozens, as unsuspecting as babies. No one paid much attention to me. The waste of it! So many lives!"

"But the Roughriders won."

"According to the history books, but historians don't see dying men; they look at final results like scorekeepers count touchdowns. The survivors came out heroes, especially Roosevelt. The dead men of San Juan Hill helped him win an election."

"I wonder if he ever felt guilty."

"I doubt it. To Roosevelt, winning was what mattered. Every man has a different outlook on things. I guess it's a matter of perspective. I was a coward, and I've had to accept that. I'm not going to lie to you and say that it's been easy. But it hasn't been all bad, either. There have been times when it has actually helped me," Grandpa said, his voice trailing off.

"How did it help?"

"Over the years I forced myself to confront situations that I would have liked to back away from. I wouldn't let myself look for an easy way out. I did that once and the price I paid was too high." Grandpa chuckled.

"Maybe I was such a big coward that I just couldn't face being a coward again."

They sat quietly for a while. Then Grandpa lifted his lame foot off the ottoman and stood up. His pulse was rapid, his hands shook. "Dale," he said, "only an idiot wouldn't be frightened in a war. You did the best you could under the circumstances. Maybe you ran into that fire for selfish reasons, but you ran without any thought of your own safety. That took courage. If your friend were here, I'm sure he'd agree. He'd understand."

Grandpa limped into the hall and paused in front of the stairs. "Why don't you come up to bed? You can unpack in the morning."

Dale didn't answer. The old man gripped the banister and started up the stairs. When he reached his room, he left the door ajar and collapsed on his bed. He lay there listening for what seemed like hours, his body shaking with tension tremors, until he heard the sound of Dale's footsteps. He held his breath, waiting…waiting. Dale's bedroom door clicked shut. Grandpa exhaled, grinning. What a night it had been, what a night!

NEIGHBORS

George Masterson came home early from a church meeting on a rainy July evening and found his youngest daughter, Emma, and the Palmer boy naked on the living room sofa. The Palmer boy saw George first; he gasped, then grabbed the nearest piece of clothing, which happened to be Emma's virginal-white brassiere, and futilely attempted to cover his engorged penis. Emma screamed and leaped off the sofa, too frightened to think of covering herself. She ran past George, a wholesome-looking, freckled girl of eighteen with full hips and breasts, and flew upstairs to her bedroom.

George left the house immediately. When his wife, Prudence, came home at ten thirty, she found him weeding the rose beds. George had worked for two hours, oblivious to the rain and the darkness. "Why are you doing this now?" Prudence said, shocked at his appearance. He wasn't wearing gardening clothes. His shirt and slacks were soaked, and his new black shoes were caked with mud; there were dirt smudges on his face and his rimless eyeglasses were streaked with rain.

"Felt like it," George said, knocking a droplet of water off the tip of his sharp nose with the back of his hand.

The next day George called his sister in Iowa and asked that Emma be allowed to visit until she started college in September. The telephone call was George's only acknowledgment of the incident. He refused to look at his daughter or speak to her. Emma tearfully boarded a train, denied the opportunity to apologize or defend herself.

She couldn't explain how difficult it was to be forbidden to attend dances and movies like the other girls; nor could she say anything about her three older sisters, all of whom had entertained boys behind closed drapes when their parents were out. George and Prudence Masterson were strict Baptists who neither drank, smoked, nor danced. They had an unblinking view of sin and considered it their moral duty to shield their daughters from the evils of temptation. While other girls dated, the Masterson daughters stayed at home under their parents' watchful eyes except for rare nights when George and Prudence were out. Emma started weeping as the train sped through Iowa farmland. For some reason the lush acres of corn, almost ready for harvest, reminded her of Jerry Palmer. But the flatness of the fields, miles and miles of unrelieved green stretching as far as her eyes could see, was so much like her father, awesome and unyielding, that she felt lost, as exposed and terrified as she did the night she ran naked through the house. There was no place to hide in that landscape; it looked like it had been leveled by the hand of God expressly to uncover shivering sinners.

George didn't tell Prudence that Emma and the Palmer boy were naked when he found them. The sight of Emma's body, her ripe breasts and triangle of pubic hair, had nearly unbalanced him. She was his child, flesh of his flesh, once his secret favorite; he could not permit himself to think of her as a sexual being. He wouldn't utter her name and averted his eyes when he walked past her bedroom, as if he were afraid he would see her standing naked in the doorway. He spent his evenings cutting the grass and working in the flower beds as he usually did, determined to eradicate the incident from his mind. Prudence didn't notice any change in his behavior; she was busy gathering items for the church rummage sale and was glad that George had the gardens to keep himself occupied.

If it weren't for Virginia Penner, George might have

been able to erase the image of Emma's nakedness from his memory. Early one evening a month after Emma left he saw Virginia coming up the street with a young boy and an unusually tall man walking a leashed dog. From a distance, she looked just like Emma. And she was unmistakably pregnant. The color drained from George's face. He stared at Virginia's belly ballooning under her loose-fitting dress, his bald head glistening with perspiration. He wanted to go into the house, but he felt weak, lightheaded. He remained kneeling on the edge of the lawn with his grass clippers, unable to move, until they were standing over him.

"Nice night," the man said, his expression friendly.

George nodded and began clipping the grass feverishly. If he didn't look up, maybe they would go away. The woman was wearing red sandals; she had slender ankles and long, fleshy toes. The man stepped closer. When his oversize brown moccasins were almost directly under George's nose, he said, "I'd like to introduce myself. My name is Saul Penner. We just moved into the corner house."

Saul. The name shot through George's head like a bullet. Jews named their sons Saul. He tried to place Penner's accent. Brooklyn. It had to be Brooklyn. Most of them came from there.

The woman spoke. "We noticed your flowers in June when we bought our house. I had never seen such magnificent irises." Her speech was different from Penner's, cultured with a trace of flatness.

George might not have gotten up if their dog, a black-and-white cocker spaniel, hadn't started sniffing around the elm. He rose stiffly, eyeing the dog with unconcealed dislike. Dogs were put on earth for no practical purpose; they were filthy creatures, excrement machines that ruined lawns.

Saul Penner pulled on the dog's leash. "Here, Buster," he said. The dog trotted to the sidewalk. Penner extended his right hand. "I can see that you don't like dogs, but don't worry about Buster. He's curb trained."

"Curb trained?" George said, ignoring Penner's outstretched hand.

"He's a New York dog, trained to go in the street."

"Is that so?" George peered up at Penner, who was nearly a full head taller. He didn't think Jews were that big. Most of them were short and had dark skin and big noses. Lillian Levinson didn't have a big nose, but she was short. So was Harry. The Rashmans, too. The men got fat in middle age. Too much money and rich food. This fellow had a ways to go. He looked to be in his early thirties. Didn't look Jewish either, except for his hair. Coarse and curly, a sure giveaway. Better shake his hand. Never want it said that George Masterson wasn't a gentleman. "The name's Masterson," George said.

George's hand was cold and-clammy. "This is my wife, Virginia, and my son, Jordan," Penner said. His friendly expression had disappeared; he looked as if he regretted that he had stopped.

George nodded at the youngster, who had curly hair like his father's, then at Virginia. He had been so preoccupied with Penner's Jewishness (of which he now had little doubt) that he had temporarily forgotten about Emma. Seeing the Penner woman up close made his vision blur. Her eyes were blue instead of gray and she didn't have freckles, but her upturned nose and high forehead were disturbingly like Emma's. There was a definite resemblance. An arrow of pain pierced George's temple. He blinked forcefully, trying to regain his composure. "Tell me," he said, focusing on Penner so he wouldn't have to look at the woman, "who cleans the street?"

"The street?" Penner said, frowning.

"You said your dog is curb trained. Who cleans up after him?"

Penner shrugged. "The city, of course."

"Not this city," George said. "The street cleaning machines come only twice a year, in the spring and again in the fall after the leaves are down."

"I didn't know."

"Well, now you do," George said with satisfaction. He walked away, leaving the Penners standing speechless on the sidewalk. The throbbing in his head began to ease. It felt good, damn good, to put that Jew in his place.

Saul was the first to speak. He had a generous nature and a gentleness common to large men who are sensitive to their intimidating size, but his temper was quick. Masterson had infuriated him. He had just moved into his house. For the first time in his life he owned a front yard and a back yard, a driveway, a garage, shrubs, and trees. He had a wife whom he adored and a son he loved with such intensity that at times it frightened him. At the age of thirty-four he had been hired by a company listed on the New York Stock Exchange for triple his salary as a professor of economics. This was his first stroll on Giffort Street. All he had wanted to do was introduce himself and his family, to announce his presence and extend his hand in friendship. Masterson's attitude toward him had been worse than an outright snub. "Jordan," he said, "I don't want you to go near that man. Stay off his lawn and out of his driveway. Look at his house and remember which one it is."

Four-year-old Jordan stared at the Mastersons' house. It was painted dark brown and had a wide front porch that was built up high on the sides. From where he stood he couldn't see the beveled-glass living room doors, which were open to let in the cooling night air. The tone of his father's voice and the blackness of the porch frightened him. "Are there ghosts in the house?" he asked, trembling.

"There are no such things as ghosts," Virginia said, cupping his face in her hands.

"But Daddy said…" He started to cry.

"Daddy doesn't want you to go on Mr. Masterson's lawn because it's so nice," she said, casting an angry look at Saul that let him know there would be trouble later.

George went into the house, washed his hands, and walked into the living room to relax for the first time in weeks. He turned a lamp on, which did nothing to add warmth to the room. The Mastersons' furniture was austere, straight-backed and stiffly upholstered. It had been purchased for function rather than beauty, as though its owners believed that bright colors and soft cushions would weaken the soul as well as the spine. George was about to pick up the evening paper when he felt lightheaded again. *Virginia.* The woman's name was Virginia. It wasn't a Jewish name. His great-grandmother's name was Virginia, and there were a couple of Virginias in Prudence's family. What if he had made a mistake about Penner? He never socialized with the neighbors anyway. They were all objectionable: either they drank or smoked or indulged in activities that were more shameless than social. Or worse, they were Catholics or Jews. There wasn't a decent Baptist family on the block. The Kenways and the Liddles were Baptists, but they kept liquor in their homes and Tom Liddle smoked. Still, he didn't want any trouble. A man had to live in peace wherever he found himself. A polite hello was better than making enemies, no matter what he really thought of them. What if Penner weren't Jewish? He had been rude. It was that woman's fault, confusing him because she looked like Emma. *Emma.*

The back of his head began to throb as painfully as his temples had throbbed earlier. Maybe aspirin would help. He would get up in a minute or two. Suddenly he felt too tired to move.

Prudence found George in the living room sleeping in a chair with his mouth open; his glasses were askew and the evening paper was folded neatly on his lap, unread. He looked tired. It was probably her fault. She had spent so much time on the rummage sale that she hadn't helped him with the yard work. It wasn't good for a man of sixty-three to push himself. George had always been healthy, but there was no sense in taking chances. She didn't relish the idea of being a widow any more than she had enjoyed her wedding night. Thank goodness that business was over! She would talk to him in the morning about slowing down.

* * *

The Penners didn't speak to each other after their encounter with Masterson. After Jordan was asleep Virginia went into the kitchen to unpack their good dishes. The dishes had belonged to her aunt; they were fine white porcelain and had wild strawberries painted in the center of each plate. Her mother owned an identical set. The dishes reminded her of Thanksgiving and Christmas dinners. She checked the gold-bordered rims for chips, then stacked the plates on the counter for washing. Her lower back ached. It had ached like that the last week she had carried Jordan, but this baby wasn't due for five weeks. For some reason she felt like crying. It was probably the dishes, bringing back memories.

It was after nine o'clock when Saul came into the kitchen. He saw the unpacked cartons and knew that she was still upset. "I'll help," he said, wanting to make peace.

"No thanks," Virginia said, pouring liquid soap into the sink.

Saul watched her hands disappear in a cloud of soap bubbles. The filled sink was an insult, a repudiation of his pride in having finally been able to give her a home with a modern kitchen. "Why don't you use the dishwasher?"

"This is fine china."

"So?" he said. There was something about the way she said *fine* that irritated him, the hint of a suggestion that he didn't know the difference between fine and ordinary.

91

His mother had never had *fine* china; she had one set of heavy blue dishes that were chipped and crazed from decades of use.

"The dishwasher could ruin them. Why did you frighten Jordan tonight?"

"I didn't mean to upset him. All I wanted to do was make him understand that he was to stay away from Masterson."

"You didn't have to be so forceful about it," she said, methodically washing and rinsing plates. "Masterson was rude, but that was no reason to terrify Jordan. You carried on as if Masterson planned to dismember him. He was afraid to go to sleep."

"He's fine now," Saul said, picking up a dish towel. "I checked on him a few minutes ago. As for Masterson, he was more than rude."

"What do you mean?"

He hesitated. She was so blond, so beautiful. And so gentile, even though she had converted for him. No one would ever look at her the way Masterson had looked at him, as if he were not quite human, as if his right to exist were questionable. "Forget it," he said.

Virginia didn't forget it. She wanted to be accepted on Giffort Street, not so much for herself and Saul as for Jordan and the baby. Saul's new job had been the fulfillment of a secret wish: that she could raise her children as she had been raised, in a gracious home on a treed street, away from the dirt and hassle of the city. Masterson had been unpleasant, but the other neighbors were probably nice. She wanted Jordan to have positive feelings about their new neighborhood. Saul had to control his temper. First impressions were important. "I think you overreacted tonight," she said while they were undressing for bed.

She had just taken off her bra; her breasts, usually small, had grown full with her pregnancy. Saul's groin ached at the sight of her; they hadn't been able to have sex for several weeks. "I'm overreacting now," he said, walking over to her.

"Be serious. I'm talking about Masterson."

Masterson again. Not only had Masterson ruined his evening, but he had invaded his bedroom. "I don't want to hear that man's name," Saul said, raising his voice. "Ever."

"You're losing your temper," she said, reprimanding him with cool blue eyes.

"You're damned right I am!"

"Because a nasty old man objected to Buster?"

"No," Saul exploded. "Because he objected to me and to my son. Masterson's anti-Semitic."

Virginia shivered, as if she'd been exposed to a cold wind. "How do you know?"

She looked so stricken that Saul didn't have the heart to tell her that Masterson had looked at him the same way her father had looked at him, with the same repugnance. They rarely discussed her father; his dislike of Saul was an unhealed wound in their marriage which they did not want to disturb. "I just know," he said.

"I'm sorry," she said, her voice barely audible.

He put his arms around her, "It's not your fault," he said. Then, because the stricken look hadn't left her face, he added, "It's Masterson's loss. He doesn't know what a great guy I am."

* * *

The following morning George asked Prudence if she knew anything about the people who had moved into the Bradleys' house. They were sitting opposite each other in the breakfast room at a rectangular table covered with an off-white tablecloth. After thirty-three years of marriage they looked more like brother and sister than husband and wife, not because they both had long faces and wore rimless eyeglasses, but because their facial expressions and mannerisms had become nearly identical. Their feet were planted firmly on the floor and white paper napkins were carefully spread on their laps. They ate slowly, methodically--chewing their bacon, swallowing their eggs, sipping their coffee--with no outward sign of enjoyment. George's inquiry about the Penners was delivered matter-of-factly, as if he were asking if she had heard the latest weather report. Her reply was equally taciturn. No, she knew nothing about them.

"I met them last night. Their name is Penner. His name is Saul," George said, watching Prudence's face intently.

Prudence's sparse eyebrows rose above her glasses. "Oh," she said.

"His wife's name is Virginia."

Prudence's eyebrows relaxed. "How old are they?"

"In their thirties, I'd guess," George said, mulling over her reaction. She had thought the same as he, that the Penners were Jewish, until she heard the Penner woman's name. He had no way of knowing for sure. Too bad he couldn't remember the boy's name. It might give him a clue.

As George drove down Giffort Street on his way to work, he mentally categorized each house by the owner's religion. By the time he reached Hewett Avenue, his face was grim. Out of thirty-six houses on the block, nineteen were owned by Protestants, eight by Catholics, and eight by Jews. If Penner were Jewish, it would be nine out of thirty-six houses that were owned by Jews. A quarter of the street. When he had bought his house there hadn't been a Jew on the block. Or in the neighborhood, for that matter. Catholics, either. They were just as bad. Giffort Street had been decent then. Civilized, like Iowa; now they were coming in in an invasion--Jews, Catholics. Thank goodness most of them were on the end toward Carlson. But it wouldn't last. Soon they'd be slithering up the street like reptiles, buying house after house. Lord knows what would come after them. Blacks, probably With Kennedy running for president anything could happen. A Catholic president. A papist! Unless Americans got some sense, the country would go straight to hell! Prudence wanted him to slow down. It might not be a bad idea. He could take an early retirement, sell the house, and move back to Iowa. They never should have left. Things would have been different if they had raised the girls there. *Emma.*

An image of Emma lying with the Palmer boy flashed through George's mind as he pulled his tan Dodge into the parking lot of Cadby and Hitchcock Engineering. There was an aura around the naked pair, a haze that remained after he purged them from his thoughts. George shook his head and blinked, trying to clear his vision, before he walked into the building to his office.

* * *

Virginia Penner gave birth to a girl the third week in September. Saul had come from a family of five boys and was delighted to have a daughter. The baby resembled her mother; she was fair and her skin turned a mottled red when she cried. They called her Rachel and somehow managed to convince Jordan that he had chosen his new sister's name.

Summer lingered that year. The elm leaves stayed green until the middle of October, and lawns thickened from heavy morning dews. Saul began walking the baby before dinner every night. He kept his left hand on the carriage, which Jordan proudly pushed, and held Buster's leash with his right. The baby carriage drew attention, and one-by-one Saul met his neighbors. Men coming home from work teased him good-naturedly about having his hands full, and women who were out calling children for dinner exclaimed over the baby. Everyone in the Penners' household benefited from the walks: the fresh air put Rachel to sleep, cutting short her fussy period; Jordan had instant status among the children on the block because he was allowed to push his sister's buggy, which helped him decide that she wasn't too bad after all; Virginia had a blissful thirty minutes without interruptions; and Saul, after his initial encounter with George Masterson, overcame his reservations about the neighborhood and concluded that it was indeed a fine place to live. The people he met were cordial, interested in him and his family without being overwhelming. They asked him polite questions about himself that were neither probing nor prying. He sensed that their easy familiarity with each other was based on mutual respect, that they were telling him by their casual manner that the word 'neighbors' meant people who live *near* each other, not *with* each other. They had bought homes on Giffort Street and were thus thrust together, but their lives were as separate as their houses; they gave each other room and because they did so, their feeling of community had flourished. Saul said nothing to the neighbors about the incident with George Masterson. As far as he could judge, Masterson was the only bad egg on the block. He wouldn't let one anti-Semite spoil the neighborhood for him. He was aware of Masterson's prejudice, and that was enough; he wasn't looking for trouble. Besides, his reaction to Masterson had disturbed him. He had always regarded anti-Semites as ignorant bigots, people to be avoided. He didn't know why he had allowed that imbecile to get to him, unless it was because Jordan was there. Jordan was sweet and innocent, too young to have developed defenses against the Mastersons of this world. He had handled the situation badly. It wouldn't happen again. He would ignore Masterson, treat him as though he didn't exist.

The Mastersons were usually eating dinner when

Saul walked the baby. They ate at five thirty every night so they could watch the evening news when they were finished. Prudence and George sat in front of the television set listening with rapt attention, as though the fate of the world were dependent upon their interest. By late October, the growing momentum of John Kennedy's presidential campaign was making George's head pound. A Catholic president—in his country! It couldn't be happening! George's headaches increased in intensity as the crowds around the youthful Kennedy grew larger. Finally, he could no longer stand it. "I'm going out to cut the grass," he said one night after they had watched Kennedy applauded by thousands in New York City.

"It's starting to get dark outside," Prudence said, looking at him with astonishment, "and the news has just begun."

"I've seen enough," George said.

Saul was talking to Stan Heussler when they heard George's reel lawn mower whirring. "Hey, George," Stan called, peering at George through the darkness, "you already have the nicest lawn on the block. You'll put us all to shame if you cut your grass in the dark."

George looked up, surprised. He hadn't noticed Stan Heussler. Although it was difficult to see, he could make out two other figures standing with Stan, a tall fellow and a youngster holding onto a carriage.

"Have you two met?" Stan said jovially, waving George over.

Stan Heusslers' wave was like a command. Heussler was a decent neighbor, a little too loud when he talked, but he minded his own business and kept up his property. George let go of the lawn mower and started walking toward them.

The street lights surged on. Saul looked at George, then took the handle of the carriage away from Jordan. "We've met," he said. "Please excuse me. We have to be getting home for dinner." He turned the carriage, tugged on Buster's leash, and started home without a backward glance.

"Strange," Stan said after Saul's abrupt departure, "he seemed like a friendly fellow."

"I wouldn't know," said George stiffly, reeling from Saul's rebuff.

"Come on, George," Stan said, "what did you say to him that scared him away?"

George didn't hear the kidding in Stan's voice. He never laughed at jokes unless he was told in advance he would be hearing one. "I talked to him about his dog," George said. "He must have taken it wrong."

"It might not be a bad idea to apologize. Sometimes people misinterpret innocent remarks," Stan said.

"Say, you wouldn't happen to know what Penner's…uh… origins are?"

"Origins?"

"His…uh…his background," George said. "You know what I mean."

Stan's dark eyes narrowed, as though he knew exactly what George meant. "I'm not sure that I do," he said. "Could you explain?"

George tried to laugh and produced a rasping sound. "It's not important," he said, starting to cough. "I guess I'd better be going in. It's chiller out here than I realized."

Stan lingered outside. It occurred to him that he didn't know George Masterson very well, although they had been neighbors for thirteen years. George's questions about Saul Penner had an unpleasantness about them that couldn't be overlooked. And Penner had left as soon as he saw George. Penner didn't look like a man who would run unless he had a damn good reason, and fear of George Masterson wouldn't be one of them. A man the size of Penner could break George in two. Personally, he didn't care what Penner was. If the man could afford to buy a house on Giffort Street, he was entitled to live in it in peace. But he did care about George. He didn't want Penner to think he was a bigot by association. He'd go out of his way to be friendly the next time he saw Penner. And he'd avoid George. A man who let feelings like that be known was looking for trouble.

George noticed a tingling in his fingers when he closed the garage door. It was that Penner! Oh, how he'd like to get his hands on him! What had Penner been saying before he walked away? Probably spreading lies. Heussler had played dumb. It figured. He couldn't count on an Episcopalian who never went to church to understand anything. That kind just went through life enjoying themselves as if heaven were a big hotel and they had reserved rooms. Maybe he'd ask Lillian Levinson about Penner. She wasn't as bad as most of them. A decent gardener too, even though she planted mostly annuals. If Penner were one of her kind, she'd know.

Saul didn't tell Virginia that he had seen Masterson. They had avoided any mention of Masterson since the night of their argument. The Penners spent a quiet evening going over estimates for a chain-link fence that included a dog run for Buster. They hadn't planned to enclose their backyard until the spring, but Virginia was finding it difficult to take the dog out since the birth of the baby. "Buster won't be happy," Saul said, reaching down to rub the dog's neck. "He's used to long walks."

"He'll adjust," Virginia said firmly.

Buster growled in dissent.

It was damp and overcast when George crossed the street early Saturday morning to talk to Lillian Levinson. As he walked across, his eyes darted up and down the curbs looking for dog droppings. He didn't see any, but he was sure they were there, hiding under leaves. Lillian was raking her lawn. She was wearing a heavy blue sweater, thick gloves, and old rubber boots. George cleared his throat to get her attention. "The leaves are late in falling this year," he said.

Lillian stopped raking and smiled at George.

"I wonder," he said, noticing that Lillian and her rake were approximately the same height, "if you've met the people who moved into the corner house."

"The Penners?"

"Yes, the Penners," George said, becoming agitated. He had mentally rehearsed his question, but now that he was about to ask it, he couldn't remember the words he wanted to use. "Would you happen to know what…what…what their persuasion is?"

Lillian looked at him, uncomprehending. "*Persuasion*? Forgive me. Sometimes I have trouble with my English."

Affiliation, that's what he meant to say. He'd forgotten she was a foreigner. "Affiliation," George said confidently. "What is their affiliation?"

Lillian's eyes narrowed. "It is impolite to ask people their politics," she said. "Democrats, Republicans, does it make a difference?"

"No, not that kind of affiliation." His voice crackled with impatience.

"I thought you were asking because of the election on Tuesday. Really, Mr. Masterson, I am surprised at you. I thought you were a gentleman."

George's mouth fell open. Lillian started jabbing at the leaves, but he remained where he was standing, as if he had been planted there. "I'm…I'm sorry," he said. "Did I say something wrong?"

Lillian continued raking. "In a great country like America, everyone is free to live," she said, keeping her eyes focused on the leaves, "without questions."

George staggered across the street. No one had ever told him that he wasn't a gentleman. He felt woozy. There were spots in front of his eyes. Maybe he'd lie down for a while. It was an effort to open the front door and climb the stairs. He collapsed on his bed and fell asleep with his shoes and jacket on.

Prudence in her wedding gown. She was beautiful, blond and freckled like Emma. Oh, how he wanted her! She stiffened, whimpering like a frightened child. He felt dirty, as if he had exposed himself in church. He disgusted her. She was a decent woman. She expected him to be a gentleman, to control himself. Undressing in the bathroom...spilling his seed in the toilet...the girls coming like surprises...Cora, Jane, Anne, Emma their healthy infant bodies clinging to him, their warm breath on his neck, fanning his darkest thoughts...teaching them to cover themselves, to keep their doors closed. All gone, even Emma. Emma...

* * *

The morning after Kennedy won the election, George told Prudence that he was going to talk to Vincent Cadby about an early retirement. "Why?" Prudence said, nearly spilling her coffee. She wanted him to slow down, but she hadn't planned on anything as drastic as retirement. He'd be constantly underfoot. With Emma gone, she had the house to herself. Being alone everyday had given her unexpected pleasure.

"I'll be sixty-four in June."

"Most men don't retire until they're sixty-five. And we have to put Emma through college."

Emma. The back of George's head began to throb. "We have enough money saved, and we can use what we get from the sale of the house to buy land in Iowa."

"Iowa? What will we do with land in Iowa?"

"Move there."

"But our home is here. Our church is here," Prudence said.

The pain in George's head started to travel toward his forehead. He had expected her cooperation. Even enthusiasm. She had cried when they left Iowa. Now it appeared that she didn't want to go back. "There are churches in Iowa. We can farm--nothing big, just a couple of acres, enough to take care of ourselves. There's no telling what will happen when Kennedy is president. It's not safe here anymore."

Prudence grasped her coffee cup with two hands, as if for support. "I don't like Kennedy any more than you do, but I see no reason to uproot our lives running away from him. Kennedy will be president of Iowa, too."

"He's a city boy, and that's where his interests are. He'll leave the farmers alone," George said, not quite believing it.

Before he left for work, George went upstairs to take two aspirin. It took him a while to reach the bathroom. For some reason he felt tired, although he had had eight hours of sleep; his head was pounding and there were spots in his vision that he couldn't blink away. He had trouble opening the aspirin bottle. A tingling in his fingers made it difficult to grasp the cap. After he swallowed the pills, he pocketed the bottle. With these headaches he'd been having, it might be a good idea to keep aspirin in his desk at work.

While he drove to the office, George thought about what he'd say to Vincent Cadby. He'd have to be careful. He didn't want Cadby to assume that he'd be quitting in June, not if Prudence was balking at the idea of moving to Iowa. It would be disastrous if they started looking for a replacement for him before he was ready to leave. There were probably dozens of young engineers who would grab his job if they had the opportunity. But they couldn't replace him. He had never missed a day of work and no one's drawings were as precise as his. There wasn't a better engineer at Cadby and Hitchcock, even if Hitchcock had become a partner. Bought his way in, Cadby said when he had asked for an explanation. Why hadn't he thought of approaching Cadby? He was ten times the engineer Hitchcock was. Then why were there rumors that Cadby had approached Hitchcock? Lies. They had to be damn lies. Those spots in his vision weren't going away. He'd better get his eyes examined.

Vincent Cadby was walking down the corridor carrying a set of plans when George entered the building. Cadby walked with the athletic stride of a man challenging old age; he had just turned sixty-six and dieted strenuously to keep trim. "George, I could set my watch by you," he said. "Do you have a minute?"

"Sure," George said, thinking that it was fortuitous that Cadby was seeking him out first thing in the morning.

They entered George's office, which was uninviting. The walls, floor, and metal furniture were beige; there were no personal items in the room, nothing to indicate that a human being inhabited the space eight hours a day except for a magnificent thick-trunked jade tree resting on a marble sill under the solitary window. "How have you been feeling?" Cadby said, setting the drawings on George's drafting table.

"Fine," George said.

"That's good. I've been concerned about you, thinking that you might be working too hard. You don't feel pressured, do you?"

"No, never have."

Cadby put on a pair of reading glasses that rested halfway down his nose and pulled a pencil out of his shirt pocket. "See here, George," he said, pointing with the pencil to the top drawing, "That armature is misaligned."

George studied the drawing in shock. He rarely made mistakes, and never such a blatant one. "I...I don't know how that happened. I'll do it over right away, stay late if I have to until it's finished."

"It isn't necessary as long as the plans are in my office by Friday. You know, George, it wouldn't be a bad idea to treat yourself to a winter vacation this year. Go to Florida, lie on the beach and watch the pretty girls in their bathing suits. It'll give you color and get your circulation going, if you get my drift," Cadby said with a grin, gently punching George's shoulder.

George stiffened. "I don't care much for the beach."

Cadby shrugged. "Every man to his own taste," he said, leaving the office.

Lecher, George thought. His head started to pound with a vengeance.

Prudence cooked chicken and rice for dinner. George asked for a small portion, which he didn't finish. "Are you feeling all right?" she said.

Was he all right? First Cadby had asked and now she was inquiring about his health as if something were obviously wrong with him. He was as competent as anyone--in control, healthy except for these headaches, which a quick trip to the eye doctor would cure. "I'm fine," he retorted angrily, "just not hungry."

George didn't consider telling Prudence what had happened at work. It would have been as unthinkable as walking down Giffort Street naked. He kept his humiliation deep inside him, buried with other emotions that might reveal weakness or vulnerability. Although they had been married for thirty-three years, they had not shared a moment of passion, the reckless and unfettered joy a man and a woman can release in each other by giving of themselves without fear of embarrassment or reprisal. Their relationship was rooted in religion, in a sense of obligation to church and family, and dedication to work for its own sake. They had taken vows that had locked their lives together and had lived peacefully, but always at a distance from each other, like the prize-winning rose bushes in their garden that existed side-by-side, protecting their delicate blooms with thorns. Yet after so many years, neither one wanted to live without the other; they were a set, like matching chairs.

By the time they went to bed in their separate rooms, Prudence's concern had grown into worry. She had watched George surreptitiously all evening and didn't like what she had seen, how he had moved his fingers and rubbed his hands every so often, as if they were numb. And there were times when he had blinked rapidly, over and over again, while he was watching television. There had to be a reason why he was doing those things; a man his age wouldn't start new habits. But he had insisted that he was fine. It had to be restlessness. He wanted to move to Iowa. Maybe he just couldn't wait. He'd sat like he was itching to go-- rubbing his hands and blinking impatiently--now that she thought about it. She'd write to Cora, Jane, and Anne tomorrow to tell them that she expected them home for Thanksgiving. Emma would be back from college. It would be nice having the house full for a few days, just like it used to be. She'd have the girls talk to him about Iowa. He might listen to them. The girls didn't seem to write much anymore. Or call, either. All the work that had gone into raising them properly and now they were too busy to be bothered with their parents. Even Emma's letters from college were infrequent, short and uninformative.

She'd be worried if she weren't sure that Emma was conducting herself with propriety, like a decent young Christian woman. There could be no doubt about that, despite her brief flirtation with the Palmer boy. Emma had been raised like her sisters.

Reassured, Prudence turned off a brass lamp next to the plain pine bed that had once been Cora's and slept in solitary comfort in her eldest daughter's room.

* * *

It was an effort for George to drive home from work on Friday. He had pushed himself to complete a new set of plans for Cadby, which he had checked and rechecked for errors. The strain had left him with a feeling of generalized fatigue, a weakness so pervasive that he wondered if he would have enough strength to slide the garage door open and closed. Somehow he managed. As he walked toward the house, he felt the need for a good night's sleep. There was a lawn full of leaves waiting to be raked in the morning.

Freak claps of thunder broke the stillness of the night and by dawn Giffort Street was covered with snow. "I don't believe it," Penner said, looking out his bedroom window at eight o'clock. He had gotten up to give Jordan breakfast.

"You don't believe what?" Virginia asked sleepily.

"Snow. There must be a foot of it, at least."

"You're not going to trick me into getting out of bed."

"Come see for yourself."

"No, thanks," she mumbled, pulling the covers under her chin.

There was no wind, nothing to divert the storm. The snow fell lazily, dense oversize flakes that buried fire hydrants and flattened shrubs. The elm trees, which still had leaves dangling from their branches, were wrapped in white. Boundaries disappeared; there were no lawns, sidewalks, driveways, nothing but fences poking through the snow. Adults turned on their radios to listen to the latest weather reports, wondering if they'd be able to get their cars out and their errands done, while children gulped their breakfasts down, eager to be outside. When the final flakes settled late in the afternoon, nearly two feet of snow had fallen. "What will we do?" Penner said, looking out the kitchen window in disbelief. "I can't see the driveway, and we don't own a snow shovel."

"I guess we'll have to scoop the snow up with our hands," Virginia said.

"What?" he said, looking at her with disbelief.

"I bought a shovel last week," she said, laughing at his reaction. Her voice was as merry as the red and yellow flowers that were splashed on the kitchen wallpaper.

He smiled. "I'll get you for that later."

"Promise?"

"Promise."

They made love after the baby had her last feeding. Their movements were slow and tender at first, as gentle as the snow that had fallen on their house. They had spent the day delighting in their children and now, in the warmth of their bed, delighted in each other.

Up the street, George Masterson gazed out his bedroom window. The street lights glowed like candlesticks on a white tablecloth, lighting the elms that stood regally in coats of snow, as if conscious of their breathtaking beauty. George blinked with irritation, unmoved by the scene. He had a lawn full of leaves under that snow; if it didn't melt soon so he could rake, he wouldn't have a blade of grass left come spring.

The Mastersons were up early as usual on Sunday morning, "I don't think we'll be able to get to church," Prudence said, looking out through the French doors in the living room. "The plows haven't come."

"It's just as well," George said. "They'll dump an extra three feet at the foot of the driveway. If I shovel there first, right after breakfast, I'll have an easier job later."

"Can't we hire someone to shovel?" she said worriedly. Every year after the first snow there were news reports of men dying of heart attacks in their driveways while shoveling.

"Who?"

Prudence thought for a moment. Most of the Giffort Street youngsters she knew had grown up--the Kenway brothers, the doctor's boy, Will. Even Tommy Heussler was away at college. She hadn't paid attention to the younger ones. "What about that Santa Maria family down the street? Don't they have a couple of boys?"

"More like a houseful," George said, grimacing. "Those Italians breed like rabbits. I'll do the shoveling myself."

After breakfast George put on long underwear and ancient corduroy pants that were almost white from years of washing. He covered his bald head with a heavy navy cap Prudence had knitted, wrapped a red plaid scarf around his neck, buttoned a gray wool jacket that was threadbare at the elbows and cuffs, and put on his heavy black galoshes, tucking his pants inside before he fastened them. When he emerged from the house, he stood in the driveway squinting for a minute or two from the glare of the sun reflecting on the snow, like an owl temporarily blinded by a sudden flash of light.

Once his eyes adjusted (except for those spots that had been plaguing him), he trudged to the garage. The snow was heavy, denser than he had expected it would be. A shovelful might weigh twenty pounds. He still felt tired. But he'd be damned before he'd hire one of those Santa Maria boys. He'd shovel it himself, every inch down to the pavement.

As George approached the foot of the driveway, he noticed animal tracks and something dark lying in the snow. He moved resolutely forward with an expression of disgust on his face. Dog droppings! Not only did he have to shovel two feet of snow, but he had to clean up excrement! In his driveway! It had to be Penner's dog with his fancy New York curb training. The paw prints were melting, but there was no doubt in his mind that they led straight to Penner's door. No Jew was going to dump on him. He'd get it back, every bit of it, on the floor of his front hall!

George carefully scooped up the droppings, making

sure that the mess was cushioned by several inches of snow so his shovel wouldn't get soiled. Then he started down the street with the load, carrying the evidence in front of him like a crusader marching to battle, sure that right and justice were on his side. His anger grew with every step he took. By the time he reached the Penners' front door, he was shaking. It was as if all the passion he had struggled to submerge, a lifetime of constraint, had finally unleashed itself in the head of that shovel. He pressed the doorbell, his gray eyes glittering with anticipation behind his glasses. Penner was going to get what he deserved!

The Penners were in the kitchen eating breakfast. "I'll get it," Saul said. He went to the front door with Jordan following close behind.

The first thing Penner saw when he opened the heavy oak door was the load on the shovel. Quickly, he grabbed the handle of the glass storm door at the same moment George's gloved hand reached for it. Then, still grasping the handle, he pushed the inner door fully open and saw that the hand and shovel belonged to Masterson. "What are you doing here?" he demanded, as if it weren't obvious from the offensive shovel.

"Just returning what's yours," George said, tugging, on the handle with one hand while balancing the shovel with the other. He was no match for Penner. The storm door didn't budge.

"You're sick," Penner said.

Furious, George heaved the contents of the shovel at the door. "Your dog left that on my property and if he does it again you'll get it back, every bit of it, right where it belongs!" he shouted, as snow and excrement slid off the glass.

Saul pushed open the storm door and grabbed the front of Masterson's jacket with his massive hand. "My dog hasn't been near your house. We keep him fenced in the back yard," he said, lifting George off the ground.

"What fence?" George squeaked.

"The fence that I had installed, you bastard!"

"Let go of me," George said, feeling helpless with his feet dangling in the air.

"Gladly."

Penner set George down squarely on the pile of excrement. "Clean up what you don't take with you on your boots," he said, "and don't come near my house again."

"Or my Daddy will beat you up," Jordan said.

The two men had been unaware of Jordan, who had been watching them with round-eyed excitement. For an instant, they both stared at the youngster, speechless. Penner recovered first. "Go to your mother," he said, stepping protectively in front of his son.

Jordan left reluctantly. Penner remained behind the glass storm door until there was no trace of Masterson except for stained footprints in the snow.

George walked up the street with a shuffling gait, trying to clean his boots. He wanted to kill Penner. He had never hated anyone as much as he hated that Jew, that kike with his filthy dog and foul-mouthed child. He'd get even if it was the last thing he ever did!

Penner went into the kitchen and told Jordan to go to his room to play. After the youngster left, he related what had happened. "The man is crazy," he said, "a nut."

Virginia was visibly upset. "Jordan said you hit him."

"I did not!" Saul said vehemently. "I only grabbed him by his jacket and set him down in the mess he brought. He was asking for it."

"But he's old and half your size. You could have hurt him."

"Are you defending that bastard?" Saul said "There must be at least a dozen dogs in the neighborhood, and that anti-Semite accused ours. What was I supposed to do, bow obsequiously and beg his pardon? Or better yet, maybe I should have called you to the door to handle the situation."

His implication was unmistakable. Virginia blanched. "I didn't mean it that way," she said.

It was too late. He had stormed out of the kitchen and was climbing the stairs, three at a time.

Penner's outbursts of temper were usually short-lived, like sudden summer showers that evaporate almost as quickly as they come, but that Sunday his anger stayed with him, festering. He and Virginia pointedly avoided each other, which affected the children; the baby howled constantly, and Jordan started to speak in a whine. It seemed to Virginia that every encounter they had with Masterson made her feel cut off from him, an outsider. A familiar nervousness attacked her, the same anxiety she always experienced when she was with his family, the fear that she might say or do the wrong thing. Even after she had converted, she knew that she was not quite acceptable to them, that embracing their faith could not correct the error of her birth, the fact that she had not been born and raised a Jew.

After they went to bed, they lay tossing until she began rubbing the back of his neck. His muscles were knotted with tension. "It was an awful day," she murmured.

"Let's end it," he said.

He fondled her breasts and moved his hands slowly over her body. But after he entered her, his movements became harsh.

"You're hurting me," she said.

Unable to control himself, Penner didn't stop until he exploded inside her.

* * *

George didn't tell Prudence that he had gone to see Penner. It hadn't turned out as he had planned, and she would be aghast if she knew he had marched down the street carrying a shovel loaded with dog shit. Besides, the only thing Prudence was interested in was Thanksgiving and having the girls home. She hadn't talked about anything else since she mailed those letters, that and his appointment with the eye doctor on Wednesday. She had made the appointment and was insisting that he go. It was a mistake telling her about his eyes. He'd have to take off from work early, which was the worst thing he could do after he'd had that trouble with those drawings.

The walls of Dr. Edwin Forrester's wood-paneled waiting room were lined with black-framed diplomas and certificates in surgery and ophthalmology. George sat on a maple deacon's bench getting angrier by the minute. All those credentials and Forrester couldn't tell time! His appointment was for two thirty. It was now four seventeen and he was still waiting. Forrester had exactly thirteen minutes. If his name wasn't called by four thirty, he would leave.

A plump nurse who had thick ankles ushered George into a narrow, windowless room at four twenty-eight. He sat in the dark in a high-backed examining chair and again waited for Forrester. When the doctor arrived ten minutes later, George was nearly apoplectic.

"Sorry you had to wait," Forrester said, extending his hand. "I had an emergency--glass in a child's eye. It was sticky, but I was able to save it."

Edwin Forrester was a short, slender man who had piercing brown eyes that required no correction. His manner was so pleasant, brisk yet low key, that George began to relax. The examination proceeded quickly. While George described his problems--the spots in front of his eyes and his blurred vision--Forrester expertly slipped lenses in and out of metal frames and put drops in George's eyes. After the doctor readjusted the frames on George's nose, he tried two lenses, asking, "Is this better? Or is this better?"

"The first one," George said, seriously doubting the doctor's ability. Not only had Forrester been late, but he had made no comment about his symptoms. "I still see spots."

Forrester studied George, who was leaning forward anxiously. "Do you ever feel lightheaded? Have you experienced a tingling sensation in your hands or blood in your urine?"

George sighed with relief. "Those are my symptoms, exactly," he said, his confidence in Forrester restored. "Even the blood in the urine. I thought I got a hernia from shoveling over the weekend."

"It sounds like you're suffering from hypertension."

"What's that?"

"High blood pressure. From the extent and frequency of your symptoms, I suggest that you see someone right away. Do you have an internist?"

"What do I need an internist for?"

"To treat you."

"You're a doctor, and you know what's wrong with me," George said, becoming agitated again. He had waited two hours in Forrester's office, and now the smart aleck was trying to get rid of him.

Forrester scribbled a name on his prescription pad, then detached the paper and handed it to George. "I'm an ophthalmologist, trained to treat eyes," he said, leaving to see his next patient. "The man I'm recommending is excellent, the best in the city."

George stared at the paper until he saw nothing but spots. The name that Edwin Forrester had written in his large scrawl was DANIEL COHEN.

Prudence was sitting on a spindly, mouse-colored chair in the living room when he came home. Her eyes were red-rimmed, and her hair, which was usually arranged in a rigid ring of curls that circled her head, was out of place. She was holding a lace-edged handkerchief and looked as if she were in mourning. "I only have high blood pressure," he said, thinking that her condition was a direct result of his appointment with Dr. Forrester. He tentatively placed his hand on her shoulder, moved by her concern.

"Cora just called," she said, as if she hadn't heard him.

"Has there been an accident? Is she all right?"

Prudence's lower lip began to quiver. "She's not coming home for Thanksgiving. She and Bill are going to Boston to be with his parents."

"Oh." George removed his hand from her shoulder.

"And these came in the mail today," she said, handing him two tear-stained envelopes.

George took the letters. The top one was from Jane, telling them that she was sorry but she had already made plans to have Thanksgiving dinner with friends in Philadelphia. George's heart lurched when he recognized the handwriting on the second envelope. It was Emma's, bold and round. He held the letter with shaking hands. Emma's words danced in front of his eyes: *I've accepted a friend's invitation to spend Thanksgiving recess with her family. They live in Des Moines. I'm sure you won't mind since the trip home from Iowa is so expensive. Have a happy holiday.*

"At least ..." George had meant to say 'At least Anne will be with us,' but he couldn't. His tongue felt thick, uncoordinated.

Prudence didn't notice. She rose slowly, holding onto the chair arms like an invalid. "We might as well have supper," she said.

The telephone rang after they were seated at the kitchen table. They simultaneously removed their napkins from their laps and walked into the hall wordlessly, each hoping that it was Cora, Jane, or Emma calling to tell them that she would be coming home after all. The telephone was resting on a small mahogany table. Prudence picked up the receiver and said hello, her voice high with expectation. It was Anne: she was sorry, but she had already made plans and would not be home for Thanksgiving. Prudence's face crumpled. She handed George the receiver and walked into the kitchen, her spine sagging with disappointment, to dutifully serve the meatloaf she had prepared. George returned to his place at the table several minutes later. He couldn't look at Prudence. His head was spinning. The meatloaf and mashed potatoes on his plate made his stomach constrict painfully. He picked up his fork and speared a piece of meatloaf.

There was really nothing else he could do.

* * *

It was clear and cold the Saturday after Thanksgiving. The snow had melted, and the branches of the elm trees were bare. George was outside before nine o'clock, glad to escape the house. Prudence had been glum since the girls had called and written. The silence of their Thanksgiving dinner, broken only by the scraping of their knives and forks, had caused another one of his headaches that aspirin hadn't touched. He held his bamboo rake and looked at the leaves matted on the grass. His head still ached, inflamed by Emma flitting in and out of his thoughts like a nymph. He felt as if he were losing control and began to breathe deeply, taking in great gulps of air as though it were a tonic that would clear his head.

Jordan Penner, dressed in a red jacket and brown corduroy pants, started riding up the street on his tricycle after George had been raking for an hour or so. Jordan was pedaling determinedly, eager to call for his friend, Tony Santa Maria. When he approached the Mastersons', he saw that the sidewalk was solidly blocked with soggy leaves. Jordan hesitated. He couldn't ride his bike through the leaves, and he was forbidden to go into the street. His father had warned him that under no circumstances could he go near the Mastersons' lawn. But he wanted to play with Tony. He had been waiting to go outside since he had gotten up. He looked around. Mr. Heussler, Mrs. Levinson, and other neighbors that his father knew and liked were out. Mr. Masterson wasn't there (George had gone into the house to urinate). If he rode on the lawn, just a little, he could get to Tony's. Mr. Masterson would never know.

George came out of the house just as Jordan was pedaling across his driveway. The sight of him made George bristle. He grabbed his rake, which he had placed against the door frame, and headed straight for the front, his head jutting forward like a crane's. Jordan was two houses away when George saw tricycle tracks striped across his lawn. "Come back here," he shouted, waving his rake.

Jordan stopped pedaling. His face, under his red knitted hat, went white with fear. Reluctantly, he turned his tricycle around.

George waited in the driveway for Jordan, holding his rake like a pitchfork. His hands tingled. He wanted to take that little Jew and his tricycle and smash them to smithereens. Bubbling with rage, he didn't notice Lillian Levinson looking apprehensively across the street or Stan Heussler approaching him.

Jordan wasn't moving fast enough. George went after him. He grasped Jordan's arms with his gloved hands and yanked the child off the tricycle. "Just a minute, George," he heard someone say.

George wheeled and saw Stan Heussler. "What's going on?" Stan said.

"This...This monster rode across my lawn," George said, pointing at Jordan.

Jordan started to cry. "I couldn't get to Tony's," he sobbed. "The leaves were there."

Heussler eased his bulk between George and

Jordan. "The boy had no other way to go," Stan said, putting a comforting hand on Jordan's shoulder.

"Then he should have waited or gone in the street," George said, trying to step around Stan so he could get at Jordan.

"I'm not allowed to go in the street," Jordan wailed, his eyes and nose running.

"You are if you're carried," Stan said. He scooped Jordan up with one arm, picked the tricycle up with the other, and walked down George's driveway to the street.

"Where do you think you're going?" George demanded, following them.

"I'm sending the boy home."

"You have no right," George shouted. He wanted to stop Heussler, but he could hardly move.

Stan set Jordan's tricycle on the sidewalk, then placed the sobbing youngster on it. "Maybe I don't," Stan said, watching Jordan ride off, "but you might have hurt the child."

George's head was reeling. "I didn't hurt him!" he yelled. "I didn't harm a hair on his body!"

"A word of advice, George," Stan said, picking up his rake. "Don't ever lay a hand on anyone in anger, especially someone who isn't your size."

"Mine...Mine..." George wanted to say 'Mind your own business,' but he couldn't get the words out. He turned and stumbled away.

Saul Penner came out of his house in a rage. He strode up the street without a hat or jacket, unaware of the wind knifing through his clothes. He didn't hear Virginia, who was standing on the front steps, calling to him to come back. There was only one thing on his mind, one person: *Masterson.*

Stan Heussler saw Penner first. He thought he might say something to avert further trouble, but when Penner came closer, he decided against it. Penner looked angry enough to uproot an elm barehanded. "MASTERSON!" Saul bellowed.

George dropped his rake, which he had been having difficulty holding. Across the street, Lillian Levinson and Frank Kenway paused for a moment, then continued working.

Penner took giant strides through the leaves, scattering them in every direction, and stopped inches from George, his fists clenched with rage. "You bastard!" he said, "You vicious bastard!"

George's nose started to bleed. His eyes rolled back and a guttural sound escaped from his lips as he slid unconscious onto the wet grass.

Penner stood helplessly, staring at George with a mixture of bewilderment and horror, as if Masterson were playing a perverse trick.

Stan came over, followed by Lillian Levinson and Frank Kenway. "What happened?" Frank asked, kneeling to feel George's pulse. "I...I was just talking to him," Penner said,

Three pairs of eyes looked at George's bloodied nose, then focused on Penner. "I didn't touch him," Penner said. "Believe me, I didn't lay a hand on him."

"Prudence had better call an ambulance right away," Frank said. "I can barely feel his pulse."

Stan Heussler went to tell Prudence. As he hurried up the driveway, he heard Saul repeating like a refrain, "You must understand: I didn't touch him. You must understand..."

WAR ON GIFFORT STREET

Meghan Danahy met Dennis Kipphut at an anti-war demonstration in the fall of 1969. Over five hundred students had congregated on the Broad Street side of the university, blocking the main entrance, to protest the Vietnam War. The roadway leading out of the school was plugged with cars, and traffic had started to back up on Broad Street. Gray-uniformed university policemen had surrounded the demonstrators, shouting into bullhorns to dispel the crowd. **"Hell, no, we won't go!"** the students shouted, unwilling to concede an inch of ground.

Neither Meghan nor Dennis were participating in the demonstration. Meghan had just left the library and, attracted by the noise and the placards bobbing above the sea of students, had started to walk across the sloping lawn toward the crowd. Sirens from city police cars pierced the air. The chanting grew louder, as rhythmic as a heartbeat. **"Hell, no, we won't go! Hell, no, we won't go!"** Spurred by the insistent cries, Meghan started to run, unaware of a tall, strapping fellow trotting behind her. Dennis Kipphut was also in a hurry. It was four fifty-five, and he wanted to catch the South Mills bus that would be stopping on Broad Street at five o'clock. He eyed her buttocks straining against her tight jeans and her dark brown hair swinging freely down her back, catching amber light from the late afternoon sun, and ran faster hoping to get a glimpse of her face before he veered left to the bus stop.

Meghan was near the fringe of the demonstration when the police riot squad alighted from their cars carrying gas masks. "Tear gas, the pigs have tear gas!" someone shouted. The chanting stopped and the crowd splintered, spilling in all directions over the lawn like a broken egg. Before she knew what hit her, Meghan was lying on the grass, dazed.

"Are you all right?" Meghan's eyelids fluttered. "Are you all right?" a bass voice repeated. She blinked, trying to focus. There was a red plaid shirt directly above her. "You better not move for a few minutes."

She had gone down almost directly in front of Dennis. He had immediately fallen on his hands and knees, using his body to protect her from students running blindly from the riot squad, although tear gas hadn't been used.

"What happened?" she asked, pushing herself up on her elbows. Her eyes were wide open; they were green and had yellow flecks in them like miniature suns.

Dennis sat back on his heels. "You were whacked on the head—a two-by-four from a sign someone was carrying." He didn't add that he knew the fellow who was carrying the sign, a slight, ferret-faced guy named Monroe who constantly espoused C. Wright Mills' theories on the power elite in an economics seminar, whether or not it was relevant to the discussion. Monroe knew he had hit her; he had glanced back as she fell, then sprinted away. Dennis had watched him escape, fighting the urge to go after Monroe to beat the shit out of him.

"What did the sign say?" Meghan asked, tentatively touching a throbbing spot on the side of her head behind her right ear. It was tender and had started to swell.

"Bomb the Pentagon, I think," Dennis said.

Meghan laughed, confirming Dennis's instinctive decision to stay with her. Although she couldn't be called beautiful—she had a stubborn chin and her cheeks, which were as round as a child's, were splashed with freckles— her face was strong, and her smile generous and disarming. "I would have liked it better if they had gotten the Pentagon," she said, struggling to get up.

Dennis rose and offered her his hand. After she was on her feet, she looked around and saw that the contents of her green book bag were scattered on the lawn; her notebooks were trampled, and torn papers carried by a light breeze were skittering across the grass, as if nature were trying to clean away the debris from the fracas that had disrupted the tranquil afternoon. "Oh, no," she said, stooping to pick up a typed piece of paper ruined by a boot print squarely in its center. "My Dante paper!"

She grabbed her book bag and ran frantically after the papers that had blown farthest away, forgetting him. When she turned to come back, he was walking toward her with her books under his arm and papers in his hand. "Thank you," she said, stuffing the papers and books into her bag. "You saved me and my paper, and I don't even know your name. I'm Meghan Danahy."

"Dennis Kipphut," he said.

"Can I buy you a beer?" she asked, unaware that she was staring at him. She had been too dazed and disconcerted to notice that he was exceptionally good looking; he had deep-set brown eyes and thick black hair, which he wore shorter than most of the boys on campus. He could be in a shirt ad, she thought, a Hathaway man without an eye patch.

Dennis glanced at his watch; it was five twenty-six. "Thanks, but I have to run to catch a five thirty bus."

"Can I give you a lift? It's the least I can do."

He hesitated. If she had her own car, she wouldn't be going anywhere near his neighborhood. The South Mills district was an isolated pocket of land tucked between the downtown business area and the waterfront. He didn't know anyone who lived close to South Mills who went to the university. Most of the fellows his age who lived there were either in Vietnam or were in trouble with the law; the remaining few were married and had children. But he had already missed the five o'clock bus and was certain to miss the next one. He couldn't afford to jeopardize his job by being late for work; men were being laid off and there were rumors that the mill was going to close. "If it won't take you too far out of your way," he said. "Are you heading south?"

"I am now," Meghan said.

The positive tone of her voice left no room for argument, although Dennis was already having doubts as they crossed the campus to the parking lot. It had gotten suddenly dark, that quick twilight which comes in autumn like a surprise. By the time they reached her car, a shiny white two-door Ford, he had decided to ask her to let him out on the corner of Broad Street and South Mills. He would run the rest of the way rather than let her drive to the waterfront. A girl alone down there in a car like hers could mean trouble.

Most of the traffic on Broad Street was heading north, away from the center of the city; the two southbound lanes were relatively free of cars. They quickly passed the South Mills bus, which was slowing to stop at the corner of Broad Street and Hewett Avenue to pick up a lone passenger standing under a street light. Dennis caught a glimpse of the woman waiting for the bus as they drove by. It was Mrs. Stone; she lived on Dennis's street. She was a stocky, tired-looking woman who worked as a domestic; her husband was an alcoholic who couldn't hold a job. Dennis shifted in the front seat so that his back was to the bus. His turning away was more of an involuntary reaction than a calculated response. He liked Mrs. Stone. She was a hardworking woman, and he wouldn't have snubbed her if they passed each other walking on the street. Still, for no reason, at least not a conscious one that he could explain, he didn't want Mrs. Stone to see him going down Broad Street in Meghan's shiny white Ford.

Meghan was relieved when Dennis threw his left arm over the back of the seat and turned toward her. She had been trying to talk to him and had elicited replies that were as sparse and perfunctory as those to a written questionnaire. In response to her questions, he had told her that he was a senior majoring in economics and that he hoped to go to law school. She wondered why he had said "hoped to go" instead of "planned to go" but did not ask, sensing that her question would be an intrusion. Instead, she volunteered that she was a sophomore, majoring in English. "What are you planning to do when you graduate?" he said.

Meghan shrugged. "Teach, I suppose," she said, feeling vaguely uncomfortable about her lack of direction for the first time. She had three years of college to complete, which seemed like forever to her. There was no reason to rush into anything. Career decisions were commitments made by adults, and she had always thought of adulthood, like gout and cataracts, as something that happened to other people.

"I was lucky you were headed in my direction," she said, wanting to change the subject. "You must have felt that you were accomplishing something until the cops came."

"I don't understand."

"The demonstration."

"Oh," Dennis said. "I wasn't in it. I just happened to be nearby."

Meghan frowned. There was more than a hint of sarcasm in his voice. Or was it condescension? "Do you have something against peace rallies?"

"Not really."

"You certainly don't sound enthusiastic."

"I'm not."

"Why?"

"I don't have the time, for one thing," he said, "and even if I did, I wouldn't waste my energy."

Meghan was flabbergasted. How could he say that

peace rallies were a waste of energy? Demonstrating was as American as apple pie; it was almost unpatriotic not to want to protest. One of her greatest joys at the university had been protesting the Vietnam War. She loved the noise and excitement of the rallies, the feeling of camaraderie and the hint of danger in the action, which was exhilarating after her years at parochial schools. Although no one seemed to notice her, she could shout until her throat was raw and feel that she was accomplishing something. "You can't be a hawk," she said, beginning to regret offering him a ride.

"No," he said. It was too dark in the car for her to see the expression on his handsome face, which was one of both bitterness and amusement.

"Then why aren't you trying to stop the war?"

"Because I can't."

"Certainly you can."

"How?"

"By protesting," she said, as if it were the most logical thing in the world.

"You don't really believe that, do you?"

"Of course, I do," she said hotly.

"Well, let me know when it works. My number will be in the lottery," he said, adding, "I'll get out at the next light."

They had just passed through the heart of the business district and were approaching the waterfront section. "There's nothing around here," Meghan said, looking at vacant lots and abandoned buildings with boarded windows.

"I'll walk the rest of the way."

"But I can drive you to where you're going."

"It's better this way," he said.

The traffic light at Broad Street and South Mills changed from amber to red. As soon as Meghan braked to a stop, Dennis opened the passenger door. "Make a U-turn and go back down Broad," he said, getting out of the car. "Thanks for the lift."

Meghan watched him run down South Mills until he was swallowed by the darkness. Then she waited for traffic to pass and swung the car around. Her U-turn was perfect, but it gave her no satisfaction. She drove up Broad Street toward Hewett Avenue thinking about Dennis Kipphut, feeling as cheated as she did on Christmas morning when she was six years old and found a doll in a carriage next to the tree instead of the puppy she had prayed for. He had escaped before she could find out anything about him. It wasn't that he was unfriendly, but there was something about him, a natural reserve like a fence with a NO TRESPASSING sign attached, that both challenged her and warned her away. She decided to ignore the warning. There was nothing she liked better than a challenge, and he had certainly given her one: it was her duty, if not her moral obligation, to convince him that the only way to end the Vietnam War was to shout it to extinction in a massive protest.

After Meghan turned left onto Hewett Avenue, her mind started searching for excuses. She was late for dinner and knew that her parents would be waiting anxiously for her. She sighed. It was the curse of being an only child. There were times when she felt the weight of their love physically, when her body grew tense under the strain of being the axis around which their lives orbited. She knew what would happen the moment she entered the house. Her father would be standing at the top of the vestibule stairs, waiting for her explanation. No matter how reasonable her excuse, he would remind her that she knew nothing of the dangers of the streets, which he had learned firsthand when he was on the police force. While they were talking, her mother would stop working in the kitchen and would listen, her eyes tearing with relief.

Meghan glanced at her book bag, which was on the

back seat. She'd tell them that she stayed late to talk to an English professor about the Dante paper, she decided as she approached Giffort Street. But she would say nothing about the demonstration or what had happened to her. It had been difficult enough getting her parents to consent to her attending the university. If her father had even an inkling that she had been near an anti-war rally, or worse, that she had been knocked to the ground running to one, she would be forced to transfer to Holy Saints. The thought of Holy Saints made her grimace. After enjoying her first freedom at the university, going back to the nuns would be like returning to prison.

* * *

Meghan looked for Dennis on the sprawling campus without success. She searched in the student union, on the paths that webbed across the lawns, in the wide corridors of the old limestone buildings, hoping to see him among the thousands of students going to and from classes. She thought he would be easy to find because of his size and several times had spotted tall, muscular youths in the distance, which had made her heart leap with expectation. But before she reached them, she saw that their hair was too long or that they weren't clean shaven. Finding him became an obsession. Finally, in desperation, she decided to go back to the place where they had met. He was probably leaving his last class, she reasoned exactly one week later as she crossed the sloping lawn to the spot where she had been hit. She withdrew a textbook from her book bag, placed the bag on the grass to use as a cushion, and checked the time. It was four o'clock.

She tried to study, but she couldn't concentrate. It was cloudy and cool, and the dampness from the wet grass was soaking through her sneakers. Whenever someone crossed the lawn, she looked up, then checked her watch.

After twenty-five minutes, she began to feel foolish and closed the book. It was too obvious; even if she did see him, she'd look like an idiot sitting here.

Dennis saw her as she was starting to leave. "Hey," he called, "returning to the scene of the crime?"

Meghan sneezed. "I guess so," she said, reaching into her shoulder bag for a tissue. Now that she had found him, she didn't know what to say.

"Do you have time for a quick cup of coffee? You look like you could use some warming up," he said.

"Sure," Meghan said, blowing her nose, which was pink from the cold.

She started walking up the lawn, assuming that they would go to the student union. "This way," he said, gesturing with his head in the opposite direction toward Broad Street. "We'll go to the Red Kitchen."

Most of the booths in the Red Kitchen were empty, but Dennis headed for the counter. Disappointed, Meghan sat down next to him on a red-upholstered stool near the front window; she would have liked to sit in a booth and linger over a cup of hot chocolate. As if responding to her thoughts, he said, "My last class on Thursday always runs over, so I have to rush to get to work on time. Today I have a few minutes."

"Where do you work?" she said.

"At a grain mill."

"Just Thursdays?"

"Every night, Monday through Friday."

"How can you work every night and go to school?" Meghan said, looking at him with amazement. Some of her friends had jobs, but they usually worked between eight and twelve hours a week.

"No work, no school," he said. "It pays for my tuition and books, among other things."

A stringy-haired blond waitress brought them coffee and hot chocolate after she served an elderly couple in a booth. Meghan spooned the whipped cream off her hot chocolate, wondering what the "other things" were. "It must be hard," she said, trying to sip the chocolate. It was too hot and burned her tongue.

"I'm used to it."

"When do you study?"

"During the day, between classes," he said, stirring cream into his coffee, "and on weekends. If I ever get rich, I'm going to have a plaque made for a carrel in the library that's on the third floor behind the stacks. I know every grain in the wood like the palm of my hand."

"Now I know where to find you," Meghan said, regretting the words as soon as they slipped out of her mouth.

Dennis saw her face flush with embarrassment. "If you're in the library on the weekend, stop by my office," he said, smiling. He stood up, reached into the pocket of his jeans for change, and picked up the bill the waitress had left. "Sorry, but I have to run."

Meghan stayed at the counter sipping her chocolate, which had finally cooled. Through the restaurant window, she watched Dennis board the South Mills bus. "Was something wrong with the coffee?" the waitress asked, removing the cup Dennis had left; it was almost full.

"No," Meghan said, as if startled out of a dream.

The next morning Meghan awakened with a head cold. Her throat was scratchy, her eyes were watering, and she sat at the breakfast room table, sneezing. "You can't go to school," Mary Danahy said, putting her hand on Meghan's forehead. "I think you have a fever. It's aspirin, juice, and bed for you."

"Tomorrow," Meghan said between sneezes. "I have a quiz today."

"You can't go," Mary said with alarm. She cast her green eyes upward, silently summoning Coyle to come downstairs to enforce her order.

Meghan saw Mary's signal and got up to leave. Even when wordless, Mary's summonses were powerful, backed as they were by a lifetime of prayer. "I'll be home before noon," Meghan promised, grabbing a box of tissues from the kitchen counter. If she didn't go immediately, she knew she'd be cornered by her parents and the ghost of her brother, Kevin, who died of cancer when he was four years old. Kevin was always there when Meghan was sick; he lived in Mary and Coyle's fear that their daughter would be taken from them, too.

"Really, it's only a cold," Meghan rasped, charging out the front door as Coyle's right foot hit the topmost stair.

Meghan spent the weekend in bed. When she wasn't blowing her nose, sleeping fitfully, and drinking freshly-squeezed orange juice brought at regular intervals by Mary, she thought of Dennis. She imagined him at his carrel in the library, his broad shoulders hunched over his books. Oh, how she would have liked to be well, and at the library, so she could stop by his "office." What rotten luck she had to catch a cold! Days later, when Dennis mentioned that he had been expecting to see her at the library, she would look back on her miserable weekend as a stroke of good fortune. If she had sought him out, he might not have looked for her.

At noon the following Wednesday, Meghan stopped outside the student union to read a hastily-lettered poster announcing a peace rally that was to take place that afternoon in front of the administration building when she heard her name called. She turned and saw Dennis climbing the concrete steps, two at a time. "Have you eaten yet?" he said.

"No," she said, trying to sound as casual as she could.

"What happened to your nose?" he said.

"I'm getting over a cold," she said self-consciously. Her nose was pink and peeling after days of constant blowing.

"Then we'd better get out of this wind," he said, pulling open the heavy glass door.

They found an unoccupied table in a corner on the far side of the basement cafeteria. It was a functional, oversize room with a drab brown tile floor; the walls were plastered with posters and announcements. Dennis had brought his lunch in a paper bag. "Can I get you something to drink?" she asked.

"Coffee, if you don't mind," he said.

Meghan stood impatiently in the cafeteria line while the women behind the long counter moved with maddening slowness, replenishing salads and sandwiches and serving bowls of soup, chili, and plates of hot roast beef grudgingly, making no attempt to conceal their dislike of their jobs and the students they served. Dennis was eating a sandwich when she returned to the table. "I thought you got lost," he said.

"The line took forever," she said, unloading her tray. She gave him his coffee, then placed her soup, salad, and tea on the table.

"You're not eating much," he said.

"I'm not hungry," she said. "There's going to be another demonstration today."

"You're not going with that cold, are you?"

"No," she said. "But I want to ask you something: Why are you so down on peace rallies?"

"I told you," he said. "They're a waste of time and energy."

"But they're not!" Meghan said, forgetting her soup. "If students hadn't protested so long and hard, Johnson might still be president."

"They stopped Johnson, but they didn't stop the war."

"This country was founded on protest. It started with the Boston Tea Party, and it hasn't stopped. It still works!" Meghan said, her cheeks getting as pink as her nose. "Washington is finally listening."

"Really?" Dennis said. "Is that why they let the military institute a lottery--so they'll have enough men to send over to 'Nam?"

"They will listen!"

"Who will make them listen?"

"We will," she said, the yellow flecks in her green eyes flashing like warning signals. "At least I will."

Dennis looked at the students surrounding them. The room was full of denim, of work shirts and faded, patched jeans worn by youths who had never done a day of hard labor in their lives. They were wearing the clothes he had worn all his life, the clothes his father had worn, but now the denim was fashion and the strategically-placed patches were signs of status, not of poverty. How could he make her understand when she was one of them? "The kids who demonstrate against the war aren't the ones who fight," he said. "They're a bunch of spoiled brats scared shitless that their daddies won't be able to pull the right strings."

"That's ridiculous!"

"The demonstrations—thcy'rc temper tantrums," Dennis said. "Rich kids screaming because they don't want to be sent to Vietnam. It's a big fraternity that anyone can join; no dues are collected, and if you're injured and need a few stitches or if you're hauled off to jail, you're an instant hero."

"You're crazy," Meghan said.

"Realistic," Dennis countered. "They can have their war at home without risking their lives and feel like men. While they're out burning their draft cards, their fathers are paying lawyers to find loopholes they can hide in."

"That's not true!"

"Where do you live?"

Meghan stared at him. Where she lived had nothing

to do with the war. He really was crazy, as nutty as he was good looking. "On Giffort Street," she said, half-afraid to tell him.

"How many guys on your block have fought in Vietnam?"

Meghan thought for a moment. "None," she said, surprised.

"A dozen guys from my neighborhood are in 'Nam now," he said. "Last year a guy from my block was killed, and two were sent home wounded: one had to have his leg amputated; the other one is a quadriplegic."

"I'm sorry," Meghan said softly. "I didn't know. I guess I never thought about it that way."

"You didn't have to," he said.

There was no resentment in his voice. He was simply acknowledging the difference in their backgrounds, in their lives. Although she wasn't aware of it then, at that moment Meghan Danahy fell in love with Dennis Kipphut.

"It can't hurt to protest, though," she said, unwilling to completely concede. "We don't belong in Vietnam. The war is unfair."

Dennis shrugged. "Life is unfair."

As they were leaving, he told her that he had looked for her over the weekend in the library. "Maybe this Saturday," she said, knowing that she would be there. Nothing, not even pneumonia, could keep her away.

When Meghan found Dennis at the library Saturday afternoon, she saw that he had put his jacket over the chair in the carrel next to his, expecting her to come. She settled into the carrel and tried to study, but it was impossible. Her eyes kept shifting away from the pages in front of her toward him, as if they had a will of their own. Dennis seemed unaware of her. His concentration was so intense that he didn't glance up when she left to roam the stacks; nor did he notice when she returned.

The afternoon dragged. Meghan began to fidget,

like a child waiting for a circus to begin. When she didn't think she could sit another minute, Dennis snapped a book shut, tilted his chair back, and stretched. "Ready to quit?" he asked.

"Hours ago," she said with relief.

The sun was setting when they left the library. The horizon was streaked with reds and pinks that looked like a wound in the gray, late autumn sky. They walked to a bar near the campus that had a flashing neon BUDWEISER sign in the window. After Dennis ordered two beers, Meghan excused herself. "Sorry," she said when she returned to the narrow booth, "I had to call home."

"Is something wrong?" he said.

"Just checking in," she said.

"You're kidding. Are you one of those precocious kids who started college at fifteen? Am I going to get in trouble for ordering beer for a minor?"

Meghan laughed ironically. "No, but sometimes I feel like one."

While they drank their beer, she told him about her parents and her dead brother, Kevin. "I was a year old when he died," she said. "It probably sounds ridiculous, but I can't get a simple cold without them treating me as if I'm terminally ill. They've told me in a thousand ways that I'm all they have—their only living child—although they've never come right out and said it. It used to bother me more than it does now, probably because I have no memory of Kevin. I felt cheated, as if I were paying for the death of a brother I never knew. I guess people can adjust to almost anything, except for my parents to Kevin's death. I always call to tell them where I am because I know they're at home, worrying. I don't think about it anymore; it's automatic, like a reflex."

"That's heavy," Dennis said.

"Maybe," she said, "but my parents aren't even aware of it. They think they're acting normally. I tried to explain it to them once, and they were so shocked I felt awful."

"*You* felt awful?" he said. "Weren't you resentful?"

"I hurt them," Meghan said.

"You're incredible," he said, looking at her as if he weren't sure she was real.

"Not really," Meghan said. "I'm Catholic, and Catholics believe that the Lord never gives you more than you can bear."

"Not all Catholics," Dennis said. "Count this one out."

He told her about himself, overcoming his natural reticence with his second beer. She learned that he was the oldest of nine children and that his father worked as a night watchman. "He used to be a scooper at the grain mill until he hurt his back and couldn't do heavy work anymore. Instead of giving him a lighter job, the company let him go. I'm working there now. I wouldn't have gotten my job if I hadn't raised hell in the front office for what they did to him."

"Is he bitter?"

Dennis picked up his glass and drained the remaining beer. "I wish he was," he said, "but he isn't. There's no fight left in him. He'll accept anything, no matter how bad it is. When they fired him, he resigned from life. He didn't even ask the union to intercede for him, not that they would have done anything. He works for pennies now—his paycheck isn't enough to feed his kids— and he doesn't seem to care. If our electricity was cut off, he probably wouldn't notice."

"And you help?" Meghan guessed, recalling the "other things" that Dennis had once mentioned.

"As much as possible. So do my brothers and sisters. We all kick in what we can, except the younger ones who don't have jobs. It's too bad my old man didn't resign from life altogether."

"That's a terrible thing to say."

"He quit in every way but one," Dennis said, his expression hardening. "They had five kids when his back went. Now there are nine. I tried to talk to him after the seventh one was born. I was fourteen and had been delivering newspapers since I was ten to pay for my clothes and save money for college. I begged him to use birth control so my mother wouldn't get pregnant again. It was the only time I got a reaction from him that showed he was alive. He hit me so hard I passed out. When I came to he was standing over me, shouting that I had better find the priest so I could make my confession."

"What did you do?" Meghan said, unable to conceal her shock.

"I took a bus to the hospital," Dennis said, rubbing his chin. "He broke my jaw."

Meghan wanted to drive Dennis home, but he refused her offer and walked her back to the campus. The night air was crisp, the sky studded with stars. They walked in silence between the limestone buildings that cast massive shadows in the moonlight, Meghan's hand enveloped in his. She could feel their history in their hands, his thickly calloused palm against her own, which was as soft and smooth as his was rough. She wanted to stay with him as long as possible. "I'll drop you off," she said as they approached the parking lot. Once he was in the car, maybe he would let her drive him home.

"At the bus stop?" he said.

Meghan gazed up at him and smiled. "At the bus stop."

"You have eyes like a cat," he said.

"Is that good or bad?"

"Cats have nine lives," he said. Then he bent down and kissed her, his calloused hand still holding hers, and Meghan felt her nine lives dissolving into one.

Dennis stood at the bus stop in front of the Red

Kitchen and watched Meghan's white Ford disappear down Broad Street. He wondered why he had told her about his family. He had never discussed his father with anyone and hadn't thought about his broken jaw in years. It was a part of his past that he wanted to forget. Meghan was unlike any girl he had ever known. Although she was obviously pampered and protected, there was nothing frivolous about her. She wasn't like the girls on campus who had made passes at him, expecting their teasing and flirting to be returned, as if sex were an endless game. The other girls he knew, the ones from South Mills, yearned for the glamour they read about in movie magazines, and made themselves over to look like cheap imitations of movie starlets with tight, suggestive clothes, thick makeup, and cheap perfume. Meghan was different from all of them, even the sound of her name...Meghan.

A number nine bus going to South Mills pulled up to the curb. It had no passengers. Dennis dropped his fare into the coin box and took a seat in the back, where he studied until he got off at the end of the line.

* * *

Meghan and Dennis saw each other as often as they could after that first Saturday at the library. They met between classes, had lunch together in the student union, and spent their weekends at the library, studying. On Saturday nights they ate hamburgers or pizza, then went to the movies or sat in one of the bars near the campus, drinking beer and talking. Later, they would get into Meghan's Ford and drive to a quiet side street where they would park until the car windows dripped with condensation before Meghan dropped him off at a bus stop.

Coyle and Mary Danahy wanted to meet Dennis. "I want to see this boy you've been disappearing with," Coyle said when Meghan came home on a Sunday night at ten thirty. "You've been gone for three weekends in a row."

The Danahys were sitting in their gold-carpeted living room on a pair of avocado-green velvet Mr.-and-Mrs. chairs that had high, tufted backs. The room was filled with the latest in Mediterranean furniture, bulky upholstered pieces and heavy, ornately-carved wood tables that vaguely resembled Spanish furniture, but without style or authenticity. "Why don't you invite him for dinner on Wednesday?" Mary suggested, trying to soften Coyle's demand. She was a slight, round-shouldered woman who looked as if she were about to disappear in the avocado velvet.

"He works during the week," Meghan said.

"Doesn't he go to school?" Coyle said, suddenly suspicious. He was a handsome, barrel-chested man who sat solidly in his chair, as if conscious of his weight. Although his black hair was gray at the temples, the pugnacious thrust of his chin denied him an appearance of distinction.

"He works nights and attends classes during the day."

"Is he Catholic?" Mary said, slipping in the question that was most important to her.

"Yes," Meghan said as quickly as she could so Mary wouldn't detect uneasiness in her voice. Her response wasn't a lie, but it wasn't exactly the truth, either. Dennis hadn't gone to church or received communion since his father had broken his jaw. Meghan knew that his being a Catholic by birth wasn't enough. Dennis had denied the church and had fallen out of grace, which to Mary was as bad as not being a Catholic at all.

"That's wonderful," Mary said, the lines on her forehead softening with relief. Her eyes were green like Meghan's, but they were perpetually clouded with worry. "Maybe he can come for dinner next Sunday after church."

"Sunday night would be better," Meghan said. "We

can have sandwiches or something light after we finish studying at the library."

After Meghan went upstairs, Coyle said, "I hope he's not one of those hippies or yippies, whatever you call them." He was thinking of the last boy Meghan had brought home, a bony youth who had shoulder-length hair and a full, unkempt brown beard; there was a patch of the American flag sewn on the left buttock of the boy's jeans that had made him livid.

"At least he's Catholic," Mary said.

Dennis didn't want to eat with the Danahys. "Can't I just meet them without dinner?" he said when Meghan invited him.

"It's a command performance," Meghan said.

"What if I use the wrong fork?"

"I told you—it's a light supper. We'll probably have soup and sandwiches. You can't mess up a sandwich."

"Wanna bet?" He crossed his eyes and put his hand to his ear, as if he were shoving something into it. "What if I miss my mouth?" he said, moving his jaw as if he were chewing.

Meghan laughed. His sense of humor was one of the things she loved most about him, unexpected flashes of biting mimicry that were unerringly accurate. He imitated his professors and the students in his classes, particularly the ones he thought pompous or affected. His impressions were devastatingly funny, especially his imitation of a fellow named Monroe. "Relax," she said. "My parents aren't fancy people."

"Giffort Street isn't what I would call a modest neighborhood."

"We've only lived there for six years. My parents were born on Catherine Street, and I grew up on Melrose Avenue, which is two blocks away. My mother didn't want to move; she talks about the old neighborhood constantly."

"Then why did you leave?"

"My father got ambitious," she said, "which reminds me: don't call the cops 'pigs.' My father will take it as a personal insult; he used to be a policeman."

The Sunday supper at the Danahys' was strained. Coyle Danahy, who believed that there were worse ways to judge a man than by his response to a firm handshake, grasped Dennis's calloused hand with unnecessary firmness, expecting the young man to either withdraw or turn the handshake into a test of strength. Instead of reacting predictably, Dennis matched Coyle's pressure with equal firmness, grasping the older man's hand until Coyle withdrew, his hand aching. They ate in the breakfast room, which had a round maple table and four maple captain's chairs. Mary served split-pea soup and club sandwiches. "It seemed silly to eat sandwiches in the dining room," she said nervously, as if she weren't sure she had made the right decision. Coyle asked Dennis what his career plans were, and Mary wanted to know what parish he belonged to. They asked him where he lived, what his father did for a living, and how many children there were in his family. Dennis answered respectfully, calling them "sir" and "ma'am," while Meghan shot them warning looks to stop asking questions. Although she interrupted as often as she could, she knew that her chances of ending the interrogation were as slim as stopping a falling star.

"I'm sorry," Meghan said to Dennis as they walked to her car. "It must have been awful for you."

Dennis shrugged. "I expected it."

"Forgive me?" she said, close to tears.

"It wasn't your fault," he said, adding, "There's only one other place I've been to that's as nice as your house."

"Where?"

"The mortuary where my grandmother was laid out," he said. "It's too bad she was dead. She would have appreciated it."

Coyle couldn't wait for Mary to finish cleaning up the kitchen. "Well, what do you think?" he said, leaning against the refrigerator. The appliances and countertops in the kitchen were all gold, a shade or two lighter than the carpeting that rippled through the house.

Mary was loading the dishwasher. "He's certainly a handsome boy," she said. "He reminds me of Errol Flynn."

"Did you notice the way Meghan was looking at him?"

Mary nodded. The way Meghan was gazing at Dennis had made her heart skip. She saw the glow of love in Meghan's eyes, the hunger that demands satisfaction.

Coyle saw something else in Meghan's eyes. "I was thinking of a different Flynn," he said. "Remember Stinky?"

"Oh, no!" Mary said, wrinkling her nose.

Meghan had found Stinky Flynn sleeping in the snow behind Queen of Martyrs church when she was seven years old. Stinky was the bum of the parish, a vile-smelling, flatulent old man whose bulbous nose was a mass of broken capillaries. Meghan had awakened him and had brought him home for dinner. Mary was aghast; Coyle was furious. "I won't have that manure pile sitting at my table!" he said. But Meghan had insisted. "It's our Christian duty," she said, parroting the nuns who taught her. "We must help those who can't help themselves." Coyle told her that Stinky didn't want help. "Everyone wants help," Meghan said. "If he can't eat at our house, then I can't eat here, either." She went outside where Stinky was slumped on the front steps in an alcoholic stupor and remained there in the biting cold, sitting next to him, until Coyle relented. It was the first of many dinners that Stinky Flynn had at the Danahys' house. Meghan watched out for the old man and brought him home for dinner as often as she could until he died of cirrhosis of the liver. Nothing Mary and Coyle said could break Meghan's attachment to Stinky; they even enlisted the help of the nuns, who, forgetting their lessons in charity, told the child that Stinky wasn't acceptable at a decent Christian table. But Meghan continued to treat Stinky with the same respect she gave the parish priest, always referring to him as "Mr. Flynn," and braved the malodorous fumes emanating from every orifice of his body without once wrinkling her nose. "You can learn to like Mr. Flynn," she argued over their objections. "All you have to do is pretend that he smells like red roses."

Coyle wanted more for his daughter than a boy from South Mills; there were bankers' sons at the university, and the sons of professional men. "Dennis Kipphut is ambitious," Coyle said, "but he has everything going against him, including the draft."

"He's Catholic," Mary offered.

"So was Stinky Flynn!" Coyle said.

The Sunday Dennis ate supper at the Danahys' began the week that the lottery to fill the draft was held. "They're going to use ping pong balls," Dennis said to Meghan. "Can you imagine--my fate decided by a ping pong ball?"

Meghan went to the library at two o'clock on Monday afternoon, where she had expected to find Dennis studying in the third-floor carrel. Instead, he was waiting for her in the reception area wearing his heavy blue jacket, his books tucked under his arm. "Let's go for a walk," he said. "I can't concentrate."

They walked hand-in-hand under a leaden early winter sky to the northern edge of the campus, which was thickly planted with pine trees. The ground under the pines was covered with brown needles that crunched softly under their feet. "You'll be lucky," Meghan said, dropping her book bag on the carpet of needles. "I just know you will."

Dennis set his books down next to hers, then put his arms around her. He loved the fragrance of her skin and hair, which was as fresh and clean-smelling as the pine.

"Maybe," he said doubtfully. "The Kipphuts aren't known for their luck."

They stayed in the grove of pines until Meghan reminded him that he had a three o'clock class. Reluctantly, Dennis stood up and pulled Meghan to her feet; their clothes and hair were covered with pine needles. "Ready?" she asked after they brushed themselves off.

Dennis glanced down at the bulge in his jeans. "Not quite," he said, grinning. "You'd better start back without me."

The final edition of the evening paper ran the complete results of the lottery. Meghan sat on the gold sofa in the living room and scanned the first column, holding her breath. If Dennis's birthdate wasn't there, she could advance to the second column, and then, if luck held, to the third column, which would mean that he was safe. She didn't reach the second column. Dennis's birthdate was forty-fifth on the list. "Goddamn ping pong balls!"

Sobbing, she ran upstairs to her bedroom.

Mary and Coyle stopped watching Walter Cronkite and looked at each other. "Poor Meghan," Mary said, almost as upset at Meghan's curse as she was with her tears. "His number must be low. It seems sort of callous to use ping pong balls."

"Straws, paper, ping pong balls—they're all pretty much the same," Coyle said. As far as he was concerned, their potential problem had been solved: Meghan's tie to Kipphut had been neatly cut with Dennis's low number.

"What do you think Dennis will do?" Mary said.

"If he's smart, he'll enlist so he can go in as an officer."

"What about Meghan? Should I go upstairs and talk to her?"

"Leave her alone," Coyle said. "She'll get over it."

"What if she doesn't? She's crazy about that boy, and you know how she feels about the war."

"There's nothing she can do about it now," Coyle said. "It isn't easy but she'll learn, like everyone else, that life is full of disappointments that she'll have to accept."

Mary sat rubbing the knuckles on her hands, a habit she had whenever she was troubled. "In the beginning, Vietnam seemed to be another Korea: someone else's war that we were fighting," she said. "I hoped it would end quickly, and that this time we'd win. But the death count keeps going up. I don't recall a daily death count with other wars, announcing enemy deaths as if we're accomplishing something. It's still killing, and that's nothing to be proud of no matter how you say it."

She paused and stared at her knuckles; her eyes were green pools of sorrow. "Night after night I watch the news and see nothing but horrors--young American boys killed and maimed, children burned alive with napalm. And those body bags, those horrible body bags! The remains of young men packaged and tagged for shipping like carcasses of meat! I think we should pull out and ignore what Nixon says about an honorable withdrawal. His way is costing too many lives."

Coyle had been listening to her with raised eyebrows. Mary was usually so busy praying that she didn't have time for the affairs of this world. "Since when are you getting political?" he said with surprise. "You sound like Meghan."

Mary sighed. "I was just thinking," she said hesitantly, "about Kevin. I wonder how we would feel if it were Kevin's birthday that was picked."

"At least we would have had him longer than we did," Coyle said. He got up abruptly and walked out of the living room into the kitchen. Eighteen years after Kevin's death, Coyle still couldn't talk about his son.

At ten o'clock Mary told Coyle that she was tired and was going to bed. She went upstairs and stopped in the hallway in front of Meghan's room. The door was closed as she expected, but she had hoped there would be a shaft of light at the bottom. The gold carpet was dark. Mary's shoulders dropped. She wished Meghan was a child again, a child with a child's hurt that could be easily soothed away, but she was an adult now, and it was impossible to protect her from life's inevitable bruises.

Mary went into the master bedroom, slipped her coral rosary beads out of a black leather case that was on a nightstand between the twin beds, and said the rosary in the darkness. Usually she lost all sense of time and place in the prayers, whispering first the Apostles' Creed on the crucifix, then Our Fathers on the large beads, Hail Marys on the small beads, and Glory Be to the Fathers after three Hail Marys in the beginning and after each group of small beads. The intricate pattern of the prayers, the ritual of pausing and reciting on each bead, always left her with a sense of inner peace. But that night she finished with a vague uneasiness. Light spilling in from the hall caused shadows in the room that felt threatening, hinting of disaster like the slipping of a stone before an avalanche. For the first time in years she thought of the people who had lived there before them—the Mastersons. She had never seen Mr. and Mrs. Masterson; he was dead when they bought the house, and Mrs. Masterson was out when the realtor took them through. A year after they moved in, a freckled, wholesome-looking young woman rang the doorbell. "I used to live here," she said. "My name is Emma Masterson." She asked if she could come in and had stood motionless for a few minutes in the living room staring in the direction of the French doors. Then she said, "Thank you" and left quickly, looking as if she had just awakened from a nightmare.

Chilled, Mary remembered what Edna Harris had told her on the Sunday following Emma Masterson's visit. She had asked Edna about the Mastersons when they were walking home from church. "There were rumors," said

Edna, who was wearing, as always, a flamboyant hat. "I heard that Prudence Masterson told the realtor she would sell only to Catholics or Jews, that they deserved to be stuck with each other because they were responsible for her husband's illness. Can you imagine? We lived on the same block with them for years and didn't know the Mastersons were bigots. Of course, there was that trouble with the Penners and George's stroke happening at the same time. I'm really not sure what it was all about. Stan Heussler knows, but he won't discuss it. George lingered for almost three years, paralyzed on one side and unable to talk. Prudence used to set him out on the front porch in his wheelchair until the elm was cut down. He'd sit there for hours, one side of his face sagging like a Halloween mask, his eyes squeezed shut as though he couldn't stand looking at the street. It was strange that their elm was the first one on the block to die. Before he had his stroke, George spent most of his time gardening; he was always fertilizing or clipping his grass or pruning his rose bushes. I guess the tree must have been as sick as George was without anyone realizing it."

Mary crossed herself, clutching the coral rosary beads tightly in her hand as if to ward off evil. They should never have moved from Melrose Avenue. She had tried to tell that to Coyle, but he had refused to listen to her. "I want to live where the houses aren't five feet apart," he had said, "where I can't hear the neighbors snoring on a hot summer night, where everyone doesn't know what's in everyone else's dresser drawers."

It was true. There were no secrets on Melrose Avenue, or on Catherine Street, or anywhere in the Third Ward. But there are no secrets between people who live and die together. They went to each other's christenings and confirmations, weddings and wakes. Whole family histories were known by every shopkeeper and tradesman. The butcher knew which families ate ham on Sunday and which families had roast beef; the owner of the hardware store knew how often people repainted their walls and replaced the washers in their faucets. She had told him she wanted to stay, that it was home and she had never lived anywhere else. "That's right," he had said, "and if we don't move, I know what will happen. You'll grow old just like the rest of the Queen of Martyrs' women: you'll wear black shoes and black dresses and live for your prayers. We're moving! I want my privacy. I've earned it!"

And the first person they saw on Giffort Street, the morning they moved in, was a woman wearing black. She was tall and gaunt, a stick clothed in a black coat, carrying a black purse and black satchel. The woman nodded at her and glared at Coyle as though he had done something obscene. That afternoon Giffort Street was filled with parked cars, and people were walking to and from a house diagonally across from theirs. Later they learned that the people were returning from the funeral of an old man named Joe Tarpin, who had lived with the Kenways.

Mary put the crucifix of the rosary to her lips, shivering with fright. How could she have missed it? The day they moved into the Mastersons' they saw the Whittakers' maid, Meddie, dressed in black, carrying a black satchel like the devil's messenger, and within hours cars that had come fresh from the cemetery were parked in front of their house. *The Mastersons, Meddie, and the old man's funeral. Three signs. The mystical number three.* Like deaths, omens came in threes. The message had been given to them, and she had read it too late.

* * *

Dennis lost his job the first week in December. He was waiting for Meghan at the third floor carrels on a gloomy Saturday morning. "Let's go for coffee," he said when she arrived, closing a thick spiral notebook.

"Is something wrong?" Meghan asked after they left the library. The muscles around Dennis's mouth were tense, and his dark eyes were unnaturally bright. "I got an early Christmas present," he said as they trudged through the snow toward Broad Street.

"What?"

"Did you see the morning paper?"

"No."

"The mill is closing. I got a notice in the envelope with my paycheck last night. They're going to keep the day shift until the end of the month, but their hours will be cut." His voice sounded tight and strained.

"Oh, no!" Meghan stood on the snow-covered lawn and stared at him with disbelief. First the lottery, now this. Why did he have such horrible luck?

Dennis had been so upset that he hadn't considered how she might react. She looked as if she were about to cry. If she broke down, he would, too. "It's bad, but it isn't a disaster," he said. "I'll survive."

"How?" Meghan said, blinking. Snow had started to fall, and a large flake had caught in her eyelashes.

"I have some money saved, enough for next semester's tuition and books. I had a feeling this was coming," he said, gently brushing the flake away. "It could be worse."

"Sure," Meghan said sarcastically.

Dennis turned away from her and swallowed hard, hoping she wouldn't notice. "Hey, do you know where we are?" he said.

Meghan's eyes darted from the limestone buildings behind them to Broad Street, then tracked their footprints in the snow. They were standing almost directly over the spot where they had first met. "The scene of the crime," she said, forcing a smile. "I had to get hit on the head to meet you."

They sat in a booth at the Red Kitchen and had

coffee and doughnuts. "What are you going to do?" she said.

"Look for another job and hope I can find one that pays more than the minimum wage."

"Full time?"

"Whatever I can get," he said.

Except for her lunches at school, which she paid for, Dennis had always insisted upon paying for both of them when they went out, even though Meghan had repeatedly offered to go Dutch. "Please, let me treat," she said, reaching for the bill the waitress had left on the table.

"No"," Dennis said, jerking the check out of her hand. His face was defensive, his neck rigid with pride.

"I'm sorry," she said. "It's just that..."

"Don't say it," he warned.

Meghan bit her lip. How could she have been so stupid? It was the worst thing she could have done. "Forgive me?" she said, fighting tears.

He slid out of the booth and bent over her, putting his face close to her ear. "I love you," he whispered, inhaling the fresh scent of her hair.

On Sunday, Meghan asked Coyle if he would give Dennis a job. The Danahys were sitting in the breakfast room eating dinner. Mary had put a glazed ham and scalloped potatoes in the oven before she and Meghan went to eleven o'clock Mass. Coyle had attended ten o'clock Mass. He was having an affair with his secretary, Mary Beth Rooney, a redhead with creamy white skin who had large breasts and skinny calves. This wasn't Coyle's first affair; he had been seeing women since Kevin's death and had rationalized his infidelities by telling himself that it wasn't hurting Mary because he was always home for dinner on time. He was uncomfortable in church with Mary, who went daily, and was grateful that she could go with Meghan. He had scrupulously avoided contemplating the time when Meghan would no longer be living with them, which would mean that Mary would look at him expectantly on Sunday mornings. Coyle didn't want Mary to know that he went to confession only once a year, before Easter, so he could receive communion.

"I thought Dennis had a job," Coyle said after Meghan asked him.

"The mill is closing. It was in yesterday's papers, and on the news."

"I'm sure he'll find something," Coyle said, sliding peas onto his fork with his knife.

"It's the height of the Christmas season; you can always use an extra man."

"I have all the men I need," Coyle said. "Besides, he has no training in security work."

"He's intelligent, and he can learn quickly," Meghan said, leaning forward.

Coyle thrust his chin out, as if to end the discussion. "I told you, I have all the men I need. Even if I didn't, I wouldn't hire him."

The yellow flecks in Meghan's green eyes grew brighter, like sparks about to burst into flame. "Why? What do you have against Dennis?"

"Nothing," Coyle said, cutting into a slice of ham. "I just don't believe in mixing my personal life with my work. It's not good business."

"You hired Frank O'Donnell."

"Frank was a cop."

"Frank is a drunk!" Meghan exploded, throwing her napkin on the table. "He trips over his own feet."

"Show some respect for your elders, young lady!" Coyle said louder than necessary.

Meghan stood up. "When they deserve it!" she said, stalking out of the room.

"Meghan, your dinner," Mary called, feeling helpless as she always did when they argued.

"I lost my appetite!" Meghan called back.

Mary started to get up when she heard the front door slam. "See what you've done," she said. "She's left without her dinner, and she had nothing but juice this morning. Why must the two of you always meet head-on? All she did was ask for your help. Did you have to dismiss her so quickly? Couldn't you try to find something for the boy?"

"I'm not an employment agency," Coyle said, spearing a scalloped potato. "Finish your dinner before it gets cold."

Dennis found a job the week before Christmas. Meghan was waiting for him at a table in the basement cafeteria of the student union. "Meet the new bouncer at Nick's Bar," he said, extending his hand.

Meghan didn't take his hand. "A bouncer? Couldn't that be dangerous? What if you get clobbered?"

Dennis took off his jacket and sat down. "I can handle myself. Anyway, the idea is to stop fights before they start."

"But Nick's is near the steel plant. A tough crowd goes there."

"It's no worse than my neighborhood," he said. "Besides, I'm getting two dollars an hour, forty cents over the minimum wage, plus beer and a sandwich on the nights that I work."

Meghan looked at him and sighed. He was wearing a denim work shirt that hugged his powerful shoulders; his rolled-up sleeves exposed his muscular forearms. He'd look ridiculous as a stock boy in a supermarket, which was the only other part-time job he'd found. "Will you get a lot of hours?" she said, blaming herself because she had convinced him to look for part-time work only.

"Every night from seven to closing until the first of the year," he said. "After that, on weekends."

"What about Christmas and New Year's Eve?"

"We'll have Christmas together," he said.

Dennis and Meghan exchanged gifts in her car the day before Christmas. She had wanted to buy him everything she saw in the stores--shirts, a suede jacket, thick wool sweaters--but had forced herself to settle for a pair of imported, hand-sewn brown leather gloves, remembering the incident at the Red Kitchen; his pride, like the tender skin of a ripe peach, was too easily bruised to risk spending more. Dennis's gift to her was a pearl held by three leaf-like gold prongs that was suspended on a delicate fourteen-carat-gold chain. Meghan was overwhelmed when she saw the necklace, which was resting on black velvet in a velvet-covered box; it was obviously expensive, much more than he could afford. "It's beautiful," she said, her voice slightly above a whisper, so moved that it was difficult to speak.

"Aren't you going to put it on?" he said, his skin flushed with the pleasure of giving. He had searched for hours for her gift, hunting for a perfect present in the nicest downtown stores, looking for something that would show how much she meant to him. Unlike Meghan, who articulated her feelings as easily as she breathed, it was hard for him to express what he felt. When he saw the necklace he knew that it would tell her, better than anything he could say, how much he cared for her, how special she was. The pearl was so perfect--lustrous and creamy white-- and it was permanent, a gift that would last.

Meghan removed the necklace from the black velvet box, undid the clasp, and raised it to her neck. "Help me," she said.

Dennis leaned forward and took the ends of the chain in his hands. After some fumbling, he managed to fasten the delicate clasp. "How do I look?" Meghan asked, touching the pearl, which had found its home beneath the hollow of her throat.

"Beautiful," he said.

Dennis ate Christmas dinner with the Danahys.

Meghan talked to Mary and Coyle before he arrived, warning them not to ask him questions. "Don't give him the third degree like you did the last time." she said. "I want him to feel comfortable."

Meghan had offered to pick Dennis up; she wanted to meet his family and had thought Christmas would be the right time. But Dennis drove to the Danahys' in his father's car, an ancient brown Plymouth that had rusting fenders and doors. Dennis had told his family practically nothing about Meghan. Except for hurried breakfasts, warmed-over suppers, and sleeping, he spent little time at home. The small house, crammed with eleven people moving in eleven different directions, was not a place conducive to sharing confidences; there was competition for seats in the tiny living room, constant noise which made it difficult to study, and overcrowded bedrooms that denied privacy. Because Dennis was the oldest and contributed money, his absence wasn't questioned; the less he was home, the more room there was for the others. His ambition set him somewhat apart from his brothers and sisters--he was the only one to go to college--but that, too, was accepted. He was twenty-one, old enough to know what he wanted, and as long as it was legal and he could do it on his own, it didn't get much more attention than one less person at the supper table.

Mary served a turkey dinner in the dining room. She had fixed enough food for three times their number: chestnut dressing, cranberry sauce, mashed potatoes and gravy, green beans topped with slivered almonds, cauliflower swimming in lemon butter, a shimmering mold of grated carrots and crushed pineapple suspended in orange gelatin, pickles and jumbo olives arranged in an oblong crystal relish dish, and for dessert, a mince pie with a lattice top that was a work of art. Dennis ate well, although his eyes never left Meghan. She was wearing a long-sleeved green wool mini-dress that she had left open at the neck to frame the pearl necklace he had given her. It was the first time Dennis saw Meghan in a dress; her legs were long and well-shaped, her ankles slender. He wished that he had money, that the future he was working toward was here, so he could take her to places where women wore dresses and men wore expensively-tailored suits. Someday, he thought determinedly. Mary watched her daughter and the strapping young man, who were clearly in love, and looked at the empty spaces around the table, imagining them filled with chattering grandchildren. Someday, she thought wistfully. Coyle ate a portion of everything on the table, partly out of gluttony, partly to keep his mouth busy so he wouldn't say the wrong thing. It was, after all, Christmas, a day of peace. He just had to be patient; it wouldn't be too long before Dennis would be drafted; then Meghan would be interested in dating other boys, the sons of doctors and lawyers. Someday, he thought impatiently. And Meghan's green eyes traveled from one to another, the yellow flecks in them glowing like the candles on the table. She had never been so happy. Oh, how she loved them all!

* * *

After final exams in January, Dennis started searching for a reserve unit he could join. (He and Meghan had both made the dean's list, Meghan for the first time, a result of the hours she had spent in the library.) Either Dennis borrowed Meghan's car or she went with him, waiting anxiously in the Ford while he talked with military personnel. The answer was the same everywhere he went: the units were full, and although he could put his name on a waiting list, the lists were so long that his name wouldn't reach the top for a minimum of two to three years.

"It's hopeless," Dennis said when he returned to the car after talking to an officer in the Coast Guard. "There's nowhere else to go."

It was a blindingly bright day; the sun, reflecting on

the snow, made Meghan squint when she faced him. She had expected the news and had been thinking of other possibilities while she waited. "Do you think you could get a physical exception?" she asked.

"Be serious." he said.

"I am being serious," she said earnestly. "They're being granted by the thousands."

"Not to me."

"Isn't there anything wrong with you--allergies, flat feet, a trick knee--anything a doctor can certify? I know someone whose brother was just rejected because he has psoriasis, and he had thought it was nothing but a bad case of dandruff. Try to think of something, no matter how insignificant it is."

"Forget it," Dennis said. "There isn't a physical that exists that I couldn't pass."

A bitter laugh escaped from Meghan's throat. "You know," she said, "the whole time you were in there, I was sitting here thinking of things that could be wrong with you. It's really sick. After a while, partial blindness, crippled limbs, missing fingers, and punctured eardrums started looking good to me."

"Would you settle for a hernia?"

Meghan's face brightened. "Do you have one?"

Dennis laughed. "No," he said, grabbing her. "But if I get one, I'll let you be the first to check it."

That night, Meghan asked Coyle if he would help Dennis get out of the draft. "There's nothing I can do for him," said Coyle, who had rushed away from Mary Beth Rooney to be home in time for dinner.

"Austin Rickard's son got an exemption last year; he's at Harvard now, getting his Master's in business. Could you talk to Mr. Rickard?"

Rickard's Department Store was Coyle's best client. Danahy Security had limped along for years until Austin Rickard hired Coyle to supply security people for his store in the early sixties,

The sit-ins in Nashville had given the city's blacks the courage to shop at Rickard's. Although they had come in hesitantly at first, a trickle of blacks moving uneasily down Rickard's wide aisles, Austin Rickard had panicked. He wanted his shoppers to feel secure in his store, which was the nicest in the city, a place where people could mingle with their own kind. Convinced the black shoppers were a threat to everything generations of his family had worked for, Rickard called private security companies to ask for bids. Coyle, who was desperate for business, submitted the lowest bid. As the civil rights movement gained momentum, other department stores hired Danahy Security. Blacks didn't cause problems in the stores. If there was trouble, it generally came from white shoplifters. But Coyle didn't mention that when he spoke to Austin Rickard. As far as Coyle was concerned, civil rights was a bonanza, and Austin Rickard was his benefactor. He had little contact with Rickard, but he referred to him constantly, as if they were intimate friends.

"Austin Rickard is a busy man," Coyle said.

"Not too busy to find a way to keep his son out of Vietnam," Meghan said.

"Dennis isn't his son," said Coyle.

"But Dennis needs help. He can't get into a reserve unit; he's tried everywhere."

"He shouldn't have waited so long. If he had any sense, he would have gotten himself on a waiting list a few years ago."

"He couldn't," Meghan said. "He had to work. He couldn't afford to take six months off and then go one night a week and two weeks in the summer. He would have lost his job. Without it, he couldn't have paid for his tuition and books."

"He can enlist as an officer."

"And get killed!" Meghan said. "Can't you ask Mr.

Rickard?”

“No. “

“A lawyer then?” Meghan said. “There are lawyers who specialize in this; they know all the loopholes.”

“Where would Dennis get the money for a lawyer?”

“We could lend it to him, or he could pay it off in installments.”

“The kind of lawyer you’re talking about doesn’t take clients on the installment plan,” Coyle said.

“Then what about us?”

“You mean ‘what about me?’” Coyle said. “Look, Meghan, Dennis isn’t my son. He has a father. Now let me eat my meal in peace.”

Meghan’s eyes widened. “I can’t believe you said that! Don’t you care about anything but your stomach? I’m talking to you about saving Dennis’s life, and you’re calmly cutting into a piece of meat as if we’re discussing the weather!”

“Dennis isn’t my responsibility,” Coyle said, spearing a piece of steak.

“I love him!”

“You think you love him,” Coyle said, punctuating his statement with his steak-laden fork. “You’re only nineteen, too young to know what love means.”

Meghan leaned forward accusingly. “When you married Mom, she was nineteen.”

“That was different.”

“Why?” Meghan demanded.

“Because it was us,” Coyle blurted, instantly aware that he had said the wrong thing. “What I mean...’”

“I know exactly what you mean,” Meghan interrupted. She pushed her chair away from the table and stood up, glaring at him. “What you’re saying is that you don’t give a damn about Dennis, that if he’s sent to Vietnam he’ll be conveniently out of the way, and if he’s slaughtered there, that’s the breaks!” she shouted, losing control. She wanted to hurt him, to hurt him as much as he was hurting her by his indifference. "If it were Kevin, you'd be running all over town trying to save him. I wish my brother were here so he could see what kind of man his father is!"

Coyle turned deathly white at Meghan's violation of the unspoken rule under which they lived: at the mention of Kevin's name he dropped his fork, which landed with a clatter on his plate. Mary was as shocked as Coyle but quicker to understand. "She's in love with Dennis," Mary said gently, putting her hand on Coyle's arm after Meghan ran out of the room. "She's afraid for him. Her fear made her speak out that way."

Coyle didn't respond. They heard Meghan's car start and the sound of her tires mashing the snow as she backed out of the driveway.

"She came to you for help and you refused her," Mary said.

"That's no excuse for what she did!" Coyle said, his color returning with a rush of anger.

"Dennis is bright and a hard worker," Mary said, adding with emphasis, "and he doesn't take drugs."

"How do you know?"

"I asked Meghan. I worry about her. Sometimes I hear stories from the women at church. So many young people from good families have gotten into trouble with drugs—marijuana. LSD, pills. The stuff is everywhere, as available as cigarettes. We've been lucky with Meghan."

"It wasn't luck," Coyle said. "We brought her up right!"

"So did a lot of other parents," Mary said, privately believing that her prayers had helped. "The Santa Marias down the street are fine people, and look at what happened to their oldest boy: he took LSD and now he's in a sanitarium, staring at the walls. Couldn't you call Mr. Rickard?"

"No!" Coyle said, his chin jutting out stubbornly.

Mary usually bent in the direction of her husband's will. Fighting Coyle was like wrestling with a tornado; once his mind had set its course, nothing could change it. But she had been uneasy for weeks, since the night of the lottery when the signs had belatedly come to her, meshing together forebodingly: the Mastersons, Meddie, and the old man's death. She had moved from Melrose Avenue to Giffort Street against her wishes, and had decorated the house like the rooms she had seen in furniture advertisements in *Better Homes and Gardens* to please him, but she hadn't felt completely comfortable in one of them. And tonight, listening to Meghan and Coyle, she knew beyond a doubt that there would be trouble. It was there, as plain to see as the fingers on her hands. She had lost one child, and had lost Coyle, too; he wasn't the same man after Kevin's death. If she had to fight with every bit of energy she possessed, she would not lose Meghan.

Mary knew Coyle better than he thought she did. "If Mr. Rickard is as nice a man as you've said he is, I'm sure he wouldn't mind discussing Dennis's problem with you," she said.

"Austin Rickard runs the biggest department store in the city. He's got enough to do without counseling a boy from South Mills."

"If he were a *friend*," Mary said pointedly, "he'd be happy to talk to you about Dennis. Isn't that what friendship is about?"

"Are you suggesting that Austin Rickard and I aren't friends?" Coyle said defensively.

"Not at all," Mary said. "What I'm saying is that it would be the easiest thing in the world for you to do. Why don't you call him tomorrow?"

"No!" Coyle banged his fist on the table. "First Meghan, then you, nagging me to help Dennis. He's an American citizen, the same as I was when I was drafted for

World War II. No one kicked and screamed when I went. I fought because it was my duty, and I was shot at the same as everyone else."

"Hitler and the Japanese wanted to destroy us," Mary said. "We were fighting for our survival then. Vietnam is different. Why should Dennis risk his life fighting in a country that isn't threatening us? The war in Vietnam is between the Vietnamese. What happens there won't affect us, even if the Communists win."

"I'm sick and tired of hearing about Vietnam and Dennis! Before Dennis, it was just Vietnam. Meghan hasn't stopped talking about that damn war since she started college. I'm sick of it! I'm sick of the hippies and yippies and the anti-war demonstrators! They're nothing but a bunch of hooligans. Look at the mess they made out of the Democratic Convention last year: it was a free-for-all, a circus run by long-haired, unshaven freaks. They have no respect. None. Not for our government, our institutions. They mock everything I believe in. They wear the flag I fought for on the seat of their pants like it's a joke. I've had all I can take!"

"But Dennis doesn't do those things," Mary said. "He's a decent Catholic boy."

"He's an American, isn't he?"

"Yes."

"Then he has to obey the law," Coyle said emphatically, "just like everyone else."

* * *

Mary and Meghan continued to pressure Coyle; the short month of February was marked by daily battling in the Danahys' house. Meghan tried every approach she could think of to change Coyle's mind, from reasoning to begging, without success. She ambushed him in the mornings when he came downstairs to eat breakfast and attacked him directly at dinner. Mary was also unrelenting, though more subtle. She mentioned Meghan's attachment to Stinky Flynn as often as she dared, reminding Coyle that his daughter's emotional attachments were fierce, and her loyalties unswayable. Other times Mary extolled Dennis's virtues, his diligence, decency, and Catholicism until he began to sound like a candidate for sainthood. Nothing worked. The harder they pressured him, the more intransigent Coyle became.

Meghan didn't tell Dennis that she had asked for her father's help. Coyle's attitude both angered and shamed her. Once she had idolized him; she had believed her father to be the strongest, brightest, kindest, most compassionate man in the world.

Now she had all she could do to conceal her contempt for him, her disgust at his indifference. Dennis had enough problems without adding Coyle's rejection to them.

Dennis was accepted to law school at the end of February; included in his acceptance was an offer of financial assistance. He made an appointment with the Dean of Admissions to discuss his draft status. "They'll keep the offer open until May," he told Meghan afterward. "It's the best they can do."

He was also having difficulty at home. "I can't contribute much now," he admitted one day, "just a couple of dollars a week. It isn't enough. I feel guilty every time I swallow a mouthful of food. If my sister Irene weren't getting married in June, it wouldn't be so bad, but she's saving every penny she can get."

His problems devastated Meghan. There were times when she couldn't look at him without choking back tears. Snatches of a Beatles song about war and destruction played in her head day after day. *It's going to be all right, it's going to be all right,* she kept telling herself. *It's going to be all right.*

But it wasn't all right, not with the cloud of Vietnam hovering over them, growing in density with each hour that brought Dennis's draft notice closer. Meghan wanted him to visit the Students for a Democratic Society headquarters on campus to get advice. Dennis thought they were a bunch of potheads and went reluctantly, at her insistence. He heard nothing but tired political rhetoric from the SDS members, who went on at length, he told her, like singers enchanted by their own voices. Meghan brought bag lunches to school to save her allowance money, which she added to her modest savings account in amounts so small that they pained her. Still, she had to try. A lawyer might accept what she saved as a down payment for counseling Dennis. And through it all the words... *it's going to be all right* rang mockingly in her ears. How could it be all right when it was as certain as the mounting daily death count that Dennis would be sent to Vietnam?

By the first week in March, Mary's nerves were as raw as the knuckles on her hands, which were red and bleeding from constant rubbing. She felt as if she were living in a war zone, that the constant battling going on in her house was destroying her family. For the first time in their married life, Coyle was coming home late for meals without offering an excuse or an apology. When they did sit down to eat together, the dinners turned into shouting matches, Meghan and Coyle screaming at each other while she pleaded with them to stop. The air in the house was electric with tension. Meghan, who was usually effervescent and affectionate, had become withdrawn and non-communicative, except when she fought with her father. "We're going to lose her," Mary warned Coyle, aching to have Meghan back, bright and bubbling, instead of the grim-faced girl who was living with them.

"That's all I hear from you! Every night you sit there rubbing your hands, saying the same thing--*we're going to lose her, we're going to lose her,*" Coyle said. "I'm telling you for the last time--we're NOT going to lose her! You're carrying on as if Meghan's eligible for the draft. She isn't going anywhere. Hell will freeze over before they draft females."

"She's drifting away from us, and you know it," Mary said as forcefully as she could.

"It's just a phase she's going through," Coyle said confidently. "Once Dennis is gone, she'll be herself again."

But privately he was beginning to have doubts. Meghan no longer called home to tell them where she was and what her plans were. She was living in the house as if it were a hotel, a place to sleep and eat occasional meals. Except for their fights, she refused to communicate with him. Feeling the chill of her icy silence physically, he started wearing sweaters in the evening like an old man. Although he wasn't introspective, he could recognize his own determination in his daughter's tenaciousness. Meghan was a fighter like him. She wouldn't give up easily, he thought with a mixture of pride and frustration; she battled like he did, so he'd have to wait it out. Dennis would be drafted when he graduated in May, Coyle reasoned, positive that time was on his side.

Mary also felt the pressure of time. It was her enemy. Life was at best a chancy business, with each tick of the clock increasing the risks. When Kevin died, she had trusted time to heal Coyle's grief, and time had failed her. She had reached out to him then for comfort and solace, but Coyle, unable to accept God's will, had turned away from her; he had numbed his grief with whisky and street fights that had led to his resignation from the police force to avoid dismissal. Alone in her sorrow, she had gone to the one place where she found comfort, to church where God had soothed her aching heart. And now, with this trouble between Meghan and Coyle, she turned to Him again. She said her rosary twice a day, every morning at church and again in the evening before she went to bed, but her fears weren't quelled. Soon she was saying the rosary four and five times a day, then more until her hours were filled with prayers. She fingered the pink coral beads constantly, unable to function without feeling them, cool and smooth, in her trembling hands.

* * *

On the second Monday in March, Mary put on her coat and boots as soon as the dinner dishes were done. "Where are you going?" Coyle said.

"To church," she said, hurrying out before he could question her further.

A cold March wind stung Mary's pale cheeks as she walked cautiously down Giffort Street, conscious of treacherous patches of ice under the wind-whipped snow. She shivered in her brown coat like a frail wren when she passed the Whittakers' house. Although new people were living there, a young couple who had twin girls, she could still feel Meddie's presence, that severe black coat and black satchel, as certainly as if Meddie had never left. Meddie, the Mastersons, and the old man's death--the omens had been there, threatening them from the day they moved in. Her pace quickened; she had to get to church on time to make her novena to St. Anne. The answer had come to her that morning. While she was dusting, she had accidently knocked her missal off her dresser. It had fallen to the floor, open to a picture of St. Anne, Mother of Our Blessed Lady. She had picked up the missal and crossed herself, then flipped to the front of the book where Meghan had written on the first page three years before:

To Mom on Easter,
May almighty God bless you and keep you always in His care.

Love,
Meghan

It was a sign, Mary thought for the hundredth time that day as she started down Carlson Street toward Our Lady of Perpetual Help. The missal had been Meghan's gift to her on Easter, the day of the resurrection of the Lord Jesus, and it had fallen open on the radiant image of St. Anne, the patroness of Christian mothers. It was as if God Himself were directing her, telling her what to do. A novena to St. Anne, nine weeks of nightly prayers, her only hope. If her petition were answered, everything would be all right: Coyle would help Dennis and the fighting would stop.

The Friday after Mary started her novena to St. Anne, Meghan withdrew the money from her savings account. She had two accounts at the bank: one with several thousand dollars in it, money Coyle had put in her name with himself as trustee until she reached the age of twenty-one; the account Meghan closed contained two hundred seventy-three dollars, money she had saved from summer jobs to spend on Christmas gifts, never thinking that she would need the money for anything else. Meghan added two dollars to the sum and walked out of the bank with a check for two hundred seventy-five dollars made out to Dennis Kipphut.

Dennis was surprised to see Meghan waiting for him when he left his last class on Friday afternoon at five o'clock. Usually he went directly from school to Nick's, where he ate before he started work at seven. "I'll drive you to Nick's," Meghan said. "We have to talk."

"Can't it wait?"

"No," she said, "it can't."

Meghan chattered nervously while she drove. When they were a few blocks away from Nick's, she pulled the check out of her coat pocket and handed it to him. "I want you to see a lawyer," she said.

Dennis studied the check, his face tight with pride. "Not with your money," he said, stuffing it back into her pocket.

Meghan nodded, as if she had expected his response. "Well, I guess this is it," she said, pulling up in front of Nick's. "I won't be seeing you again."

"You're kidding," he said, staring at her as if he were the victim of a sudden cruel joke.

"No, I mean it."

Dennis reached over to turn off the ignition and grabbed her by the shoulders. "Why?" he said.

"I can't stand it anymore! Every time I'm with you I feel like crying. You're going to be sent to Vietnam, and you're not doing a damn thing about it."

"I tried to get into every reserve unit in the county," he said. "I even wasted my time with those SDS jerks. There's nothing else I can do except leave the country."

"You can go to a lawyer."

"Not with your money!"

"Think of it as a loan. You can pay me back."

"No."

"If that's your decision," she said, "I can't see you again."

"C'mon, Meghan," he said, drawing her to him, "be reasonable."

It took every bit of strength Meghan possessed to push him away. "Good-by," she said, starting the car. Then she waited for him to leave, gripping the steering wheel as if it were a life preserver, until the car door slammed shut.

Pale and perspiring, Meghan drove home in a trance, automatically stopping for lights and breaking in traffic like a robot. When she entered the house, her nostrils were assailed with the odor of frying fish, a smell she detested. Suppressing an urge to gag, she told Mary that she wasn't hungry and went upstairs, where she removed her clammy clothes and showered. She went to bed immediately afterward, thoughts of Dennis circling in her head until they became a whirlpool, dragging her down, down into a restless sleep.

Meghan stayed in her bedroom on Saturday gazing out the back window at the rose bushes George Masterson had planted years before. It seemed impossible to her that those brittle, dead-looking twigs poking through the snow contained life, that in three months they would burst into flower--pale pinks and yellows, white, red, and magenta roses. How simple it was to be a plant, she thought enviously, to blossom and wither and be reborn again, season after season. She pictured Dennis sitting at his carrel in the library. What if he didn't call? What if she had made a dreadful mistake forcing the money on him with an ultimatum? Suddenly her plan seemed stupid and cruel. He was so proud. It was the worst thing she could have done. Or was it?

By mid-afternoon, the slightest sound in the house made Meghan jump. When the anguish of waiting became unendurable, she hurried downstairs, put on a suede jacket, and drove to the campus. She parked the Ford and ran to the library unsure of what she would say, knowing only that she could not imagine her life without him.

He wasn't there. She searched every floor of the building, then went to the student union and raced to the Red Kitchen without finding him. Desperate, she called his house. A boy with a squeaky adolescent voice answered. No, he told her, Dennis wasn't there.

Mary was waiting for Meghan when she came home. "Dennis called," she said, noticing that Meghan's eyelids were pink and puffy. "I wrote his number on the pad. Is something wrong?"

"No," Meghan said, running to the telephone.

They met at noon on Sunday in front of the Red Kitchen and clung to each other, oblivious to the traffic going up and down Broad Street. "I'm sorry," Meghan said over and over again, her arms encircling his neck, holding onto him as if she were afraid he'd evaporate.

"It's all right," Dennis said, stroking her hair as if comforting a child. His body was tense with desire; he wished that he had a place to take her where they could make love.

"I went crazy when you didn't show up at the library," he said after they ordered coffee. "Finally I got the hell out of there and started walking. I didn't know where I was going. I just walked. When I passed the VA Hospital, I remembered the guy from my block, the one I told you about whose spine was severed in 'Nam. He was sent there from San Diego last month. I went up to see him."

Dennis shook his head and swallowed hard. "Oh, God," he said, averting his face.

Meghan reached across the table and squeezed his arm. "You don't have to talk about it."

He clenched his hands into fists, as if he were fighting what he had seen. "Christ!" he said. "The guy's a head without a body. He hears, he sees, he thinks. The rest of him is dead. His arms and legs are withering into sticks. Sticks under a hospital sheet, that's all that is left of him. He was bigger than I am. When he was in high school, he boxed in the Golden Glove matches. He had a left hook that was lethal. Now he can't wipe his nose. His goddamn nose was running and he couldn't wipe it!"

Meghan listened to him, horrified. He was describing her nightmare, only the body in her dream was his: Dennis mutilated in Vietnam. Her eyes glistened with tears, the vivid green of leaves soaked in a heavy summer rain.

"Don't cry," he said, his voice breaking. "Please don't cry. "

"I can't help it," she sobbed.

"I'll go to a lawyer," he said, willing to do anything

to make her stop crying. "But I'll pay you back, every cent of it."

"Forget about the money," she said, giving him a glorious, wet-cheeked smile. "All I care about is you."

Finding a lawyer wasn't as easy as they had anticipated. After a number of telephone calls, they learned that most attorneys didn't handle Selective Service cases. The lawyers' secretaries told them draft cases were a specialized area of the law, and the tone of their voices made it clear that it wasn't a particularly desirable one. Finally, Dennis asked around the campus, obtained some names, and made an appointment with the first attorney who would see him. He left the lawyer's office both angry and depressed.

"It was a waste of money," Dennis said with disgust when he met Meghan later in the student union. "He told me to get a full-time job and claim an exemption as the sole support of my family. Where in the hell can I get a job that will support eleven people? And even if I get one, what will I do about my father? Tell him to quit his job? He'd personally escort me to my draft board before he'd do that."

"Did you explain about your father?" Meghan said.

"I practically spelled it out for him. What an idiot! Once he got the idea in his head, he couldn't think of anything else. 'Nine kids, nine kids,' he kept saying over and over again," Dennis mimicked, raising his eyebrows so that his face had an expression of stupid surprise. "He acted like he had never heard of a family that had nine kids. If that's going to be my competition, I can't wait to go to law school."

"You have to take care of Vietnam first," Meghan said. She secretly agreed with his assessment of the lawyer's suggestion, but it was something to think about. A doubtful chance was better than none. And if it didn't work, they could get some of the lawyer's retainer back and go to another attorney. "What if you can get a job, a good one? With your degree in economics, you could get into an executive training program."

"Most executive training programs are high in prestige and low in pay."

"Then what about a job in heavy industry? You have experience from the grain mill..."

"As an unskilled laborer," Dennis interrupted. "Forget it, Meghan."

"You have to try," she said determinedly. "I'm not going to visit you in some VA hospital."

"What about my father? He'll never go for it."

"Get the job first," she said. "Then we'll worry about him."

Dennis borrowed Meghan's car between classes and drove to area plants where he filled out job applications. To his amazement, he was offered an opportunity to enter a management-training program after several interviews at a steel company. "I don't believe it," he told Meghan on the Wednesday before Easter. "They want to hire me at ten thousand dollars a year to start. They're even willing to subsidize any graduate work I do. I can take night courses at law school and get my degree. It's almost too good to be true."

Meghan was ecstatic. "Not really," she said. "You're graduating with an A average."

"But I applied as a laborer. I was willing to do anything, even work in the blast furnace." Dennis thought for a moment, then smiled ironically. "I've always had jobs where I used my back instead of my brain. I don't even own a suit."

"I can't wait to see you in one," Meghan said, imagining him stunningly handsome in a gray flannel suit.

"Not so fast," he warned. "I have to convince my father first."

"When are you going to talk to him?"

"Tomorrow morning when he gets home from work."

"Maybe you should wait," she said uneasily.

"Why?"

"Tomorrow is Holy Thursday."

"So what," he said.

Thursday was the first day of the university's spring recess. Meghan waited nervously at home for Dennis's call. By the time the telephone rang late in the afternoon, she was beside herself with worry. "Where have you been?" she said, both furious and relieved.

"My father threw me out."

"Oh, no!"

"I'm at Nick's now. He's letting me stay in a room above the bar. "

"When can I see you?"

"I have to work until ten tonight."

"I'll be there at ten thirty," she said, hanging up before he could argue.

Meghan left the house a few minutes after ten. "Where are you going?" Coyle asked when he saw her start down the vestibule stairs.

"Out," she said.

"Not at this hour," Coyle said, rising out of his chair.

The front door slammed. Coyle stood in the living room, debating whether he should go after her. Suddenly he felt tired, tangled in a blanket of weariness that he couldn't escape. He sank back into his chair. Mary shot him an 'I told you so' look. "Don't say a word," he warned, thrusting his chin out as if to reinforce his order. "I heard enough at dinner from the two of you to ruin my digestion. I'm sick of Dennis and that damn war! I can't wait until May when he graduates so I can have a little peace around here."

Dennis was waiting for Meghan in front of Nick's. He got into the car and drove it to a private parking area behind the building. "Do you want to have a drink in the bar or go upstairs?" he said.

"Upstairs," Meghan said, curious to see where he was living.

The room, which was off a dingy hallway, was sparsely furnished with an old iron bed that had peeling blue paint the same color as the walls, an ancient oak dresser, a small table that served as a nightstand, and a single straight-backed chair; there was a faded, blue-striped curtain hung across a closet and a door that opened into a small bathroom. "It's not much," Dennis said, "but it's better than the street. Nick said I can live here rent-free and have my meals in the kitchen for helping him out in the bar when he needs me. He's a nice guy, a Greek. They're good-hearted people."

Meghan didn't know what to say. The bleakness of the room depressed her. Although it was clean, it had the sharp smell of poverty, of harsh soap and hopeless scrubbing. "It could be worse," he said, trying to mollify her wordless reaction. "At least I have a place to stay."

"What happened with your father?"

Dennis sat down on the bed, which was covered with a worn red-and-white quilt. "If you're called to serve your country, you serve," Dennis said, mimicking his father's guttural speech. "I won't have a coward living in my house!"

His imitation of his father was so precise that she could see the man vividly. "Maybe he didn't understand. Could I talk to him?" she said, chilled.

"No," Dennis said. "We gave it our best shot and we lost. It's over."

Meghan sat down beside him; her eyes were a kaleidoscope of love and fear. "Now what?"

"We'll think of something," he said, putting his arms around her.

Until that night, the only privacy they'd had was in

Meghan's Ford, where they were always watchful for the intrusion of cruising policemen and the headlights from passing cars. Finally alone together in the shabby room, they could relax and let desire lead them. A virgin, Meghan had often wondered what it would be like. What he would be like. She hadn't imagined that a man's body could be as beautiful as his, all muscle under firm flesh like a sculpture come to life. And Dennis, sensitive to her inexperience, moved his calloused hands over her body, milky-white as the pearl suspended on the chain around her neck, until she was ready for him. Then he leaned over and pulled his wallet from his jeans, which were on the floor next to the bed. Startled at the interruption, she saw him open a foil wrapper and asked him what he was doing. He told her it was a safety. "No," she cried, feeling that the magic web that held them had been broken, "it's a sin."

He cradled her face in his hands. "Meghan," he said, "love is never a sin; it's a responsibility." Then he put his mouth on hers and eased himself onto her, and after a moment of pain her body opened to him and she knew what he meant.

On Giffort Street, Coyle and Mary lay sleepless in their twin beds, Mary praying for Meghan's safe return while Coyle stared at the illuminated oval face of the alarm clock, nearly feverish with anger and worry. It was twelve forty-five. She's with that Dennis, he thought. God knows what they're doing. Those people from South Mills have no morals; they fuck their lives away. Why did she have to pick that boy out of a university full of young men from fine homes? First Stinky Flynn, now Dennis Kipphut-- charity cases, both of them. It was the nuns. They did it with their talk about Christian charity, pumping children's minds full of saints and do-gooders. What a self-serving bunch they were, living in their convents with their needs paid for out of parishioners' pockets: charity was their meal ticket, and they got Meghan hooked like a junkie, the same as her mother. Mary running out to church every night and Meghan running to that Dennis, both pleading Kipphut's case like a pair of born do-gooders. They were brainwashed. Or was it a weakness in their genes?

"What time is it?" Mary said in a trembling voice.

"One o'clock," Coyle said.

"It's Good Friday," she said, feeling an overwhelming need to hear his voice, warm and reassuring, in the darkness. If he talked to her, it might calm the wild beating of her heart.

"Mmmhh," Coyle grunted, remembering that he had to make his confession. Why did she have to remind him? He had a closet full of mortal sins. He thought of the hours he had spent fornicating with Mary Beth Rooney as the words he uttered once a year droned in his head: *Receive my confession, O most loving and gracious Lord Jesus Christ, only hope for the salvation of my soul.*

Mary listened to Coyle tossing in his bed and groped in the darkness for her rosary. Holding the crucifix, she prayed silently: *I believe in God, the Father Almighty, Creator of heaven and earth...*

They didn't sleep until they heard Meghan's car pull into the driveway at three o'clock in the morning.

* * *

On the Monday after Easter Meghan went to see Dennis's parents. She drove down unfamiliar South Mills streets, narrow and winding, like gnarled fingers extending from the palm of the waterfront, until she reached Groat Street. She was glad to be out of the house, away from Mary's gaze, which was full of hurt and reproach. For the first time in her life, she hadn't gone to Easter Mass with her parents. Instead, she had gotten up early on Easter morning and had left the house while they were sleeping to attend eight o'clock mass, where she had sat alone in the back of the church, unable to receive communion. The wafer and the wine, the body and the blood of Christ on the holiest of days, the celebration of His Resurrection. She couldn't open her mouth to receive the wafer because she hadn't fulfilled her Easter duty. She was unworthy; her soul hadn't received absolution. She had gone to church on Saturday to make her confession, but when she had entered the confessional, she couldn't speak. Her body still tingled from the touch of Dennis's hands; she could feel his arms around her and hear him saying…*love is never a sin; it's a responsibility.* Everything she had been taught, all that she knew became jumbled in her mind. How could their union have been a sin when they had joined together in love? Could anything that had brought her so much joy be wrong? Even the protection they had used, how could that have been a sin when they had no right to bring a child into the world that they couldn't provide for? She had run out of the confessional, her head reeling. After hours of driving aimlessly, she had stood at the foot of her brother Kevin's grave, staring at the simple marble headstone, hoping for a sign from him that would tell her what to do. The air was warm and balmy, more like the end of April than late March. She looked for a robin, a squirrel, a rabbit hopping on the soggy grass. There were no signs of life. "Oh, Kevin," she had whispered to the headstone before she left, "will I see your shining face in heaven or are you forever lost to me?"

The cottage-size houses on Groat Street were built close to the curbs, without garages, driveways, or lawns; their sagging front steps and weathered wood siding gave them a look of impermanence, as if they had out-lived their original purpose and were collapsing steadily, just hours ahead of a wrecking ball. The Kipphuts' house was in the center of the block, gray and cheerless. Meghan knocked on the front door, wondering how eleven people could live in a house that was narrower than her garage on Giffort

Street. A dark-haired boy of ten or eleven answered; he looked so much like Dennis that Meghan stared at him, open-mouthed. She tried to recall the names and ages of Dennis's brothers and sisters to place the youngster. "Are you Bill?" she guessed.

"Yeah," he said, smiling shyly. "How did you know?"

"Dennis told me. I'm Meghan Danahy, a friend of his. Is your father home? I'd like to talk to him."

"He's sleeping."

"Your mother, then?"

"C'mon in," he said.

The door opened directly into the living room. Meghan stepped inside, where the air was thick with the smell of bacon grease. Youngsters ranging in age from five to fifteen were clustered on a threadbare carpet watching a black-and-white television set. Meghan eased herself around them, brushing against a small sofa covered with a flower-print throw that ran the length of the beige wall; there were two chairs in the crowded room, also covered with print throws, and several tables and lamps. The kitchen and eating area were directly behind the living room. Mrs. Kipphut was folding laundry on a large table that had a chipped white enamel top and chrome legs; the chairs around the table were mismatched, no two alike. "Mom," the boy said, "this is..." He glanced at Meghan and blushed, embarrassed that he had forgotten her name.

"Meghan Danahy," Meghan said. "I'm Dennis's...uh...friend."

Mrs. Kipphut nodded and straightened her apron. She was a woman of medium height, her body broad and sagging from a lifetime of eating starchy foods and bearing children. When she told her son to go back into the living room, Meghan noticed that most of her side teeth were missing.

"I came to talk to your husband about Dennis,"

Meghan said hesitantly.

"He's sleeping," Mrs. Kipphut said, appraising the young woman. "Just as well, if you've come to talk about the draft. His mind's set on that."

"But Dennis can get out of the draft legally. He's found a job--ten thousand dollars a year, more than double your present income. He can take care of you."

Mrs. Kipphut's eyes flashed, dark and proud. "We ain't complaining."

"I know you're not," Meghan said. "I didn't mean it that way. This is a chance for Dennis, his only hope. He'll be able to go to law school. He's worked so hard. If he's sent to Vietnam, he may be killed or..." She couldn't finish.

"It's a war," Mrs. Kipphut said, as though the fact, with all of its ramifications and probabilities, needed no further elaboration.

"It's an unfair war, a wrong war! Please, Mrs. Kipphut, will you talk to your husband? If he'll quit his job, just for a year or two, the war will be over and Dennis will be safe."

Mrs. Kipphut shook her head. "His mind's made up. We ain't got much, but there has never been no cowards in the Kipphut family."

"Dennis isn't a coward!" Meghan said, trying desperately to reach the woman. "He isn't doing anything that's illegal. He's following the advice given to him by an attorney."

"Where did he get the money for a lawyer?" Mrs. Kipphut said, her voice sharp.

"I...I loaned it to him. He didn't want to take the money, but I insisted," Meghan said. "Please, Mrs. Kipphut, can't you talk to your husband?"

The expression on Mrs. Kipphut's face softened. "You love Dennis, don't you?"

"Yes," Meghan said, "and I'll do anything I can to

save him. "

"I'm sorry," Mrs. Kipphut said, leaning wearily against the table. "I can't ask my husband to quit his job. A man needs to work so he can hold his head up. Then there's the neighbors. Why should Dennis be spared when their boys have gone?"

"He's your son!" Meghan said, unaware of tears that were rolling down her cheeks.

Mrs. Kipphut looked at Meghan and nodded; the woman's prematurely aged face gave testament to a life of resigned acceptance. "Don't take it personal. You seem like a decent enough girl." She reached into her apron pocket, withdrew an envelope and handed it to Meghan. "This came in today's mail. Give it to Dennis when you see him."

There was a return address on the upper left hand corner of the envelope; it was from Dennis's draft board.

Meghan's face was ashen when she left the Kipphuts' house. She stopped at a drug store and called Dennis at Nick's to tell him that she couldn't meet him at the library and would see him later. Then, because she couldn't face Mary at home and had nowhere else to go, she drove to a park and walked aimlessly down muddy paths, carefully holding her shoulder bag with the letter tucked inside as if it contained a vial of nitroglycerin that was about to explode. The trees and grass in the park, brown and dismal-looking after the long winter, seemed to reflect her thoughts. There was no way she could give Dennis the letter without him knowing that she had gone to his house to talk to his parents. He had never offered to introduce her to his family; she had interfered without his consent and dreaded his reaction. And, if that weren't bad enough, there was the letter itself. Giving it to him would be like handing him his death warrant. Maybe this had happened because she hadn't made her Easter duty. There was a period of grace in which she could still make her confession. It wasn't too late. She would go to Dennis's room just once more and wouldn't go again.

The Danahys ate dinner in silence. Meghan and Mary picked at their food, avoiding each other's eyes. Coyle, who was delighted at first to be able to eat a meal in peace, soon felt the strain and lost his appetite. By the time the dishes were cleared, he was almost wishing they were bombarding him with pleas to help Dennis. As bad as that was, it was better than facing two females who looked like they were at a wake.

Mary left for church at seven o'clock with a heavy heart. Her novena to St. Anne wouldn't be finished until May, and so far her prayers seemed to be unheard. Meghan was slipping away from them faster than sand running through an hourglass. She hadn't gone to church with them on Easter Sunday, which could only mean one thing: Meghan had neglected her Easter duty, a mortal sin. She had always been a headstrong child but faithful to the church and conscientious about her prayers. How could this have happened? It was the war, Mary thought as she hurried down Giffort Street to Our Lady of Perpetual Help. Destruction breeds destruction, and the trouble in Vietnam was a plague that had spread half-way around the world into her house.

Through the window at the landing, Meghan glimpsed Mary and fought an impulse to run after her to ask for forgiveness. With the exception of Dennis, she loved no one on earth more than her mother, who, like the Blessed Virgin, was the embodiment of goodness. The telephone rang. Meghan ran up the stairs and picked up the receiver before Coyle could answer. It was Dennis; he had finished work early and would be waiting for her in front of Nick's.

Dennis took Meghan into the bar for a beer before they went upstairs to his room. "It's quiet in there now," he said. "There's always a lull between the after-work crowd and the late-night drinkers."

Meghan's eyes had to adjust to the dimly lighted interior of Nick's. The walls were paneled in an undistinguishable wood that had darkened to a chocolate brown from years of exposure to cigarette smoke and pollution from the steel plant. Meghan sat at a table that had a scarred butcher-block top while Dennis went to the bar to get their drinks. He returned with two beers and a short, thickset man who had jet black hair. "Meghan, this is Nick Papadakis," he said.

"Pleased to meet you," Nick said, bowing slightly like an old-world gallant. Then he straightened and smiled broadly, revealing strong white teeth. "I see that Dennis has picked himself a beauty."

"Thank you," Meghan said, flustered. His open appraisal was startling in its directness, but it was unaffected. She could understand why Dennis liked him. The man had an appealing, earthy charm.

Nick reached up and threw his arm around Dennis's shoulders.

"Dennis is a fine young man, strong and ambitious. Sometimes I look at him and think he must be Greek," Nick said, chuckling before he became serious. "Maybe this is the wrong time to mention it, but we talked today about Canada. I've been against the war from the beginning and want to help. I have relatives in Toronto. If he goes there, they will treat him like he is the son of Nicholas Papadakis."

Meghan's eyes locked with Dennis's. Deserting was the one alternative they had avoided discussing. "He won't be able to come back," Meghan said, clutching her shoulder bag with the letter inside.

"Toronto is a beautiful city, young and growing," Nick said. "He can make a life there for himself, and for you if you follow him."

No one spoke. Nick watched Meghan and Dennis, his face full of compassion, until he excused himself to serve customers waiting at the bar.

Meghan gave Dennis the letter after they went upstairs to his room. "Where did you get this?" he said, ripping the envelope open.

"Your mother gave it to me," she said, steeling herself for his reaction.

Dennis scanned the letter quickly.

"Is it your draft notice?" she asked anxiously.

"It's an advance warning. They want to know my graduation date. I didn't give it to them when I sent in my grade-point average in January. The notice will probably come the day after I graduate. They don't waste time."

"But it's only March thirtieth. Why are they hounding you?"

"It's not just me," Dennis said, crumpling the letter. "They treat everyone from South Mills the same. We're like cattle to them: they corral us and ship us off as fast as they can, as if they're being paid by the head. If this fucking war continues, they'll get my brother John when he graduates from high school next year. The poor kid will have seven days after he gets his notice; then he'll have to sign up so he can be slaughtered! Happy graduation!"

"We'll call the lawyer tomorrow."

"Forget about the lawyer! When did my mother give this to you?" he said, thrusting the crumpled letter at her.

Meghan could feel the force of his anger physically and stepped back. "Today," she said nervously. "Please don't be upset."

"You went to my house?"

"Yes."

"What the hell were you doing there?"

Meghan had never seen him so furious. Suddenly she wasn't sure that she knew him; his personality had become dark and ugly. "I...I went to talk to your father. I hoped I could get him to change his mind."

"What did he say?"

"He was sleeping. I talked to your mother. She said there was nothing she could do. Then she gave me the letter and I left."

"Is that all?" he said, his eyes flashing.

"She told me not to take it personally. She said that I seemed like a decent girl."

The air in the dismal room crackled with tension. Meghan stood uncomfortably while Dennis glowered at her. "Maybe I should leave," she said finally, not knowing what else to do.

"Sure," he said. "You've probably had enough slumming today."

Meghan gasped. "You can't mean that!"

"Decent girls from Giffort Street don't go visiting in South Mills," he said coldly. "It must have been a shock."

His remark, like a brisk wind, cleared away clouds of hurt and misunderstanding in Meghan's mind. She knew then that his anger was a defense mechanism: he was ashamed of his home and family, of how they would appear to her. For months she had believed the opposite to be true, that he hadn't introduced her to them because they might reject her as an outsider, unfit for their son. "There was only one shock," she said, "when I saw your brother, Bill. He looks so much like you that I wanted to hug him."

"Really?" he said, as though he wanted to believe her but couldn't.

"Really," she said.

Soon they were making love on the narrow bed, the war and the draft and their families temporarily forgotten. Meghan called the lawyer's office Tuesday morning. His secretary told her that he was in Florida and wouldn't be back until the end of April. Meghan asked if Dennis could see someone else in the firm or get his retainer back. The secretary said she was sorry, but no one else in the firm handled Selective Service cases and only Mr. Kipphut's attorney could return the retainer. Meghan replaced the receiver, her body shaking with dry sobs.

She told Dennis later when they met at the library. "It figures," he said. "Don't worry, I'll get the money back."

"We need the money now for another attorney," she said, fighting panic that was growing in her like a tumor. She started to shake again.

"C'mon," he said, picking up her books, "we'll go for coffee."

They walked across the campus to the Red Kitchen, holding hands. It was mild and sunny; the air was sweet with the fragrance of spring. They talked about their papers that were due at the end of the spring break--Dennis's senior thesis and Meghan's term paper on Chaucer-- carefully avoiding the topic that was on both of their minds: Canada. But they each knew what the other was thinking and both secretly wished that things were different, that time would miraculously stop so they could be together, holding hands on a beautiful spring day, until they ceased to exist.

Meghan went to Dennis's room again on Tuesday night, and on Wednesday and Thursday nights. She ate supper with him at the back of the barroom, then went upstairs and waited for him to finish working. It was easy to rationalize that since she wasn't going to go to confession until Friday, her Monday resolution not to be with him again was pointless. But with each night they spent together, she became less sure that what they were doing was a mortal sin. When his body entered hers, she knew the meaning of ecstasy; it was beyond anything she had ever imagined, so right, so perfect that it couldn't be wrong. The love she had had for him before was nothing compared to what she felt now. She waited in his room on Thursday night consumed with desire, knowing finally that it could be no other way.

While Meghan waited for Dennis, Mary and Coyle sat opposite each other in the breakfast room, both painfully conscious of Meghan's empty place at the table. "It's the third night in a row that she hasn't eaten at home," Coyle said. "If you don't put a stop to her gallivanting, I will."

"How?" Mary said.

"I'll take her car away!"

"It won't help," Mary said as matter-of-factly as she could. She'd had a sob caught in her throat all week. The house had been so empty and cheerless without Meghan. She had walked from room to room in despair, conscious of her own heartbeat in the intense quiet. It was as if no one lived there anymore, that she was alone in an oversize box padded with gold carpeting,

"It certainly will!" Coyle said louder than necessary.

"She'll take a bus or walk. She wants to be with him and nothing will stop her."

Coyle scowled.

"This morning I asked her to invite him to eat with us tonight, but she said no. I really don't blame her." Mary paused, gathering courage. "I don't think he is living at home."

"WHAT?"

"I overheard her the other morning on the telephone. She called him at the place where he works. Bars like Nick's usually don't open before noon."

"That does it!" Coyle said, slamming his fist on the table. "I'm going to forbid her to see him."

"It will only make things worse. She's going to be twenty in June. You can't forbid her to do anything anymore. She's a young woman, not a child you can put a harness on."

"As long as she lives in this house, she has to answer to me!"

Mary looked at him, red-faced and bullheaded. Although she had never used physical force on another human being, not even a light tap on her children's behinds when they were little, she wanted to grab him by the shoulders and shake him until his head wobbled. "You fool!" she said with such passion that even she was shocked. "Why can't you understand? She's in love with Dennis Kipphut; he means more to her than anyone in this world. If you force her to make a choice between you and him, she'll choose him.

"And that isn't all," Mary said, propelled by courage she didn't know she possessed. "If that boy is sent to Vietnam and something happens to him, she'll never forgive you!"

Coyle stared at her as though he couldn't believe what he was hearing. Mary, who was always sweet and soft-spoken, was yelling at him like his old desk sergeant. "What's gotten into you?" he said.

"Nothing but common sense," Mary said, trembling. "It's time you got some!"

"I won't sit here and be insulted!"

Mary picked up her plate. "Excuse me," she said.

She went into the living room and turned on the television. There, in living color, she watched Vietnamese running from their burning village; a young woman Meghan's age was crying and jabbering hysterically while she pointed to a hut engulfed in flames. After that, she saw Vietnamese children lying on crude cots in a makeshift clinic, whimpering in pain from wounds. The room swirled. Unable to move, Mary sat in her avocado-green chair weeping while she listened to a special news report on deserters living in Canada and Sweden.

Alone in the breakfast room, Coyle sat staring at Meghan's empty chair. God, how he missed her! He was so damned sick of love, prayers, and politics, one battle after another. He wanted peace. Maybe Mary was right. Maybe he should ask Austin Rickard. But Rickard might think he was presumptuous. What if he got annoyed and canceled his contract with Danahy Security? The other stores would follow Rickard's like dogs chasing a bitch in heat. Kipphut wasn't worth the risk. "Just one more month," Coyle muttered to himself, getting up to go to the liquor cabinet for a whiskey.

Meghan went to church on Friday and confessed venial sins. She was determined to resolve the rules of the church with what she knew to be right in her heart. She didn't believe that what she had done with Dennis was a sin She could no longer believe that her days on earth were an insignificant prelude to everlasting life in heaven, that perfect happiness could come to her only through salvation. There could be no greater happiness than what she was feeling now, with Dennis, and no greater pain than her fear for him. But when she went to church with Mary on Sunday and received communion, the wafer stuck to the roof of her mouth like a scab. Even after it dissolved, she could still feel it clinging to her palate, hard and dry. The dryness didn't go away until hours later, when Dennis put his arms around her and thrust his tongue into her mouth.

* * *

Meghan continued to go to Nick's several times a week after spring recess ended. She and Dennis left the university together when their classes were finished and drove to the bar in Meghan's Ford, where they were joined by Nick while they ate supper. No matter what they talked about, the conversation inevitably turned to what was utmost on their minds—the draft. They discussed rumors that were circulating about boys who had tried to fail their physicals by taking digitalis or consuming enormous quantities of sugar. "They're on to all the tricks," Dennis said. "Now they put you in the hospital for observation for a couple of days. As soon as your heartbeat is normal and your piss passes, they induct you. They're even hassling the guys who show up in lace pants and lipstick. The ones who do that are jerks."

"Maybe not," Nick said. "Wearing lipstick for a few hours is better than being sent to Vietnam. You could try it. What do you have to lose?"

"Everything!" Dennis said. "It would go on my record. I'd be labeled for the rest of my life."

On the second Monday in April, Nick suggested that Meghan and Dennis drive to Toronto. "Skip your classes for a day and go up there to look around. It's an easy trip from the Peace Bridge, all straight driving."

Neither Meghan nor Dennis replied. Nick gulped down his coffee. "It was just a thought," he said, the tone of his voice apologetic. He got up to tend the bar. "The offer I made is still open."

While Meghan waited for Dennis in his room, she forced herself to think about Toronto. It was almost too painful to contemplate. Deserting was the last resort, an irrevocable alternative as final as a prison sentence. If Dennis left the United States to avoid the draft he could never come back, except as a criminal. He would be forced to make a life for himself that wouldn't include her unless she went with him. What if he didn't ask her to join him? What if he did? How could she leave her parents, especially her mother? She was their only child, the life in which their hopes were invested. But she wanted Dennis. He was her present and her future and he would be safe in Toronto. But how could she live in Canada with him when she was an American down to the marrow in her bones? If she came back to visit, she'd feel like a foreigner in her own country.

Meghan heard Dennis's footsteps on the stairs and ran to meet him. "Hold me," she said, feeling lost and scared.

Later, when Dennis withdrew from her, the condom

he was wearing was coated with blood. *Oh God, my period,* Meghan thought, wanting to disappear. She slid out of bed, hurried to the bathroom, turned on the shower, and stood under the spray, dreading the moment she would have to come out and face him. He knocked on the bathroom door and called to her, asking if she was all right. She leaned against the cold white tile, too embarrassed to reply. Within seconds, he was pulling back the blue plastic shower curtain. "I'm sorry," she managed to say, "I didn't know... I'm a few days early...this has never happened before..."

"You thought you turned me off?"

She nodded, unable to look at him.

He stepped into the mist and drew her to him. She felt the spray from the shower, warm and wet against her back, and his penis growing hard against her belly. "You thought wrong," he said.

The next day Dennis was unusually quiet. After they ate lunch on the steps of the student union where they watched students gathering noisily for an anti-war demonstration, they walked to the pine grove at the northern edge of the campus, both oblivious to the sparkling spring day. Disturbed by his silence, Meghan began to dwell uneasily upon what had happened, although he had proved beyond any doubt that she hadn't repulsed him. *Maybe he forced himself,* she thought illogically while Dennis walked beside her, wondering when and how he could broach the subject of Toronto. He had read somewhere that upsetting a woman could make her bleed early. She had been upset when he had come back to the room. It had to be the talk about Toronto.

They sat on the grass at the edge of the pines, facing the sun. "Is something bothering you?" Meghan said. "Is it me?"

"I got my exam schedule this morning. My last final is on May sixth."

Three weeks from tomorrow. Meghan shivered as if

she had been hit by a blast of cold wind.

He reached over and stroked her hair, gleaming in the sunlight. "I've been thinking," he said. "Would you like to take a short vacation?"

Meghan's pulse quickened. "Where?"

"Toronto" he said. "Nick's been talking about it so much that I'd like to go up there for a day just to look around."

"Are...Are you going..."

"I don't think I can desert," he said, answering the question she couldn't ask. "I hate this fucking war! It's wrong and I don't want to fight in it, but I'm not a coward."

The yellow flecks in Meghan's eyes blazed through her tears as bright as the sun overhead. "I know," she said, "I know."

They decided to skip their classes the following Monday and drive to Toronto. Meghan didn't go to Nick's for the remainder of the week. Instead, she went directly home from school and waited for Coyle, determined to make him help Dennis. She tried every argument she could think of, but Coyle was immovable. "It's not our war!" she said to him in exasperation on Saturday night. "It's between North and South Vietnam. The United States has no business there. Even the French pulled out when they saw they couldn't win. I bet if you asked a Vietnamese, he'd tell you that he wants the war to end so he can grow his rice in peace."

"I don't know any Vietnamese," Coyle said, confident that he would have the last word. She had been at him night after night and she hadn't worn him down.

"That's my point!" Meghan said. "You don't know any and you don't want to know any! So why won't you help Dennis?"

"Dennis had the same chance in the lottery as everyone else."

"But he could be killed or crippled!"

"I didn't start the war, and I can't stop it."

"No one from our block has fought in Vietnam."

"I guess the boys on Giffort Street have better luck than Dennis," Coyle said, feeling like he held all the aces in a poker game. There was no way he could lose.

"You don't believe that!" Meghan shouted, nearly choking with rage.

"I have no reason not to," Coyle said with the smugness of a man cashing in a bucket full of poker chips.

Meghan ran out of the living room. "I hate him! I hate him! I hate him!" she muttered to herself, running upstairs to her bedroom.

"Well, I hope that's the last of it," Coyle said to Mary, who was slumped in her chair, exhausted from their battling.

"No, you don't," Mary said, her fingers creeping inside her skirt pocket for her rosary beads. "If Meghan stops asking you to help Dennis, it will mean that they've found another way."

"There is no other way," Coyle said. "He'll be drafted and he'll go."

Mary squeezed the crucifix; the edges of the cross dug deeply into her palm. "What if he deserts and she leaves with him?"

"He won't desert," Coyle said. "I know the stock he comes from--people who have nothing but their pride. His kind are all alike. They won't give anyone reason to call them cowards, even if they have to die to prove it."

"Are you sure?" Mary said, wanting to believe him.

"Positive," Coyle said. But his voice lacked conviction. He remembered Dennis's handshake the first time they met, how Dennis had returned his pressure with equal pressure, no more, no less. Coyle shifted uncomfortably in his chair, feeling as if he had been dealt a new hand in which none of the cards matched.

Meghan was shocked when she met Dennis at the

library on Sunday. His left eye was swollen shut. "What happened?" she said, wincing as she looked at his bruised skin, which was a livid purple.

"There was a fight at the bar," he said. "I forgot to duck."

"It's not funny," she said. "Where else were you hurt?"

"Isn't this enough?"

"Be serious!"

"I am," he said. "It's nothing, really. It'll be gone in a week."

"You told me your job wasn't dangerous."

"It isn't," Dennis said. "I didn't expect the guy to act up. He threw a lucky punch, that's all."

Although she asked him several times, he wouldn't discuss what had happened, "There's nothing to tell," he said, dismissing her questions. "If I had known you'd get this hyper, I would have worn an eye patch."

"Mmmm," she said. "You'd look like the Hathaway man."

"Who?"

"A man in a shirt ad," she said, still mesmerized after so many months by his incredible good looks.

Dennis didn't want her to know about the incident, which had disturbed him more than his black eye. He had been hit by a Vietnam vet who had gone berserk in the bar. Since he had been working at Nick's he had become more aware of vets. They came into the bar occasionally, almost always alone, and drank prodigious amounts of liquor as if it were medicine that would cure what was ailing them. Nick had warned him about them his first night on the job. "Watch out for the vets. They can be very quiet, then explode like bombs. They act like the war is still inside them and they're fighting it."

The vets were relatively easy to spot. They were all in their late teens and early twenties, young men with wary faces, veiled and defensive. The other customers shied away from them. They sat by themselves and drank until they either passed out or became abusive or violent. The vet who had hit Dennis had slipped quietly into the bar, a rail-thin blond fellow of about twenty dressed in jeans and a denim jacket. The place was packed with neighborhood regulars out for a few drinks on a Saturday night. Dennis didn't notice him at the far end of the bar until he heard the crash of bar stools and bodies hitting the wooden floor. A woman screamed, then another. Dennis pushed his way to the back of the bar. The vet was straddling a middle-aged steelworker twice his weight; the vet's hands were on the man's throat, choking him. Dennis grabbed the vet from behind, reaching under his arms to pull him off. With amazing strength and speed the vet broke free, leaped up and punched Dennis in the face. Stunned, Dennis staggered backward. The vet hesitated for a moment, wild-eyed, between Dennis and the gasping man on the floor. Dennis recovered and hit the vet in the solar plexus, temporarily knocking the wind out of him. It took three men to subdue the vet; he was a human grenade exploding in their midst— kicking, punching, and cursing until they were able to carry him out to the street. No one knew what had set him off, and no one seemed to care. After the customers went back to their drinks, Dennis stood near the front door, haunted by the vet's pale blue eyes, wild and tortured looking. What had he seen in 'Nam? What goddamn horrors had that poor guy witnessed?

* * *

Meghan left the house Monday morning at seven thirty wearing jeans and a yellow blouse. She had packed a navy blue mini-skirt and sandals in her book bag, planning to change in Dennis's room. Mary came down the stairs as she was leaving. "Where are you going so early?" Mary said. She had slept poorly and had dark circles under her eyes.

"To the library," Meghan said. "I have some work to do before my first class."

"Will you be home for dinner?"

"I don't think so," Meghan said, feeling guilty as Mary seemed to shrink, white and frail, in her blue bathrobe. "I'll call you later."

Dennis was waiting for Meghan dressed in a plaid shirt and chinos. After Meghan changed, he put on a pair of sunglasses to hide his black eye. "I don't want to get hassled at the bridge," he said.

They decided that Meghan should drive in case the ownership of the car was questioned at the Peace Bridge. Their fears were groundless. After they paid a twenty-five-cent toll and drove across to the Canadian side of the bridge, a customs inspector asked them what their citizenship was, where they were going in Canada, and how long they would be staying. "Okay," he said, waving them on after they answered.

"I can't believe it was so simple," Meghan said, following signs directing them to the Queen Elizabeth Way.

"It was as easy as crossing the street," Dennis agreed.

It was overcast in Toronto when they got off the Gardiner Expressway. The city was bustling, full of traffic and well-dressed people walking purposefully on crowded sidewalks. They drove up Yonge Street past miles of stores selling every kind of merchandise imaginable, then turned onto Bloor Street and were surprised by elegant shops and restaurants. "There is a bank on almost every corner," Meghan said with amazement.

Toronto continued to amaze them. Instead of finding the backwoods, unattractive city they expected, they discovered a sophisticated, sparkling metropolis.

Toward late afternoon they drove to the University of Toronto. There were no reminders of Vietnam on the campus--no anti-war signs posted anywhere, no flag-burnings, no demonstrations. The faces of the Canadian students were unmarked by tension; they were getting their educations and dreaming about their futures, their lives untouched by the threat of the draft and the war.

It was raining when they arrived at a Greek restaurant on Eglinton Avenue owned by Nick's relatives. Kostas Papadakis, a compactly-built man who had large, expressive features, sat with them while they ate. "What do you think of Toronto?" he said.

"It's wonderful," Meghan said, enjoying a Greek salad that was smothered with feta cheese.

Kostas Papadakis beamed with pride, as though he had built the city with his own hands. "Then you've decided to come and stay?"

Meghan looked at Dennis expectantly. "I'm not sure," Dennis said.

Papadakis nodded. "I understand. It's a big decision. But I want you to know that if you come, I'll help in any way I can."

Dennis drove the car back to the United States. It was still raining. The constant movement of the windshield wipers, clicking back and forth like a metronome, put Meghan to sleep. Dennis turned on the radio for company. A Beatles song was playing about a girl with kaleidoscope eyes:

He glanced sideways at Meghan, sleeping peacefully next to him. He couldn't do it, he couldn't leave her and he couldn't let her come with him. She still had two years of college to finish. If she went with him, she'd have nothing. It would kill her parents. He didn't give a shit about her father, but her mother was a nice woman. Then there were his parents—his father, the stupid bastard. His father would call him a coward for as long as he lived.

He'd be damned before he'd give him that satisfaction. He was no coward.

The rain started to increase in intensity. Soon it was coming down hard and fast. It was difficult to see; the windshield was a blur of movement, of overworked wipers and running water. Dennis concentrated on his driving, letting Meghan sleep until they reached the Peace Bridge.

* * *

Meghan went to Dennis's room on Wednesday night. "I don't understand you," she said with frustration. "It's been two days since we've come back and you still won't talk about Toronto. Why?"

"There's nothing to talk about," he said, starting to unbutton her blouse.

She pushed his hands away. "Yes, there is!"

"We'll discuss it later," he said, peeling off his T-shirt.

"Now," she said, adding, "It was your idea to go."

"It was a stupid idea."

"Didn't you like it there?"

"Sure, it was a nice place to visit."

"That's not what I mean."

"I'm not a coward, Meghan."

"Going to Toronto has nothing to do with being a coward. It's stupid to risk your life in an unfair war."

"The United States government doesn't see it that way."

"Well, I do," she said. "I've thought about it: it takes more courage to leave the country knowing you can't come back than it does to let them draft you."

Dennis stretched out on the bed and stared at the ceiling. In a way she was right: it almost did take more courage to leave the country. "Maybe," he said.

Meghan sat down next to him. "Is it me?" she said.

"Am I the reason you won't go?"

He hesitated. Being labeled a coward wasn't all that was troubling him. After growing up in a large family, he had been lonely staying in the small room. He was accustomed to having people around, to falling asleep listening to the rhythm of his brothers' breathing, like an audible pulse in the darkness. If he deserted, he didn't want to go alone. He wanted her with him; meeting her was the best thing that had ever happened to him, the only piece of luck he had ever had. He had nothing to offer her. The decent thing to do, if he did desert, would be to leave at the last minute without telling her. She could visit him later, after he was settled.

"Why won't you answer me?"

"I can't," he said, torn between doing what was best for her and what he wanted. Since Sunday, he had been reminded of the vet who had hit him when he shaved every morning. He'd rather die than come back carrying nightmares he couldn't live with, or return like his friend, a head without a body. But he didn't want to die, and not in a meaningless war. Going to Vietnam was as senseless as stepping in the path of a speeding car.

"Then it is me," she said.

"Partly," he said.

She wished she could tell him to forget about her, but she couldn't. Yet she couldn't force herself on him either, not if he didn't want her. "There isn't much time. Your last final is three weeks from today," she reminded him, tracing the hair on his chest with her fingertips as it narrowed into a line on his stomach.

"Keep going," he said, guiding her hand with one of his, while with his other hand he undid his jeans.

Meghan reluctantly got out of bed when it was time for her to leave. "What are you going to do?" she said, stepping into a pair of pink underpants.

He lay naked on the red-and-white quilt, watching

her. "I'm not sure," he said.

"I need to know."

The uncompromising tone of her voice demanded an answer. Although he wanted to have the strength to do what was right, to release her so she could stay where she belonged, he knew then that he was going to desert and take her with him. "Meghan," he said, hating himself for his weakness, "I can't promise you anything if you come with me."

"I don't want anything," she said, "except you."

They decided to leave at noon on May seventh after Meghan's last exam. Dennis wrote to the law school declining his acceptance and the offer of financial aid. Sending the letter didn't bother him as much as he had anticipated it would; law school had become a fantasy, an impossible dream that couldn't be fulfilled. He had pushed himself for four years, working nights so he could go to school, but now his efforts seemed insignificant. After months of agonizing over the draft, he was escaping with his life, which was all that mattered. And it would be bearable because Meghan would be with him. He arranged to have his diploma sent to Nick, who promised to forward it to Canada. He didn't regret missing his graduation ceremony; the diploma with honors was his, regardless of whether or not he spent an afternoon sweating in a cap and gown. If he hadn't completed what he had set out to do, at least he had accomplished something. He decided to postpone telling his family until the night before he left when his father would be at work. Once his father was told, he knew he would no longer be welcome in the house, not even as a visitor. He tried not to think about being banished from his family and his country, but when he walked down familiar streets he was seized with a sense of loss, emptiness deep in his gut like a hollow pain, reminding him that what he was seeing would soon be forbidden to him. Although he couldn't come back without facing a prison sentence, he didn't believe he was a criminal for refusing to participate in his government's mistake. He was still an American and always would be, no matter where he lived. Nothing could change that. Nothing ever would.

The first days after Dennis's decision, Meghan felt as if she had been released from a prison of uncertainty. She hummed the Beatles' song that had played mockingly in her head for months--*Don't you know it's going to be alright*--after she bought an oversize green-and-blue plaid canvas suitcase which she put in the trunk of her car. Everything was going to be all right, she thought, packing her book bag with clothes to smuggle to the car. Most of her winter things had already been cleaned and put away in the cedar closet, so her mother wouldn't miss them. She hummed to herself while she shopped for underwear, bras, jeans, and summer clothes, charging the items to her parents' accounts. She had always had free use of the charges and knew the bills wouldn't come until after she was gone. Still, she purchased only what she felt she would need, resisting the temptation to be extravagant. She hummed while she placed the clothes in the canvas suitcase, thinking of them as her trousseau. She didn't stop humming until Sunday, when she went to church with Mary. "Edna Harris called this morning while you were in the shower," Mary said as they walked down Giffort Street. "Patty got engaged last night to that boy from Buffalo she's been seeing. Edna went to eight o'clock mass. She's so happy and excited, she's been up since dawn."

"That's wonderful," Meghan said, glad for Patty and Edna. Poor Patty had always been overweight and unattractive to boys, and Edna, ever vocal, had worried aloud for years that her daughter might be an old maid.

"They're going to have a big church wedding," Mary said. Then she sighed. "I can't wait to plan your wedding. We'll fill the church with roses and baby's breath and white ribbon. We'll..."

Meghan couldn't listen. She let Mary talk, rambling on about the food and the flowers, while she blinked back tears. She would never be married at Our Lady of Perpetual Help. After this Sunday, she would enter the church with Mary only one more time. She thought of the suitcase in the trunk of her car. How could she leave? First Kevin, now her. But then she thought of Dennis. Somehow it would be all right. It would have to be all right.

Kneeling in church next to Mary, Meghan tried to pray. She felt nothing but her bones pressing uncomfortably against the wood kneeler. Her mouth was dry when she accepted the wafer. When it finally dissolved, pieces stuck to her tongue like gritty particles of sand. As they were leaving, light pouring through a stained-glass window illuminated Mary's face. Again, Meghan choked back tears. For a moment her mother's face seemed to glow with unnatural radiance. How could she ever leave her?

Meghan met Dennis at the library early in the afternoon. "I can't have supper with you at Nick's," she said.

"Why?"

"I want to spend as much time with my parents as I can before we go."

The color left Dennis's face except for the skin around his bruised eye, which had turned a greenish-yellow. There was still time, twelve days in which she could change her mind. ''Are you having second thoughts?" he said, shaken. He looked as if he were about to crack.

"Don't worry," Meghan said, "I'm going with you."

Coyle drove home at the end of the week more relaxed than he had been in months. He felt generous, magnanimous. He would eat the fish dinner he knew was waiting for him without complaining as he had for four years that even the Pope ate meat on Fridays. He could afford to be overlooking. Here it was, the first of May, and

Meghan had eaten at home all week without mentioning Kipphut or Vietnam once.

"It's over," he said to Mary when she returned from church, the expression on his face one of supreme satisfaction.

"What's over?"

"That business with Dennis. Haven't you noticed? Meghan hasn't pleaded his case all week."

Mary sank wearily into her chair. She had stayed in church longer than necessary, praying to St. Anne until her body had started to shake. Her novena wouldn't be finished for a week, the Friday following this one, and she had felt time, the signs, Meghan's sudden silence, and Coyle's obstinacy closing in on her like walls of granite. "It's happening," she said, "just like I told you it would."

"Are you going to start that losing her nonsense again? The whole world could be enjoying a perfect summer day, and you'd be out looking for rain clouds," Coyle said. "Meghan has finally come to her senses. You're acting like you left all of yours in church."

"Have you asked her if she's still seeing him?"

"No."

"Well, she is!" Mary said, leaning toward him. "It can only mean one thing: he's deserting!"

"I told you: his kind don't desert."

"Where is it written?" Mary said. "What kind of guarantee do you have?"

"Trust me. I know."

"You don't know! If Dennis found a way out, Meghan would tell us. She'd be explaining it down to the last detail. Instead, she hasn't said a word, not one word!"

"His kind..." Coyle started to say.

"Stop talking about Dennis as if he belongs to a different species! He's a fine young man. What do you have against him?"

"Meghan can do better."

"Meghan will do what she wants. She's just like you!" Mary said, her eyes swimming in tears of frustration.

"What's that supposed to mean?"

"Remember Stinky Flynn," Mary said, thrusting Stinky's name at him like a weapon.

"Oh, God," Coyle groaned, shuddering as if he'd been lanced.

Later that night, tossing in his bed, Coyle considered the possibility that Mary was right. It couldn't hurt to ask Rickard if the opportunity presented itself. He'd be casual about it, pretend he was inquiring to help a nephew. But he hadn't spoken to Rickard in a couple of years. He'd have to go to the store and push his way past Rickard's secretary. Damn that Kipphut! Why the hell should he save that kid's ass? Mary predicted doom like she was forecasting the weather. It was a way of life with that woman, looking for trouble so she could pray it away. Prophecies and prayers since they'd been married, just like the other Queen of Martyrs' women. If he'd moved her to China instead of Giffort Street, she would still be the same. Meghan was his daughter, too. She had good sense, not a head full of prayers like her mother. She wouldn't leave the country with a penniless kid, not when she had everything she could possibly want at home. It would be stupid, plain stupid! Or would she?

He kicked off his covers, groped in the darkness for his slippers, and went downstairs for a drink.

On Wednesday, Coyle went to see Austin Rickard. He might have procrastinated longer if it hadn't been for the shootings at Kent State on Monday. Pictures of National Guardsmen firing at unarmed college students as if they were the enemy were on television and on the front pages of all the newspapers. The photographs of students lying dead on the grass sickened him. God forbid, one of those kids could have been Meghan. If he could keep Dennis out of Vietnam, Meghan wouldn't have anything to protest, and he'd make her promise to stay away from those anti-war demonstrations.

Austin Rickard wasn't in. "He usually leaves early on Wednesdays," his secretary said. She was a stylishly dressed, anemic-looking woman whose arched eyebrows and sharp nose gave her face an expression of frozen condescension.

Probably playing golf, Coyle thought as he stood uncomfortably in Rickard's outer office. The place smelled of money—walls covered with paper that looked like dead grass and the brown wall-to-wall carpeting so thick it curled over the tops of his shoes. "Will he be in tomorrow morning?" he said, hating Dennis for putting him in this position. Here he was, the owner and president of Danahy Security with a full payroll of his own, practically bowing to a woman who looked as dead as the wallpaper so he could talk to her boss.

"Would you like to make an, appointment?" she asked with frosty politeness.

"Yes," Coyle said, disliking her as much as he did Dennis.

She checked Rickard's appointment book. "How is ten thirty?"

"Fine," he said.

Coyle took the elevator up to the eighth floor of the store at ten twenty-five on Thursday morning dressed in his best suit, a brown plaid that was a little too bold to be considered in good taste. He felt as if he were wasting his time. Meghan had finally come around. At breakfast she'd been studying at the table as if she had had nothing on her mind but her final exam. And she had kissed him good-by when he left, just like she did when she was a little girl. The elevator door opened. Coyle stepped forward reluctantly. It was too late to break the appointment now.

Austin Rickard was visibly flattered. He sat behind his desk in an impeccably tailored navy blue suit, white shirt, and burgundy-and-white rep tie, a balding man whose cold gray eyes softened as Coyle spoke. He had assumed Danahy had come to renegotiate a new contract at a higher rate. Instead, the man was asking him for advice. "Actually, it's quite simple," he said in a cultivated voice. "Advise your nephew to have braces put on his teeth."

"Braces?" Coyle repeated, dumbfounded.

"My son is at Harvard now, safe and sound, with a full set of wires and bands on his teeth," Rickard said, smiling at Coyle's reaction. "The Army won't touch him."

Coyle's chest was puffed up like a pigeon's when he left Austin Rickard's office; he had gotten the information he had come for in less than ten minutes. It certainly paid to know the right people. Braces, a goddamn mouthful of metal! He couldn't wait to see the expression on Meghan's face when he told her at dinner. Mary's, too. He'd even spring for the dentist. The whole business shouldn't cost more than a thousand bucks. It would be worth every penny of it to teach Mary a lesson. She'd been running to church every night for weeks, and he could buy the miracle she wanted for a thousand bucks. It was about time she learned that money works a helluva lot better than prayers.

* * *

Meghan and Dennis crossed the Peace Bridge at one thirty in the afternoon. The American and Canadian flags, standing at attention in the center of the long span, waved vigorously in a strong breeze. Below, the Niagara River moved swiftly between the banks of the two countries, carrying the waters of four Great Lakes. Sitting quietly on the passenger side of the front seat in jeans and white cotton blouse, Meghan couldn't stop thinking of the note she had placed on her mother's pillow, slipping it under the gold bedspread before she had left the house. Her parents would wait for her, worrying, until they finally went to bed. Then they would find the note...

Dennis steered the Ford toward an empty customs booth. He had been talking about the money they had with them--two hundred dollars they had gotten back from the attorney and two hundred fifty Nick had given them-- wanting to plan a tentative budget until he found a job. "Are you all right?" he asked, glancing anxiously at her when she didn't respond.

Meghan looked straight ahead at a WELCOME TO CANADA sign. "Yes," she said, the sign blurring with tears, "I'm all right."

HARRY DANCED DIVINELY

Lillian Levinson unscrewed the lid of an old peanut butter jar that was partially filled with money and carefully emptied the jar in the center of the kitchen table, watching that the change didn't roll onto the floor. Then she began to count slowly, smoothing each rumpled bill flat as she set it aside. "Six," she said aloud, sighing as she started working on the coins. She counted the quarters first, then the dimes, nickels and pennies, separating the coins into piles totaling one dollar. There were two groups of quarters, one of dimes, and the rest were puddles of nickels and pennies.

"Fourteen dollars," she said, picking up a few loose pennies which she dropped back into the jar. "A month I saved, and all I have is fourteen dollars." She picked up the bills, put them in her wallet, then opened a large black change purse and slid the coins inside. That done, she recapped the jar, returned it to a cupboard next to the sink, and started upstairs to bathe and dress, noting with resignation as she did each time she climbed the stairs that jute backing was exposed on every carpeted stair tread. At least the backing blended with what was left of the beige carpet; it would have been worse if she had picked green.

The carpeting was expensive, as were the other furnishings in the Levinson house, but it had worn away under twenty-four years of use. Harry Levinson had always insisted upon buying the best. "You get what you pay for," he often said in his accented English, "so it pays to buy the best." Harry liked to express himself in clichés; they made him feel more American. He also liked to spend his money where it showed, and to Harry, a beautifully-appointed home was as important as a new Cadillac every year and a trip to Florida in the winter. When a large piece of charcoal-broiled filet mignon became lodged in his windpipe during the Levinsons' last trip to Florida together, Harry died with an expression of amazement on his face, a man betrayed by the most expensive cut of meat on the menu.

Lillian thought of Harry after she descended the worn staircase an hour later. She was dressed to go out and stepped in front of the gilt-framed hall mirror for a final look at herself. She turned, first to one side, then the other, gazing into the mirror critically. At sixty-five, her figure was still trim. She felt lucky to have inherited her mother's small bones; her wool suit in a flattering soft rust color fitted perfectly. But then she remembered that the suit had been purchased several months before Harry's death and the corners of her mouth fell.

She went into the kitchen and put her wallet and change purse into the brown leather handbag she was carrying. As she snapped the bag shut, she noticed a spot in a corner where the leather was worn and cracked. Her chin trembled, as though she'd been insulted. Then, biting her lower lip, she recalled that Harry had kept tins of shoe polish in the basement. She went downstairs and returned with cordovan brown shoe crème, which she rubbed on the worn spot with a moist rag, determined not to let this spoil her day. The cracks in the leather remained, but the worn spot was darkened sufficiently so that it was hardly noticeable. Lillian wasn't satisfied, but she was a realist. It was the best she could do, so she returned the polish to the basement and left the house, locking the front door behind her.

It was a magnificent fall day, one special to the month of October when the sky seems bluer than at any other time of year. A strong sun had evaporated the heavy early morning dew from Giffort Street lawns, and the neat patches of grass appeared dark and lush in a final growth spurt before winter. Lillian walked up the street briskly, so intent on reaching her destination that she didn't lament the passing of the elm trees as was her custom.

When Harry bought their home, Giffort Street was lined with mature elms. He was pleased with the house because it was one of the few on the street that was constructed entirely of brick. "It's a good investment," Harry said at the time. "Low maintenance. Only the trim will need painting."

Lillian wasn't interested in the trim. She had fallen in love with the Giffort Street elms. Through the years she came to measure the seasons by them, by their spring budding and summer leafing. Each fall she took pleasure in raking leaves into neat piles at the curb, which irritated Harry. "Why do you rake?" he said. "For this I pay a gardener. In the summer he cuts, and in the fall he rakes. It is natural." Lillian ignored him and continued her annual leaf raking until their tree succumbed to Dutch elm disease. When men from the city forestry department came with chain saws to cut the tree down, she stayed inside the house and wept, holding her hands over her ears to muffle the angry sound of the saws. For weeks afterward she mourned the tree as if it had been human. She bristled at the sight of the spindly maple planted later by the city as an intruder on her lawn; no tree could replace her elm. Her devotion to the elm was not unlike her devotion to Harry--spontaneous and unquestioning. Not once did it occur to Lillian that her leaf raking was the only action she had taken during the years of their marriage that was contrary to Harry's wishes.

At the intersection of Giffort Street and Hewett Avenue, Lillian crossed the street and walked into Van Horn's drug store, which was on the corner. The owner, Perry Van Horn, was behind the cash register. He was a man close to Lillian in age. After a lifetime spent in the store dispensing prescriptions, his color was perhaps a shade darker than his immaculate white jacket; silver-rimmed glasses and thinning gray hair accentuated his whiteness. "I haven't seen you in a while, Mrs. Levinson," he said, smiling. His voice was deep and warm, surprising in contrast to his ghostlike appearance. "Beautiful day, isn't it? It reminds me of those Indian summers we used to have when I was a boy."

"Yes," Lillian replied, flustered. She had expected a girl to be behind the cash register, one of Mr. Van Horn's part-time clerks who wouldn't know her.

"Is there something I can help you with?" he asked kindly, noticing that she seemed ill at ease. Perry Van Horn was fond of Lillian Levinson. She had traded in his store for years and was always pleasant, unlike her late husband, whose manner had sometimes been abrupt and demanding. The Levinson boy, Edward, had been more irritating than the father. He was one of the few neighborhood youngsters Perry Van Horn had actively disliked. Edward Levinson was arrogant and indulged, particularly by his father, who bought him whatever he wanted when they stopped at Van Horn's store.

Lillian picked up a pack of peppermint Life Savers. "I'll take these," she said, handing them to Mr. Van Horn. Then, hesitating: "Would you mind…? Would it be too much trouble…?" She clutched her handbag, embarrassed. "Would you change some money for me?" she finally managed to ask.

"I don't have any hundred dollar bills," he joked, disturbed by her discomfiture, "but I'll be glad to help you if I can."

"Oh, no," said Lillian gratefully. She opened her handbag, removed the bulging change purse, and emptied it on the glass counter. "It's just some extra change. I hope you don't mind. I counted eight dollars, but you should count for yourself to make sure."

"If you say it's eight dollars, then it's eight dollars. I

can always use change," said Van Horn, deftly separating the coins. He opened the cash register. "Would you like singles or a five and three ones?"

"A five and three ones," Lillian said, her quiet dignity somewhat restored. She paid Van Horn for the Life Savers, thanked him, and went to the back of the store to use a pay phone. As she walked past him on her way out, Lillian thanked Van Horn again, wishing him a pleasant day.

Perry Van Horn watched her waiting at the corner until a taxi came to pick her up, wondering about the money, which had come, as he knew it would, to exactly eight dollars. He recalled Harry Levinson's gleaming Cadillacs. It was odd that she was fussing over change. She should be well-fixed. A nice lady. One of his favorite customers, although he hadn't seen her in a while. Looked well, too. An attractive woman, Mrs. Levinson. Maybe he would ask her out to dinner. It was lonely eating alone since his wife had died. No, she might be offended. Jewish people were sometimes funny that way--not the young ones, just the older ones. Wasn't it the Levinson boy who had gotten serious with the O'Brien girl? There had been a fuss, but he couldn't remember exactly. Strange how she had acted about changing her money.

Perry Van Horn would have continued thinking about Lillian if his clerk hadn't returned. When he had last checked, there were close to a dozen prescriptions in the back waiting to be filled.

Inside the cab, Lillian began to relax. She had been anticipating this day since Ida Jacobs had called her, a month before, to tell her that Rose and Sam Falk were retiring to Florida. Ida, Rose, and Lillian were all that remained of a group of eight women who had joined together better than thirty years ago to play mah-jongg. The game had later changed to bridge, more social than serious, but it didn't change the nature of the group. The women met every Tuesday night. They played cards, exchanged gossip and recipes, celebrated together in times of joy, and helped each other in times of need. Generous graduation, shower, and wedding gifts were purchased collectively through the years, the cards signed *The Tuesday Night Group*. When there was a death in a woman's family, the others worked quietly in her kitchen, supplying and preparing food for the traditional meal after the funeral. Twice the women had stood weeping in the familiar kitchen of a member, peeling hard-boiled eggs and arranging rolls, while she was being lowered into the ground.

The group hadn't met regularly for quite some time. Besides the two members who had died, three women retired with their husbands to Florida; of the three that remained, only Lillian lived in the city. The others had moved in the mid-sixties, part of what seemed like a mass exodus to the suburbs. Harry had planned to move, also. "I'll put the house on the market in the spring," he said during their last trip to Florida. "We can build from scratch--everything brand new on one floor." He returned from Florida in a coffin, and Lillian remained on Giffort Street. She would have been lost living anywhere else. Lillian had never learned how to drive, and there was no public transportation outside the city. If she moved into an apartment to live near her friends, she would be dependent upon them for rides. Lillian was too proud to be dependent upon anyone.

Usually Lillian walked or took a bus wherever she went, but today was an exception. When Ida had called her, they had discussed Rose's move and had decided to take her out to lunch and to buy her a small gift as a going-away present. Lillian hadn't seen the two women in over a year and had been so delighted at the prospect of being with them again that she had accepted Ida's suggestion to meet at a suburban restaurant. It was only after she had put the receiver down that she had realized she would have to take a taxi. A taxi meant money, as did lunch and a gift, and Lillian had been living penuriously. Harry had left a sizeable estate--it totaled close to five hundred thousand dollars after his clothing store and other assets were liquidated--but the money was not left directly to Lillian. Instead, it had been put in trust for her with their son, Edward, named as trustee. Legally the money was Lillian's, but in reality it was Edward's: every nickel that was spent had to pass through his hands. Rather than call her son to ask for cash that was rightfully hers, Lillian ate omelets for dinner almost every night for a month. She reused tea bags until they no longer colored the hot water in her cup, watered the milk she poured over her cereal, and shredded a head of lettuce into slivers of salad that lasted for a week. At no time during that stringent period did she feel martyred or resentful; nor did she think unkindly of Harry or their son. Lillian was a pragmatist; she was merely doing what was necessary to go out with her friends.

Antonio's was located deep within the suburb where Ida and Rose lived. It was new and garish. The owner, mistaking excess for elegance, had cluttered the front of the premises with enough statuary to amply fill a small cemetery. As the taxi turned into a winding roadway leading to the building, Lillian spotted Rose and Ida waiting for her under a red canopy that covered the front entrance. She waved to her friends excitedly. "Is it okay to let you out here?" the driver said, anxious to avoid the line of cars ahead of them.

"Yes," Lillian said, still waving.

"That'll be four eighty-five," said the driver, shutting off the meter.

Lillian's arm dropped. *Four dollars and eighty-five cents.*

She should have paid attention to the meter. Her heart started racing. She had only twenty dollars--six plus the fourteen she had saved. There was the gift and the luncheon to pay for. She opened her purse and withdrew her wallet while trying to calculate the man's tip. If she gave him six dollars, she'd have only fourteen dollars left. She hesitated, recalling Harry's heavy tipping, then handed the driver a five dollar bill. He accepted it, his hand still outstretched. Nervously, she snapped open the-change section of her wallet and withdrew two quarters. She thrust them into the man's palm, almost beside herself with the certainty that she had given him too little, and practically leaped out of the cab. "Fourteen dollars and fifty cents," she said to herself, walking toward her friends.

"You look marvelous," gushed Ida, a coarse-featured, matronly woman whose hair was dyed platinum blond. "You're as slender as a girl of sixteen."

"I could hate you for being so skinny if you weren't one of my oldest friends," said Rose, who was sweet-faced and sixty pounds overweight.

The interior of Antonio's was coated with red fuzz--red-flocked wallpaper, red-velvet drapes and chair cushions, and plush red carpeting. The three women entered the dining room chatting warmly, clearly glad to see each other. They continued to talk while the maître d' seated them and were so engrossed in conversation that a waiter had to return to their table twice to remind them to order. When they finally opened their menus, Lillian's eyes traveled directly to the right hand column, drawn immediately to the price list. The lowest figure was two dollars and ninety-five cents for chicken salad Italianne. Lillian chuckled. "I think I'll have the chicken salad," she said. "I want to see what they can do with it to make it Italian."

"Chicken salad is chicken salad," Rose agreed, laughing.

"I'm sure they'll do something creative with it," said Ida defensively, fingering a gold chain resting on her ample bosom. "Everyone says Antonio's is THE place to eat."

"Then, it is," said Lillian. She had forgotten how sensitive Ida was; of the eight women in the group, Ida had been the most difficult, the first to take offense and the last to forgive.

When the group had first formed, Ida's husband was floundering from job to job; the husbands of the other women had already begun establishing themselves. Ida's life was a constant struggle to save face until her husband achieved a modest success in the real estate business. He was in his late fifties then, which was too late for Ida. Although she finally had the means to live like her friends, she could not relate to them differently than she had in the past; money cured neither her envy nor her insecurity. Ida's eyes were quick, and her memory infallible. She could remember items of clothing, jewelry, and accessories worn by her friends twenty years ago, and could recount trips they had taken and cars they had owned with total recall. Lillian's remark about the chicken salad offended Ida; she felt that Lillian was criticizing her choice of restaurant. She looked at her friend critically and silently noted that Lillian was wearing a suit purchased before Harry's untimely death. Her quick eyes also spotted the camouflaged worn spot on Lillian's handbag, which was resting on the red tablecloth.

After that brief moment of discord, the women resumed their nonstop conversation. They reminisced, exchanging anecdotes from their shared past. "Do you remember...?" one would ask, and the other two would nod, then contribute to the story. They laughed and wept in unison as if in a chorus, deeply moved, each aware that this was possibly the last time they would be together.

Lillian's chicken salad was a disappointing mixture of diced chicken and mayonnaise set on a bed of lettuce. Slivered almonds were sprinkled sparingly on top, and

Lillian, who had a dry sense of humor, was tempted to muse aloud as to whether the almonds were Italian. But she happened to glance at Ida and decided to keep her observation to herself. She was glad later that she had kept quiet, for the salad had an off, slightly-spoiled taste; because she said nothing, she was able to maneuver half of it under the lettuce without her friends noticing.

The women talked and ate while their second cups of coffee grew cold. When the waiter approached their table, Rose was describing a wedding she had recently attended. "It was so lavish," she said, "that they had two bands--one for the old fogies like us and a disco band in a separate room for the young people. You know, Lillian, I thought of Harry that night. He was such a marvelous dancer, a regular Fred Astaire. I thought to myself: if Harry was here, he would be the best dancer in both rooms."

The waiter, who had been waiting impatiently for a break in their conversation, cleared his throat and placed a bill-covered tray on the table. "Oh, my," said Rose, looking around, "we're the last ones in the restaurant."

Ida picked up the bill and handed it to Lillian. Their lunch, including tax, had come to thirteen dollars and twenty-one cents. The waiter stepped back discreetly and Rose, who was fussing with her napkin self-consciously, excused herself to go to the ladies' room.

"I think fifteen dollars should take care of it," Ida said after Rose left.

Lillian opened her purse and extracted seven dollars and fifty cents from her wallet. She gave the cash to Ida, who then added her own money, placing it on the tray. The waiter stepped forward, mumbled his thanks, and disappeared.

"I bought Rose a scarf," said Ida, removing a slender, wrapped box from her oversize purse. "She's gotten so heavy that I didn't know what else to get her."

"How much do I owe you?" asked Lillian, who had

started to perspire. She had only seven dollars left.

"Four dollars. I have the receipt." Ida started hunting through her purse.

"That isn't necessary, Ida," said Lillian, handing her four singles. "After all these years, who can I trust if not you?"

Ida smiled, clearly touched by the compliment. She reached across the table and covered Lillian's hand with her own. "Really, it's been so wonderful seeing you again. If only you didn't live in the city. It's such a distance to travel. But we must make the effort to get together. With Rose gone, we are all that is left of the group. Let's set a date now to meet next month so we don't lose touch and let a year go by again."

Lillian didn't respond to Ida's invitation; her mind was frozen on the remaining three dollars in her wallet. How would she get home? She couldn't ask her friends to drive her into the city; nor could she borrow money from them. Both alternatives crumpled instantly under the pressure of her pride, and unhearing, she sat in silent panic while Ida waited for her response.

As Lillian's silence continued, Ida drew her shoulders back and her warm expression vanished.

When Rose returned to the table, she opened her gift and thanked Lillian and Ida effusively. "It's beautiful," she said. Then she began to cry. "You are such wonderful friends. As much as I'm looking forward to living in Florida, I hate the thought of leaving because of old friends like you. Al says we'll make new friends, but it won't be the same. We three share a lifetime of memories"

"Yes," said Ida, "but we must part on a happy note. And it's late. I have to be home to fix dinner."

The three women rose from the table. Lillian hung back while Ida and Rose started toward the door, "Aren't you coming, Lillian?" asked Rose, her round face mottled and swollen from crying,

"I have to call for a taxi," said Lillian. "Let's say good-by here."

Rose embraced Lillian, weeping anew. "Come, Rose," said Ida impatiently. Lillian disentangled herself and watched them leave the restaurant.

After they were outside, Rose said, "Doesn't Lillian look wonderful? All these years and she hasn't gained an ounce!"

"Maybe she can't afford to," said Ida, still bristling from Lillian's silence at her suggestion that they meet next month. "When we were talking about our latest activities, Lillian didn't have too much to say. All she talked about was Edward running for county comptroller. And did you notice that she was wearing a suit she bought before Harry died?"

"No," said Rose. "Who can remember from that long ago? It didn't look old, and if it was, I'm sure that Lillian was wearing it because she wanted to. I wish I could wear a suit from seven years ago, from even two years ago. Besides, Harry left a large estate. It was big enough to be reported in the paper. Lillian has never flaunted what she has. She's always been a lady."

"Well, Harry flaunted," Ida said as they walked to the car, recalling the years Harry Levinson had made her husband feel insignificant. Whenever the Jacobs went out with the Levinsons, Harry had always insisted upon driving his Cadillac rather than going in the Jacobs' Chevrolet.

"He was flashy," said Rose, disturbed by Ida's venom, "but Harry danced divinely."

Ida couldn't argue with that, so she started talking about the late afternoon traffic while she waited to pull onto the highway.

The restaurant was empty except for Lillian and several busboys, who were setting up tables for the dinner hour. She lingered in the dimly-lighted room uncertain of what to do, wanting only to avoid Ida and Rose so they would not witness her panic. She struggled to think of a way out of her predicament but couldn't, and when the maître d'--a tall, heavy-set man dressed in a tuxedo-- approached her from behind, asking if he could be of assistance, Lillian jumped with fright.

"I'm sorry, I didn't mean to startle you," he said, towering over her. "Are you waiting for someone?"

"I...I have to make a telephone call," Lillian said, "for...for a cab."

"There is a pay phone in the outer vestibule," he said crisply, eager to be rid of her. The varicose veins in his legs were throbbing despite his support socks, and he wanted to sit with his feet up until the dinner crowd started.

Lillian thanked him and left. When he could no longer see her, he sat down at a back table and pulled a chair up to elevate his aching legs, resenting women for the hundredth time that day. "Men kill themselves working so their wives can go out to lunch," he muttered to himself, leaning forward to rub his calves.

Like the main dining room of the restaurant, the telephone booth was decorated in a style best described as late bordello. Lillian closed the frosted-glass door of the booth, sat down on a seat covered with a scarlet-velvet cushion from which dangled gold tassels, and probed the change section of her wallet for dimes. She was lucky. There were two dimes wedged in a corner. She removed them with her forefinger. Then, chewing her lip, she called her son's house. A young, unfamiliar female voice answered, "The Levinson residence."

"May I please speak to Mrs. Levinson?" Lillian asked.

"Who is this?"

"This is Mrs. Levinson's mother-in-law."

"Oh. She's not here."

"Do you know when she'll be back?" Lillian said. The booth was uncomfortably warm, and she had begun to perspire again.

"No, she's playing tennis," the girl said. Then, without asking if Lillian wanted to leave a message, she hung up.

Lillian replaced the receiver and wiped her perspiring face with a lace-edged handkerchief, too upset by her daughter-in-law's absence to be angered at the sitter's rudeness. She opened the cover of her watch, which was set into a heavily-engraved gold bracelet, Harry's gift to her for their twenty-fifth wedding anniversary. It was four thirty. Her son Edward was still downtown in his office. There was no one else to call, so with shaking fingers Lillian put her last dime into the slot and dialed for a cab.

The day had turned cool. There was a distinct chill of winter in the air that went unnoticed by Lillian as she waited for the taxi. She was still perspiring, this time with worry over how she could pay for a five-dollar taxi ride and give the driver a tip with three dollars. She couldn't ask him to take her home and wait outside while she went in to get the rest of the money. There was no money in the house except for some pennies in the peanut-butter jar

The taxi was late in coming, and Lillian, beside herself, realized that she had to urinate. But she couldn't go back into the restaurant to use the ladies' room. If she did she might miss the taxi, and she didn't have another dime. Her face was creased with discomfort and unshed tears by the time the cab pulled in front of the statue-cluttered entrance of Antonio's. The faces of the plaster monstrosities appeared grim, almost mocking to her as she climbed into the cab.

"Where to?" the driver said. He was a young man who had a long, narrow face and a neat reddish-brown beard.

"Giffort Street in the city," Lillian said, "but I might want to get out sooner."

"It's your ride," he said, turning on the meter. It registered one dollar and sixty-five cents.

Lillian sat stiffly in the back seat, wincing each time a new number appeared on the meter. The driver tried to talk to her. He commented on the rush-hour traffic and told her that his grandmother lived three streets over from Giffort. Maybe she knew his grandmother, he wondered aloud.

But Lillian didn't hear him. Her eyes were riveted on the meter: $1.95, $2.00, $2.05, $2.10, $2.15, $2.20. When the meter clicked $2.50, Lillian tapped the young man on the shoulder. "Please, I'll get out here," she said. They were stopped at a light on Sherman Drive, the main artery that pumped cars in and out of the city. The taxi was in the center lane, one of a growing mass of vehicles waiting' for the signal to turn green. "I can't let you out here," he said, turning to face Lillian. "You'll get killed."

"Then let me out over there," Lillian said, pointing to a small plaza on the other side of the intersection.

"All right lady, it's your ride, but I hope you don't get us both killed," he said, hunching his body over the wheel. He turned his blinker on and waited for an opening so he could switch lanes while Lillian watched the meter, oblivious to the cars zooming past them.

The meter registered two dollars and sixty cents by the time they reached the plaza. Lillian handed the young man her last three dollars, thanked him for his trouble, and got out of the cab. He watched her walk to the corner from his rear-view mirror, a small, slender woman with sagging shoulders, wondering why the hell anyone would want to be let out here.

Lillian waited at the busy intersection for the light to change so she could cross. The sky was overcast, the clouds heavily bordered in charcoal. She wrinkled her nose when the fumes from car exhausts reached her nostrils; her clothes felt damp and she shuddered, chilled by the early evening air. The light changed. She stepped off the curb and crossed the six lane highway, barely making it to the other side before the light turned again, releasing a torrent of traffic.

There were no sidewalks. Unlike the city, which had been built for people, the suburb had been constructed for cars. Lillian walked along the concrete edges of plazas and gas stations, and in open, weed-choked fields filled with rubble, broken bottles, and empty beer cans. She kept her eyes fixed straight ahead after she spotted a used condom draped obscenely over the curb. Her feet ached. Her shoes had grown tight from sitting all afternoon, and a corn on the little toe of her left foot was rubbing painfully against the inside of her brown pump. The pressure from her full bladder was so great that she could feel the strain to contain it in her back teeth.

When she had walked perhaps a mile, Lillian tripped over a crumbling cinder block in an open field. She fell, landing hard on her hands and knees, but no one in the cars whizzing past noticed her. She remained there, too shaken to rise. Finally, she pulled herself erect. There was a long gash on her right leg, and the skin on her knees had been scraped; cinders were embedded in the palms of her hands. She brushed them off as best she could and wiped her knees, seeing with dismay that her skirt was ripped. She could do nothing about it; nor could she treat the gash on her leg, which was steadily oozing blood, soaking her torn stocking.

Each step Lillian took after her fall was an effort. She forced herself to think, to concentrate on something outside of her bruised and bleeding body so she could make it home. Harry, she'd think about Harry. He never let anything stop him.

Her thoughts wandered back to the day they met in a park in Bucharest: Harry, the son of a poor tailor, and she, the daughter of a philosophy professor. They were so young. Harry had always insisted that he loved her from the moment he first saw her. "You were the most beautiful girl in the park," he often said, "the most beautiful girl in Bucharest! A picture, you were so pretty."

Her father had objected to their marriage. Harry was a nothing, a nobody with no education, the professor told her. But she loved Harry. He was slender then, an attractive young man with high color in his cheeks, eager blue eyes, and a quick smile. Harry had a wonderful smile. He had large, even teeth that were the whitest she had ever seen. A girl couldn't help loving Harry when he smiled.

Harry courted her as he courted life, with the brashness of a young man who had nothing to lose and the assurance of one lacking peripheral vision. Harry was a man who kept his eyes fixed straight ahead. "There is no point in looking anywhere but up front," he often said. "Only a fool looks from his behind."

Up front to Harry meant the future. He was a dreamer, a planner, a man who prepared himself for contingencies before they occurred. When her father wept uncontrollably at their wedding, shaking his head in bewilderment at how such an improbable event could actually be taking place, Harry said: "There is nothing as shocking as a shock. Your father had his eyes in the wrong place. He should have looked up from his books." Her mother had left her a modest inheritance. As she walked, her knees throbbing, she recalled the day less than a week after their wedding when Harry told her they were leaving for America. She remembered weeping, imploring Harry to let them remain where they were, near their families and friends in Bucharest. "No," Harry said adamantly, "we're going. A man can make something of himself in America." She reminded him that America was in the depths of a depression. "Better a depression in America than Hitler in Europe," Harry said, anticipating problems while his neighbors, untroubled, conducted their daily lives.

She was frightened in America, a new bride who could neither cook nor clean, for she had lived all her life in a house kept by servants. Harry taught her what he knew about such matters and sent her to school to learn English. "You'll teach me," he said. "We can't leave New York City until I can talk like an American."

Lillian blinked hard, as if to quell the excruciating pressure emanating from her full bladder, and recalled her days in school. She had a fine ear, her teacher said. Soon she was speaking in almost unaccented English. Harry's ear wasn't as good as hers, but his mind was quick. He absorbed everything she taught him, insisting that they speak only in the tongue of their new country. It was difficult, but their efforts were rewarded. Within a year they were ready to move to upstate New York.

Harry worked at odd jobs, at anything he could find to sustain them. They survived the depression, and after World War II began, he had enough money saved to open a small men's clothing store. Harry took her for a walk to show her the store he had decided to rent. She was against it. "You're all the time so scared," Harry said, "like a frightened rabbit."

"No," she said, "not scared. The store is on the wrong side of the street. There is no parking on this side."

"So people will walk across," Harry said, dismissing her observation with a wave of his hand. But he didn't rent the store. Instead, he waited until one was available on the other side of the street, although they never discussed the location again.

The store was a success. So was she. In 1942 she gave birth to their only child, named Edward after her mother, Esther. Harry was ecstatic. Every dream he had ever had had come true in America. Hers was a grateful happiness. From her body had come a new life at a time when it was certain that the family she had left behind were doomed. When a nurse handed her the baby, she wept.

Lillian clenched her teeth. The gash on her leg had started to swell, and the open flesh was pressing painfully against her blood-soaked stocking. Her thoughts turned to Edward. He was a beautiful child, blond and blue-eyed. "He even looks like an American," Harry bragged, beaming.

Nothing was too good for Edward. Harry bought him a tricycle before he could walk, a baseball mitt before he could throw a ball, books before he could read. "You're spoiling him," she said.

"What is a son for, if not to spoil?" Harry retorted, lifting Edward high into the air.

She limped past a sign-post marking the city limits. She spoiled Edward, too. She never insisted that he do anything. She treated him like a little prince, picking up his dirty clothes wherever he left them, making his bed even in high school, clearing his dishes from the table when he had legs strong enough to play ball for hours without getting tired. But it was a pleasure doing for him. And the women in the Tuesday Night Group did the same for their sons, who weren't nearly as bright and handsome as Edward.

So what if she and Harry listened to everything he said like he was a *maven*. She felt herself becoming defensive. Edward knew something about everything. He was so American. And friends, he had so many friends. But then she remembered how he had often neglected to introduce her to the boys he brought home, how he had led them past her into the kitchen or living room without so much as a hello. The memory was more painful to her than her aching feet. Edward had made her feel self-conscious. Maybe her accent had embarrassed him, but her teacher had said that she had hardly any accent at all.

Dragging her right leg as she approached Hewett Avenue, she forced herself to think positively, which didn't require as much effort as did walking. Edward had been a good son. The presents he had given her--lopsided clay flower pots he had made in school and awkward, handmade cards for Mother's Day when he was a little boy, barely able to hold a crayon that said I LOVE YOU on them. She had saved every card; they were tied together with a blue ribbon and tucked away in her top dresser drawer. Those cards with the big clumsy letters meant more to her than the presents he had given to her when he was grown, expensive bottles of perfume and frilly, impractical housecoats that were always several sizes too big. And he had never brought grief into their house. Only once had Harry been upset with Edward. He was dating the O'Brien girl, Katy. Such a sweet child. Harry had fussed and fumed, arguing and threatening until she was positive that he would work himself into a stroke. Harry had gotten heavy, and his blood pressure was dangerously high. "Stop already," she implored him. "Edward is only eighteen. He's young yet. He's not getting married to the girl. Besides, would it be so terrible if he did? She's sweet and bright in school. He could do worse. Maybe she would convert."

"My son marry a *shiksa*? My grandchildren wouldn't be Jewish!" Harry said. "Nothing could be worse!"

Then, magically, the problem was solved. Harry congratulated himself, saying: "Given a choice, what healthy Jewish American boy wouldn't pick a shiny new red convertible over a *shiksa*?"

She remembered how overjoyed they were when Edward graduated from the university, an accountant. Harry was so proud. So was she, but she wasn't as happy as Harry when Edward brought Diana Fishbein home to meet them. Diana was Jewish, the daughter of an attorney yet, but she wasn't as nice as the O'Brien girl. "So," Harry said defensively when she commented on the girl's coldness, "at least the girl is Jewish. Pretty, too. My son has as good an eye as his father."

And Harry, who was not an overlooking man, paid

for the wedding when the Fishbeins confessed that they didn't have the money for anything but a small affair limited to fifty guests. She didn't care for the Fishbeins. They lived in a fancy house and wore expensive clothes, but she sensed that they looked down on the Levinsons as being socially beneath them. "Why should we pay?" she said. "It isn't our place. I read in a book on etiquette that the bride's family is responsible for the wedding. You're letting the Fishbeins put on a show with your money."

"We have only one son," Harry reminded her. "Edward is a good boy; he'll remember what we did for him. And the girl will know, too. Think of the wedding as an investment."

Some investment, she thought bitterly, willing herself down Hewett Avenue, step by painful step. Diana invited us to dinner only twice a year, on Rosh Hashanah and for the first seder. And when our grandsons were born, she named both boys for her relatives, ignoring our dead as if they didn't matter. Such awful names--Derek and Shane. Who ever heard of Jewish boys with such names? But Harry was generous with the birth of each child. "Boys," he beamed, opening his checkbook, "to carry on the Levinson name."

It was after the birth of their second grandson that Harry decided to have a will made, she recalled, now several blocks away from Hewett and Giffort. The pressure radiating from her full bladder had become exquisite. She prayed that she would make it home before she lost control.

The will. Harry told her that everything would he left to her. "It's all yours," he said, "in trust."

"What's trust?"

"In case something should happen to me, my assets will be put into a special account," Harry said. "Edward will be the trustee to manage things. After all, he's a CPA now. What better manager could you have than a CPA who happens to be your son?"

"I could always manage very nicely. Even when we had nothing, I managed. I have never been from the spenders," she reminded him, her syntax suffering as it always did when she was upset.

"I know," said Harry, patting her on the shoulder. "You have been a wonderful wife, more than a man could ask."

"Then why don't you trust me?"

"It's not you that I don't trust," he said. "It's the men who will chase you that I don't trust!"

"What men?" she said, deeply wounded. "There has never been another man but you. I have never given you a moment of worry on that score."

"That's the point!" said Harry, waving his right index finger in the air. "You don't know from such things. But if something should happen to me, men will flock around you like flies around a honey jar. You're still a beautiful woman, Lillian. One of those men will chase you until he wears you down, and then what? He will have you and my money! How could I rest in peace?"

"You could trust me, Harry," she replied stiffly.

"A trust makes for better trust," said Harry, so accustomed to planning for contingencies that it was only natural for him to plan beyond his death.

Lillian was grateful for the darkness as she approached the intersection of Giffort Street and Hewett Avenue. Mr. Van Horn was leaving his store to go to his car, which was parked on Giffort Street. It would be terrible for Mr. Van Horn to see her in such a state. She stepped into the recessed doorway of Jimmy's Shoe Repair Shop and waited until she saw Mr. Van Horn's car start up Hewett Avenue. The corn on her little toe was festering, and her bruised knees had stiffened; the gash on her leg was throbbing constantly, as if the nerves inside were exposed. But the pain from her lower limbs could be borne. It was the insistent pressure from her bladder that strained the very fiber of her being, the terrible realization that she could not contain its contents much longer.

She limped to the corner of Hewett and Giffort, thinking about Harry and Edward and the trust. "Don't worry," Edward assured her after the funeral. "You'll never want for a thing. Dad left more than enough to provide for you for the rest of your life." She wept at his words, both moved by his tender concern and reminded anew that she had years left without Harry. How could she live without Harry?

She managed. It was difficult at first, but as the days blended into weeks and the weeks into months, she became whole again. She started to do volunteer work at the Veterans' Hospital, which Harry had forbidden when he was alive. He wouldn't listen when she explained that she wanted to help the soldiers who had fought to save their families. "I don't want you should work in a hospital for men," Harry said, "and that's final."

She also began making frequent trips to the neighborhood library. Since English was now her language, it was a good time to begin reading English literature. Harry wasn't a reader, and he had always made her feel uncomfortable when he found her absorbed in a book. "I hope you're reading recipes," he would say, letting her know exactly how he felt about her cooking and her reading. After years of effort in the kitchen, all that could be said for her meals was that they were adequate. She had given up trying to compete with the ghost of Harry's mother who, Harry often told her, had made feasts from scraps.

She had started reading the works of Charles Dickens when the checks from the trust stopped coming regularly. There was one missed check, then a few months later, another. When she could no longer blame the postal service, she called Edward. He was busy and didn't she know better than to call him it the office? Embarrassed, she reminded him that the first of the month had passed. Well, he was building a house and he had just come back from a trip and he hadn't noticed and please don't call him again at work. But she hadn't talked to him in weeks. She knew he wasn't one to call, but he hadn't stopped to visit her, either. She missed him. "It would be nice to see you," she said, hoping her voice sounded suggesting rather than pleading.

"As soon as I get a chance," was his reply before hanging up.

But Edward didn't seem to get a chance. He called her rarely and was impatient when she called him, so she stopped calling. She had questions about the trust. She wondered what had happened to the money--so much from the store, the savings accounts, Harry's stocks and bonds-- but dared not question him. If she did, she might lose Edward altogether. Doubts started sprouting in her head like the weeds that were forever threatening her flower garden. Angry after a missed check, she decided to see an attorney: she wanted an accounting. But she cancelled her appointment with the attorney the same day she made it. How could she even hint to a total stranger that her son might be less than an honorable man? Some things she could not say, even to herself.

There were more tight months, months without a check. But how could she feel sorry for herself, safe and warm in her house on Giffort Street, when the people in Dicken's books were starving on London streets? She would make do with what she had. There was still some money in a savings account she had started years ago from what was left of the weekly house money Harry had given her. She wouldn't bother Edward. He was a busy man, an accountant with his own family, and he didn't neglect her completely. He wrote checks to pay the property taxes on the house. The water bills, too.

At the thought of water, she grimaced. One block more and she would be home. Control, she had to have control. So he didn't call. She could be overlooking. And then Social Security started to help, a check coming regularly every month. But things were getting more expensive. Excuses, always excuses. She was too busy. She had too many things to do. Maybe some other time. Now she went only to the library and to the Veterans' Hospital and twice a year to Edward's house. Such a gorgeous house, such luxury. Six bedrooms for four people. A swimming pool. Then an article appeared in the paper with his picture. *Edward Levinson Running for County Comptroller*, it said. To hear news of her son she had to read the morning paper. Oh, how that hurt! Hadn't she always loved him and tried her best to please him? She called his office. Maybe she would tell him that he had hurt her. She would wish him well. His secretary asked her to hold. She heard a click, then Edward's voice. "Tell her I'm not here," he said. "I have to leave for a meeting in a few minutes."

"But she knows you're here," the secretary said.

"Then tell her I had to rush out. You know how Jewish mothers are--they'll run your life if you let them," he said, laughing as if Jewish mothers were a joke, comic book characters that were all alike.

The secretary got back on the line. She was sorry, but he wasn't there. She had made a mistake. Perhaps Mrs. Levinson would call back later.

She put the receiver down and sobbed.

Thank God, only two houses more. She had tried so hard not to interfere with his life, not to be a burden. She wanted only the best for him--health and happiness and success in whatever he chose to do. He had made her sound like a monster, and to a stranger yet, a woman she had never seen. What had she done to deserve such treatment?

Up the front steps. Legs aching painfully. Bladder stretched to bursting. Key in the door. Inside. Just a few more steps.

Lillian Levinson sat on the toilet and relieved herself at last. Then she wept.

She went to bed after soaking in the tub. She had cleaned and bandaged the gash on her leg and removed the cinders imbedded in her hands and knees as best she could. Before she fell asleep, Lillian thought of Edward once again. It occurred to her that other than a mild reprimand, neither she nor Harry had ever punished him for bad behavior.

It was after midnight when Lillian awakened with severe abdominal cramps. She dragged herself out of bed and groped her way to the bathroom. There was no time to turn on a light. Pale and shaking, Lillian made the first of many trips to the toilet that long night, her suspicion about Antonio's chicken salad painfully confirmed.

She slept intermittently, dreaming of Harry. Harry was dancing. He was gliding through a tango and whirling around in a Lindy. His body bounced to the rhythms of a cha-cha, never missing a beat: one, two, one-two-three, one, two, one-two-three. He waltzed with effortless grace, spinning in and out of her dreams. Harry danced with a carefree abandon that exhausted her.

The morning dawned cold and gray. Lillian put on a bathrobe and descended the worn staircase, gripping the banister for support. She moved slowly, aching and stiff-muscled, weak from a lack of food and the ravages of Antonio's tainted chicken salad. She knew she needed nourishment, but her stomach rebelled at the thought of anything heavier than a cup of tea. After filling the kettle and putting it on the stove to boil, she opened a yellow ceramic canister on the kitchen counter marked TEA and reached inside. The movement of her hand, which had been automatic--a straightforward reaching to grasp--become frantic. Her fingers fluttered inside the canister, searching the bottom for a tea bag. She felt nothing but the glazed ceramic surface, cool to her touch. She picked up the canister and overturned it. A fine brown powder that had collected on the bottom flew out, dusting the front of her robe. No tea bags. She slammed the canister down on the counter, cracking it. Her lower lip quivered with anger, and the lids of her deep-set brown eyes tightened. Wisps of steam began to thread their way through the kettle spout. Lillian ignored them. She stood grim-faced while the water boiled until it jetted forth with such strength that a cloud of steam formed over the stove. When she finally shut the burner off, she made a cup of bouillon and, carrying it with her, limped determinedly upstairs to dress.

It was drizzling outside when Lillian left the house. She tightened the belt of her beige raincoat against the chill and, her shoulders set, started up Giffort Street. She looked neither to the left nor to the right. As she neared the end of the first block, Edna Harris, who had just opened her living room drapes, spotted Lillian and waved. Lillian didn't return her greeting. Edna thought it strange and wondered, as she watched the retreating figure, why Lillian was out walking with a limp on such a nasty morning. She talked about it at great length in the weeks to come.

When Lillian reached Hewett Avenue, she turned right. She walked past Van Horn's Drugstore, Creigle's Bakery, Simpson's Stationary Store, Jimmy's Shoe Repair Shop, an expanse of sidewalk rimming a parking lot, and stopped in front of the Blue Star Supermarket. Then, pursing her lips, she stood in front of the electric-eye door, waiting for it to open. The door beckoned her silently to enter.

Inside, Lillian walked directly to aisle nine. There, on the second and third shelves, were cellophane-wrapped boxes of tea bags. Lillian removed a box of Tetley tea bags, marked one dollar and fifty-nine cents, from the third shelf. She held it close to her chest in plain view, walked back down the aisle past the check-out registers where two clerks were ringing up customers' orders, waited for the electric-eye door to open, and left the store.

She stood in front of the supermarket, her heart pounding under the strain of what she had done. Her eyelids fluttered. She told herself to be calm. She had to handle this act of dishonesty with dignity.

Five minutes lapsed. Lillian began to shiver in what was now a light rain and waited, clutching the box of tea bags, but nothing happened. She started to pace the sidewalk nervously, hoping to catch the attention of someone inside. No one noticed her. Finally she stopped and, struggling for composure, again stood in front of the supermarket door. It swung open. Lillian hesitated, then stepped resolutely forward, chin high, still clutching the box of tea bags to her breast. She went immediately to the manager's office, an enclosed, elevated area in the front of the store.

Calvin Ernst, the manager of the Blue Star Supermarket, was standing in the back of the enclosure checking invoices he had received with early morning shipments. A sallow-complexioned clerk came to the window. "May I help you?" she said.

"I would like to speak to the manager, please," said Lillian, "but don't interrupt him. I can see that he is busy. I'll wait."

Calvin Ernst looked up. He was a robust, broad-faced man in his early fifties, and when he saw Lillian, he smiled.

"This woman says she'd like to talk to you, Mr. Ernst," explained the clerk, who had been recently transferred from another store.

"Certainly," said Calvin Ernst, walking to the window. "Mrs. Levinson is one of our oldest, nicest customers. What can I do for you today, Mrs. Levinson?"

"I took this," said Lillian, holding up the box of tea bags with shaking hands.

Calvin Ernst frowned. "Was there something wrong

with the tea? We'll be happy to replace it for you."

"No, nothing was wrong. I *took* the tea," said Lillian, her voice quavering.

"I don't understand," he replied, frowning.

Unable to utter the word stole, Lillian said agitatedly, "Mr. Ernst, I want you should call the police."

Calvin Ernst unlocked the door to the booth and stepped onto the selling floor. "Mrs. Levinson," he said quietly, "sometimes people forget to bring their money with them. Usually we hold their groceries until they come back with the cash, but in your case that isn't necessary. I'll write your name and the price of the tea on a memo, and you can bring the money in the next time you do your shopping."

"No, thank you, Mr. Ernst," Lillian said. "I appreciate that you want to be kind, but I would appreciate it more if you would please call the police."

"Oh, I couldn't do that, not to you." He reached into the pocket of his khakis. "I'll lend you the money myself if you'll be more comfortable."

"Thank you, that's very nice," Lillian said, ignoring the dollar bills in his outstretched hand. "Please, could I use your telephone?"

Customers were not allowed inside the booth, but Calvin Ernst was sincerely fond of Mrs. Levinson. She was such a gracious lady, and she seemed so upset. He would bend the rules, just this once. "Certainly," he said, wondering if she were planning to call someone to take her home.

Lillian climbed the two steep steps into the enclosure. She went directly to the telephone and dialed 911, cradling the box of tea bags.

Ernst gasped when he heard her ask to be connected with Precinct 14. Still holding his money, he quickly entered the booth, intending to break the connection. Lillian faced him squarely. She pulled herself up to her full height, a fraction less than five feet tall. He listened helplessly while she spoke into the receiver: "This is Mrs. Lillian Levinson. I am at the Blue Star Supermarket on Hewett Avenue near Giffort Street. I took a box of tea bags and didn't pay. I want you should come and arrest me."

* * *

Edward Levinson left his office at five-thirty. He had had a fruitful day. His meeting with the county chairman of the Democratic Party had been successful beyond his expectations. His campaign was going well. While he waited for the elevator to take him to the lobby, he engaged in a private daydream that had become a recurrent favorite. First, he would be elected county comptroller. Then he would run for county executive, which was just a reach away from state comptroller. The elevator door opened. Levinson stepped inside. The door closed. It had been such a satisfying day. It wouldn't be farfetched to think about eventually running for governor.

When the elevator arrived on the first floor, Levinson stepped into the lobby, an attractive sandy-haired man who had eager blue eyes. He walked automatically to the newsstand to pick up an evening paper.

It was a while before Levinson reached the revolving doors. He stood still as a plaster statue in the marble lobby, staring at his mother's picture in the center of the front page. There, in bold letters, he read: MOTHER OF WOULD-BE COUNTY EXECUTIVE ASKS TO BE ARRESTED. The text began:

Lillian Levinson, widow of prominent businessman Harry Levinson, and mother of Edward Levinson, currently running for the office of county comptroller, called Precinct 14 today from the Blue Star Supermarket on Hewett Avenue, asking to be arrested.

According to Patrolman Brian Halloran, who responded to the call, Mrs. Levinson explained that she wanted a cup of tea and didn't have enough money to buy a tea bag. She was holding a box of tea bags valued at $1.59 for which she didn't have a receipt.

AUTHOR'S NOTE

When I conceived the idea for this book, I thought it would be interesting to use the physical setting in which I was raised--the gracious homes and magnificent elms that graced my childhood. I wanted to plant the trees again, to walk under the elms in my imagination as they once were, stark and lofty as the skeleton of a cathedral in the winter, rustling green umbrellas of shade in the summer, dripping gold in the fall. Once planted, however, it was inevitable that I would have to witness their death and hear the painful sound of the chain saws cutting the elms down. It was the price to be paid, I suppose, for interfering with nature's verdict.

I have read that no self-respecting writer would admit to having had a happy childhood. At the risk of losing mine, I admit to having grown up in a home that was secure, sealed with love and the strong bonds of family. As a child, I innocently believed that all the families on the block were as happy as ours. But when I populated the houses with characters born in my imagination, I discovered that this was not the case. Perhaps it is no accident, then, that the stories in this book are tales of loss of innocence, some of the innocence mine. The characters in ***Harry Danced Divinely*** are precious to me nonetheless, and I would like to believe that the people who lived on my block, wherever they are today, were as happy as I remember them.

Marian D. Schwartz

www.mariandschwartz.com